SPEAKING OF THE FANTASTIC IV

Interviews with Science Fiction and Fantasy Writers

Conducted by
DARRELL SCHWEITZER

WILDSIDE PRESS

Vernor Vinge appeared in *Orson Scott Card's Intergalactic Medicine Show* 15 and 16, November 2009, January 2010. Copyright © 2009 by Darrell Schweitzer. *Paolo Bacigalupi* appeared in *Orson Scott Card's Intergalactic Medicine Show* 42, November 2014. Copyright © 2014 by Darrell Schweitzer. *Paul Di Fillippo* appeared in *Orson Scott Card's Intergalactic Medicine Show* 17, June 2010. Copyright © 2010 by Darrell Schweitzer. *Tanith Lee* appeared in *Orson Scott Card's Intergalactic Medicine Show* 11, March 2009. Copyright © 2009 by Darrell Schweitzer. *Patricia McKillip* appeared in *Orson Scott Card's Intergalactic Medicine Show* 21, February 2011. Copyright © 2011 by Darrell Schweitzer. *Robert Silverberg* appeared in *Orson Scott Card's Intergalactic Medicine Show* 22, April 2011. Copyright © 2011 by Darrell Schweitzer. *Allen Steele* appeared in *Orson Scott Card's Intergalactic Medicine Show* 38, March 2014. Copyright © 2014 by Darrell Schweitzer. *John Clute* appeared at full length in *Science Fiction Commentary*. A shorter version appeared *Orson Scott Card's Intergalactic Medicine Show* 25, November 2011. Copyright © 2011 by Darrell Schweitzer. *Elizabeth Hand* appeared in *Orson Scott Card's Intergalactic Medicine Show* 33, April 2013. Copyright © 2013 by Darrell Schweitzer. *Maurice Broaddus* appeared in *Orson Scott Card's Intergalactic Medicine Show* 41, September 2014. Copyright © 2014 by Darrell Schweitzer. *James Blaylock* appeared in *Orson Scott Card's Intergalactic Medicine Show* 32, February 2013. Copyright © 2013 by Darrell Schweitzer. *Theodora Goss* appeared in *Orson Scott Card's Intergalactic Medicine Show* 27, March 2012. Copyright © 2012 by Darrell Schweitzer. *Ben Bova* appeared in *Orson Scott Card's Intergalactic Medicine Show* 24, August 2011. Copyright © 2011 by Darrell Schweitzer. *Richard Lupoff* appeared in *Orson Scott Card's Intergalactic Medicine Show* 18, August 2010. Copyright © 2010 by Darrell Schweitzer. *Jay Lake* first appeared in *Dark Discoveries* #10, Summer d2007. Copyright © 2010 by Dark Discoveries Publications. *William Tenn* first appeared in *The New York Review of Science Fiction* #260, April 2010. Copyright © 2009 by Dragon Press. *Kim Stanley Robinson* originally appeared on the *Amazing Stories* website. Copyright © 2016 by Darrell Schweitzer. *Stanley Schmidt* appeared in *Orson Scott Card's Intergalactic Medicine Show* 30, September 2012. Copyright © 2012 by Darrell Schweitzer. *Larry Niven* appeared in *Orson Scott Card's Intergalactic Medicine Show* 23, June 2011. Copyright © 2011 by Darrell Schweitzer.

SPEAKING OF THE FANTASTIC IV

DARRELL SCHWEITZER INTERVIEWS:

VERNOR VINGE

PAOLO BACIGALUPI

PAUL DI FILLIPPO

TANITH LEE

PATRICIA McKILLIP

ROBERT SILVERBERG

ALLEN STEELE

JOHN CLUTE

ELIZABETH HAND

MAURICE BROADDUS

JAMES P. BLAYLOCK

THEODORA GOSS

BEN BOVA

RICHARD A. LUPOFF

JAY LAKE

WILLIAM TENN (Philip Klass)

KIM STANLEY ROBINSON

STANLEY SCHMIDT

LARRY NIVEN

Contents

FORWARD: WHY THERE ARE INTRODUCTIONS

This is not my first interview book by any means, folks, not by a long shot. In fact my very first book was a collection of interviews, *SF Voices*, published by T.K. Graphics in 1976. Not a hugely catchy title that. People asked me if it was about San Francisco writers. But it did spawn a whole series of future *SF Voices* volumes, by myself and Jeffrey Elliott, from Borgo Press. The title worked if you were entirely *inside* the science fiction field, so that the initials could only have one meaning. T.K. Graphics had very little distribution outside of the convention scene, and Borgo Press sold mostly to libraries, so it probably didn't matter.

Which brings up the question of why there are introductions to the individual interviews in this volume. The simple answer is that at some point the editor of *Orson Scott Card's Intergalactic Medicine Show*, where a good number of these interviews first appeared, started asking me for introductions. They probably would have been a good idea all along. It is a matter of accessibility, of not taking too much for granted. If one of these books falls into the hands of someone who might not automatically assume that "SF" always means "science fiction" and not "San Francisco," it might be practical, not to mention good manners to give them *some* orientation regarding these interviews, when and where they were done and in what context, and who the interviewees are. Yes, we do live in the age of Wikipedia, but if you paid for this book, you are entitled to a little information without working for it. So there are introductions. I think there will be introductions in my future interview books.

Meanwhile, what I usually say in introductions … yadda, yadda, yadda. Welcome to my equivalent of a talk show. This is the kind of talk show where the *guest* is featured, of interest for the sake of him or herself, not just as a foil for my own brilliant wit. There has been no attempt to update these interviews, because, as I see it, interviews (at least after they have been published for the first time) are not news. They are cultural context, the raw material of history or biography. They record what so-and-so said and felt at a precise moment in time, rather than the long view of retrospect. I've joke about this before. The point is to interview Homer when he's just finished the *Iliad* and it's a smash hit, and he is just thinking about maybe doing a sequel, about the homecoming of one of the minor characters in his first epic. What are his ideas about is writing just then? That is why Zeus invented tape recorders, or, more recently, the Internet. I never would be able to get this kind of detail in shorthand with a reed pen on a scroll of papyrus.

A talk show. It's about talk, theirs more than mine. My job is to get them going, to poke and pry and lead, then shut up and listen. Enjoy.

—Darrell Schweitzer, July 1, 2017

VERNOR VINGE

Note: The starting point for this interview is an article called "The Coming Technological Singularity" which you may quickly find by doing an internet search on Vernor Vinge's name. It was presented at the VISION-21 Symposium sponsored by NASA Lewis Research Center and the Ohio Aerospace Institute, March 30-31, 1993. A slightly changed version appeared in the Winter 1993 issue of *Whole Earth Review*. Otherwise, what you need to know by way of an introduction is that Vernor Vinge has been publishing science fiction since 1965. One early story of his, "The Accomplice" (1967) is remarkably prophetic. Not only does it describe desktop computers and CGI animation, but suggests that this could use used to make a movie out of *The Lord of the Rings*. His "True Names" (1981) is one of the first stories about cyberspace, hackers, and virtual reality. He has won Hugo Awards for *A Fire upon the Deep* (1992), *A Deepness in the Sky* (1999), "Fast Times at Fairmont High" (2002), "The Cookie Monster" (2004) and *Rainbows End* (2006). *Marooned in* Realtime (1996) won the Prometheus Award. He is a retired professor of mathematics from San Diego State University.

At the beginning of the Wikipedia entry about him, he is quoted from the Singularity article as saying, "Within thirty years, we will have the technological means to create superhuman intelligence. Shortly after, the human era will be ended."

←*―··―*→

Q: I've read your 1993 paper about the Singularity online. The first question that occurs to me is this: If the future will soon become unforeseeable and unknowable, what is the science fiction writer to write about?

Vinge: I've maintained that actually science fiction writers are the first human occupational group to be impacted by the Singularity, whether or not the Singularity actually happens. The reason is what you just said in your question, if the proviso is that after some point in time the universe is not just unpredictable but it is unintelligible. I think that if you look at science fiction from the 1990s on, in particularly science fiction like space opera. Here, by the way, I am not claiming any credit. These are ideas that everybody is going to have. But if you look at a lot of science fiction that takes place after the point in time after which there would otherwise be this

Singularity, you will find that the author has imposed some sort of explanation for why the Singularity did not happen, or why, if the Singularity did happen, the story as told is still an intelligible story.

This is true even for science fiction writers who are adamantly convinced that there is no possibility that the Singularity is going to happen. There are such writers. But even those writers, for purely commercial reasons, may feel the need to say why it never happened. It doesn't have to be explicit, but it has to be something expressed, even structural in the story. So that is the way that a lot of science fiction has possibilities. Science fiction is in the business of what-ifs, so there certainly a lot of reasons why you could explain in retrospect that the Singularity didn't happen or if it did that meant you could still have stories.

Q: If only Philip K. Dick were alive today. He might argue that the Singularity has already happened, but it has been concealed from us, so we'll never know.

Vinge: The idea that the Singularity has already happened or that it has been concealed from us actually is a fairly common one. Giving this sort of talk, I get that explanation a lot. In fact the very first time I ever used the term Singularity in this way was in 1983 at an AI conference at Carnegie-Mellon, and afterwards this fellow came up to me and said, "You know, I think the Singularity has happened already, and it happened several thousand years ago." He said this was because, "Nation states are superhuman entities and the first nation states are several thousand years old, so there is nothing new here."

That's an interesting point of view. I don't think it has quite the actionability that what we're running up on in our near future has.

Q: Before we proceed further, please define for the readers exactly what you mean by the Singularity.

Vinge: By Singularity, I am talking about the likelihood that in the relatively near historical future, we humans, using technology, will either create or become creatures that are superhumanly intelligent. This is an event with few analogues in the past, one being the rise of humanity within the animal kingdom. Perhaps another would be the Cambrian Explosion. It is a technological event, but it is different from previous technological events, because you could explain things like the telegraph or television to people from earlier eras, and you could even explain the social consequences of such technological progress; but you could not have an equivalent conversation of explanation with a goldfish or a flatworm. So in the same sense, when we talk about what things will be like after the Singularity, we are talking about things that are ordered by creatures that are significantly smarter than human. Trying to explain that is a qualitatively different problem than trying to explain past technologies to earlier humans.

Q: Wouldn't an equivalent of this be trying to explain written language to a pre-literate? Among other things, written language is alleged to have changed certain brain processes, particularly the way people remember. That was how in the old days people could memorize all of Homer, for example.

Vinge: The invention of written language. I like that one better. I get occasionally fire or the invention of agriculture. Written language, that does have intellectual content. I think that, unless you feel there was some profound psycho change, like a bicameral mind type thing, you could *explain* the consequences of writing, verbally, to someone from before writing. They might not believe you. In their heart they might not see that it would have that much of an effect. But you could do that.

One thing I like about writing, but writing has a place in a trend that I see. That is, to me, the biggest difference between us and the dumb animals is none of the things I've seen others talk about. The difference between us and the dumb animals, is that, more than any other attribute that is advertised, we are the critter that externalizes cognitive function. Writing *is* an externalization of memory. So I regard writing as a data point on this progression. Maybe writing and computers are two data points in this progression. Maybe writing and computers are two data points.

Q: Isn't painting on the cave wall another one?

Vinge: Only if you regard it as a form of writing. In that case, yes. There are people who always like to find animals doing things. A bear scraping up a tree—"Oh, that's like writing. It's bear writing." On the other hand, I don't think it actually is in a class with the writing that we talk about.

On the other hand, chimpanzees make tools, which are elaborated for particular functions—that does look like tool-making to me. I don't think tool-making is nearly as good a differentiating feature as our occasional externalizations of cognitive function.

Q: If we have artificially-enhanced intelligence in humans, or human-computer interfaces, or anything like that, aren't these advantages only for the *rich?* You and I may be talking about this, but there are illiterate stone-age farmers in Borneo or someplace like that. They don't have electricity or running water. They've never heard of a computer. How does this concern them? Aren't these enhancements only going to be for a small segment of the total population?

Vinge: The general issue of whether technology and high-tech computer technology is a tool of social division, for the enhancement of rich people to the detriment of poor people is something I have heard over the years quite often. But technology in general and computer technology in particular is much more of an egalitarian thing, or at least a meritocratic thing. It is more egalitarian than most stuff that affects human welfare. The old story that you get is that the first inventions are very expensive. Hopefully the rich people do get their hands on them, because there are more rich people than there are governments. That means there is the prospect of making still more money by making them a little bit cheaper.

The current, most beautiful example of this is the cell phone explosion. We—humans—are selling the quantity of cell phones to other humans that are beginning to be the same as the number of humans in the world. We are selling hundreds of millions of these devices a year, and they are not all a matter of a smart phone replacing someone's stupider phone. Cell phones have revolutionized many of the poorest parts of the world, because they give farmers the ability to get market intelligence about stuff that is happening two or three days' walk away. This is just one thing that has changed lives more than any number of dam projects—or damn projects.

Q: I think what they're doing in the Third World is just bypassing the need to put in land lines.

Vinge: Yes, but also the facility—who can talk on the phone—have gotten to be at an extremely diversified level. First of all, many people can afford the phone. Also get villages that are so poor that there may be only enough money for one phone. So you will get some old lady who gets a phone and then rents it. If you want a minute of phone time to call your market place, okay.

This and some other technological developments have been to me heartwarming to the point of being poster-boy ripostes to the question about, "Isn't technology just going to make poor people poorer?"

Q: If enhancements get to the point where they makes some people significantly smarter—not just a matter of better tools, but a significant increase in intelligence—won't this create, for the first time in history, a superior race? Won't the people who have greater abilities inherently take over and lord it over their inferiors?

Vinge: Unlike the cell phone thing, I cannot say with certainty, "No, that is obviously not true!" I think that there are various questions to raise, though. How much advantage does a smart person have to being the *only* smart person? The answer may not be as obviously that that is what you want to do. So, there are many variables: exactly how the change comes online, exactly what the perceived self-interests of the various players are, whether the players are willing to use force or threats to prevent other players from getting super-intelligence—if that's the case, then this is just another form of the AIs take over the world.

In fact I have friends who would prefer to have a pure AI rather than intelligence amplification. They say that we're carrying fifty million years of biological bloody baggage in the back of our heads and you just couldn't trust somebody not to use that in a non-killer way, the way you could trust a machine that doesn't have that instinctual load. The friends of mine who make this argument then pat themselves on the chest and say, "In fact, there is only one person I would trust to undertake this responsibility."

So, a lot of people regard intelligence amplification as the most mellow of the possibilities. If, on the other hand, they think that the preponderance of the evidence indicates the possibility that you just said, or like my friend they think that the first person who gets it is going to become god and reduce us all to serfs—those viewpoints are not going to regard intelligence amplification with an entirely calm demeanor.

Q: It might not be a matter of active malevolence, but of a lot of people being left behind. The nation or social group which enhances itself first will inevitably win. If we can make ourselves ten times smarter, immune to most diseases, and much stronger, then the people who have *not* become supermen are much less employable. Let us throw into this the idea that the enhanced people can interact with machines in a way that unaltered people cannot. The science fiction precedent I see for this is Asimov's division, in his robot novels, of the human race into short-lived people and the long-lived spacers, who are almost two different species. Couldn't we see the human race divided into two species, those who are enhanced and those who are left behind?

Vinge: I am not saying that is not going to happen. What you've described is a plausible scenario. I think that there are very plausible scenarios in which there is not that much advantage to ruling over a group of poor people who live in squalor and aren't as smart as you. It is entirely plausible that the idea of being inclusive would actually be the most profitable.

This is a relative scenario: there could well be large groups of people who say, "Hell, no! I've paid off my mortgage, my I.Q. is 130, and I'm satisfied. I have legal title to this property. So you guys that are smarter, I don't want to buy into what you have. I'll just where I am, and you will have to find somewhere else to play your game."

The idea of stay-at-homes rather than put-downs is, I think plausible. There will be a certain percentage of people who are rejectors of the technology. There are several scenarios there, and I certainly grant that the negative one that you're talking about is one that should be explored, both seriously and in fiction.

Q: So some people opt out, and they're still the equivalent of stone-age farmers plowing a field behind a mule. Everybody else goes high-tech. The inferiors just get ignored.

Vinge: If part of your scenario is *not* that the smart people are actively suppressing, that they just don't care, I would say that at most you have just slowed things down a bit for the rest. There would be an intermediate level of entrepreneurs who would be quite happy to use the cheapest forms of stuff that exist, which probably would be pretty good, if we are that far into the future and the entrepreneurs have access to design studios that are run by smart people. If there is no active measure to keep people down, then the ones who stay behind are those who made the moral decision to stay behind.

Q: You realize, of course, that a good deal of the population of the world has no idea what you are talking about, because they have never seen a computer.

Vinge: In the last ten years, that is drifting over into negative territory, if you count cell phones, which certainly have powerful computers in them. Look at cell phone penetration right now. There are very few places that are not riddled with cell phones, and they are used by these people to enrich themselves.

Q: They're also used with those previously mentioned killer instincts to set off remote-controlled bombs. Maybe nothing has really changed since the discovery of fire, or before.

Vinge: There is a long-term question about whether technology is going to kill us before it saves us. I think there are some questions that probably never will be answered, because anything that looks like a definitive answer is necessarily confined in space and time.

Q: Can't we argue that the first step in this future evolution of mankind is science fiction itself, in the sense that you and I are using a science-fictional method of thinking even to have this discussion?

Vinge: Yes. I think that, really, science fiction plays for the body politic, or for the social body of humans, the role that dreaming does for the individual. Most dreams are nonsense. Some dreams clue you in to things that you might want to be thinking about, like, my God, maybe I should be paying that particular bill, because that particular bill has a cascade of negative consequences. So, in the later Twentieth Century, the notion of thinking out scenarios, which we have been doing in science fiction since forever, began to begin to be an actual serious bureaucratic planning tool. I think it is far superior to predictions and even trend-lines—people who study trends and that sort of thing. In fact, no one knows what the future is going to be like. So, earlier in this interview where you were talking about the dystopian possibility of what happens with intelligence amplification, for example. It is important for people to work their way through all sorts of scenarios like this. I am mainly for science fiction for doing this.

When it's done more seriously and with a less entertaining effect, one thing to do with it is to come up with a scenario and then work backwards from that, and think, if that's really how things turned out, what would be the ongoing symptoms that you would see as you fall toward that scenario? Do that with a lot of different scenarios. Then you have these families of symptoms for different sorts of outcomes. This is to me a far more important planning tool than some trend-line of where you think oil prices are going to be in five years. You can watch these symptoms, and even have notions of planning. You can say, well, if such-and-such happens, that makes it really likely that we are in Scenario A or Scenario C, in which case it would be good to spend some money on such-and-such.

So I think I agree with you about the power of science fiction and the overall power that I think that society is acquiring by taking scenarios very seriously.

Q: Does this then give the science fiction writer a certain responsibility to be realistic?

Vinge: [Laughs.]

Q: You're talking about science fiction as a kind of dreaming. A lot of science fiction makes no attempt to be realistic. Think of van Vogt's *The World of Null-A*. It was supposed to be a big revelation, but there is nothing realistic in it at all.

Vinge: That's an external judgment on your part. [Laughs.]

Q: Aren't we describing only a specific type of science fiction, if the subject of realism comes up?

Vinge: It probably it isn't that healthy to try to confine valuable science fiction to science fiction writers who are serious. Taking science fiction writers as a whole, there is no reason why they have to take themselves seriously. Now, the people who read their stories get various different things out of them. I read some people's stories for reasons that may be fairly serious, but for many, the more crazy it is, the better, if they can handle it cleverly. I don't think that any internal categorization is worth very much, partly because we're inside the system, we don't know what the future is going to be. On the other hand, people who *do* take thinking about the future seriously, when they look at this stuff, they may actually get something of value out of it, using in it more serious scenarios of their own making, where it can be quite helpful. Various science fiction writers get invited to be the loose cannon at meetings of that sort, somebody who is crazy enough to jerk everybody's chain without turning the boat over. That is good and I am content not to be seriously trying to claim more for my fiction.

Q: I am thinking of the Balonium Factor.

Vinge: [Laughs.]

Q: Balonium is that substance or field effect which suspends the laws of the universe as needed for the plot. Doesn't any given science fiction contain something which is probably impossible? If Wells had known how to build a time machine, he wouldn't have written a story about it. He would have done so, and collected his Nobel Prize. What he was actually doing was *pretending* that someone had discovered a new scientific principle which made this possible. So, in a science fiction story, how much extrapolative realism is required, and how much balonium is desirable.

Vinge: I think your point that if you actually knew enough about the idea, you could do it now, is a fairly important reducto-ad-absurdum argument. It also may be one of the reasons for the explosive run-up in technology in the last three or four hundred years. That is, we have achieved this change in mindset, which was that if you can imagine something, that's the first big step in being able to do it, that imagined things can often be done. As soon as you have that, you have a real-world adaptation of the reducto-ad-absurdum that you just said.

In other words, you get this tumbling forward into the future because people realize that if they can think of it, they may be able to do it. Or they may not be able to do it. Or they may not be able to do it in this generation. It may take twenty or thirty years. In fact that principle of thinking of what may be possible and using that as the reason for going ahead and doing it is very powerful. My limited reading of the history of the atomic bomb espionage leads me to the conclusion that the Soviets did not actually get facts, engineering facts that were especially important to them. What they got were statements that, yes, this approach works. You can do it this way. That information by itself was enough to allow brilliant people to go ahead and do it.

There's balonium and balonium, obviously. There are stories that are patentable. But there is a spectrum of balonium. I think that it is unwise to say, ah, beyond this point the balonium is pure. [Laughs.] It is amazing how often you get something that *is* pure balonium, but the consequences are worked out and if you look at that story in the right way, you say, "Oh, Jesus Christ, those consequences could be caused by X," which has nothing to do with balonium, but has similar effects. I believe that a person could dig up a lot of examples of that sort of situation. The area of computers may be the most fertile, because there is a lot of stuff in the area of magic and the properties of magic, that you can easily simulate if you have a proper distributive system set up.

Q: The idea that what you can imagine might actually become possible most have itself only been possible when people became aware that the past was different from the present.

Vinge: Yes, that's *the* ur-version.

Q: But, for example, Lucian of Samosata could imagine going to the Moon. He made a joke out of it. He wrote something like a Douglas Adams story. But for thousands of years thereafter there was *no* feeling that merely because you could imagine going to the Moon that one day it would be possible. Maybe somewhere around the 18th century did this begin to change. People had imagined flying for a very long time, but only about then did more than a very few people realize that they actually could. There was Leonardo back around 1500, but he was way ahead of his time and pretty much alone.

Vinge: Franklin apparently wrote an essay in which he said that within about two hundred years or so, we would have prolongevity. If he actually said that, that's certainly a perfect example of what you're saying, a guy who says, "Yes, the world could be different."

I remember as a child that the thing that first attracted me to science fiction before I even had a name for it was that occasionally I would read a story or see a movie where the world was different at the end than it was at the at the beginning. Also, I didn't have wide horizons because I seven or eight years old, but in the early 1950s I found that it was very rare that I could find a story—I didn't have access to magazines—in which the world was different at the end of the story, unless it turned out to be a dream, and then it's really different because you wake up from a dream.

Then someone, probably one of my parents, pointed out, "You know, there's a name for that. It's called science fiction." I though, Oh, I think I know want to do.

Q: Even then, particularly in the movies, there was a lot of science fiction which put the world back in order at the end. Consider *Odd John,* for example. In most of the early superman stories, the superman has to die at the end. I suppose the most extreme example is C.S. Lewis's *Out of the Silent Planet,* where they fly to Mars and at the end decide never to do *that* again. It was even a change in science fiction that writers started to leave the world in a different condition at the end.

Vinge: Yes, and for a different audience, I think. I have to say that the perspective of my autobiographical example there is of a six or seven or eight year old. I obviously was not aware that there were stories that were quite open about the future, and also stories that closed themselves off. In some cases, I think, for purely artistic reasons, they closed themselves off. I really loved "Flowers for Algernon," and I don't think the ending is dictated by the sort of social background reasons that you were talking about with *Odd John,* but I think the ending was chosen for its emotional impact.

Q: Well it certainly closed things off for the individuals in the story. Certainly for the mouse.

Vinge: [Laughs.]

Q: So, when did you first realize that you wanted to write science fiction, and what did you do about it.

Vinge: I have very weak childhood memories, but I can remember that the first book I ever read was Heinlein's *Between Planets.* That is in the second grade. So my parents were getting worried. Was this kid ever going to learn to read? The first story I ever tried to write was "Rocketship X-54."

What year do you think that was written in?

Q: About the same time *Rocketship XLM* came out, which would make it about 1949.

Vinge: No, I would say 1954.

Q: Then the movie was a couple years old when you saw it.

Vinge: I doubt I ever saw the movie, because my parents wouldn't let me go *The War of the Worlds.*

Q: *Rocketship XLM* was a knockoff of *Destination Moon,* which the producers got into theaters first.

Vinge: Wow, I am ignorant of that. However, in looking at my little efforts over the years, they are pretty obviously derivative. I spent two years writing what turned out to be Campbell's "Forgetfulness." I am *so* glad I never sent that in to him. It was not deliberate. I was just immersed in the culture of science fiction, so I was just recapitulating all this stuff, which I should have known better than to do. But I was just not that aware of what was going on. I was never able to finish a story until the tenth or eleventh grade. Then I wrote that story which was probably very similar to "Forgetfulness." I don't mean it was plagiarized, but that thematically, and the point of the story turned out to be the same. This is not surprising because I was reading *Astounding* all the time that I would do that. So then in high school I was writing science fiction. A story I wrote the summer after I graduated from high school was the first story I ever wrote that sold. It was not the first story I ever sold.

Q: Maybe if you had submitted that story to John Campbell, he might have been flattered.

Vinge: If I had been John, I would have said, "Boy, this is really a derivative story. The guy obviously worked very hard on it, but I hope he can come up with more original ideas in the future."

Q: Where did you sell your first story? Was it to *Analog?*

Vinge: The first sale, which was the second story I wrote, which was "Apartness," sold to *New Worlds* when Michael Moorcock was the editor. So this was the one about the South African forced colonization of the Palmer Peninsula in Antarctica. Then the first story I ever wrote that sold was the monkey intelligence amplification story, and that was to John Campbell. That was really an ego-trip, because he rejected the story with this long letter about what was wrong with the story. Well, I recognized what *that* was. I dutifully revised the story, and I think he rejected it again with another long letter. I still am extraordinarily proud of that interchange and the fact that he eventually bought the story.

Q: Were you primarily an *Astounding* reader all this time, not a *Galaxy* reader or a *Fantasy & Science Fiction* reader?

Vinge: Eventually I became very, very enamored with *Galaxy* and with

F&SF, and I had very good collections of them, but as a child from 1956 or 1957, up to about the tenth grade, I would say my magazine reading was pretty much exclusively *Astounding*. Then I was reading, from the library, Heinlein juveniles and Asimov and Clarke, the canon of the time.

Q: One of the interesting things about the canon of that time was that for people who grew up in the '50s or the '60s, what we were reading, at first, was very likely science fiction that was written before we were born, not the contemporary stuff. Kids today don't seem to do that.

Vinge: Well the stuff I was reading in *Astounding* was of course contemporary.

Q: But before you got to the magazines, you would have been reading earlier Heinlein, or whatever. I figured this out for myself once. Of the first ten science fiction books I read, only one was first published within my lifetime. That was James Blish's *The Seedling Stars,* which came out when I was three. (1955).

Vinge: Most of what I was reading was not that old.

Q: I mean the Golden Age *Astounding* stuff from the early '40s.

Vinge: Yeah, but I was born in '44.

Q: But by the time you were old enough to read, say, *Beyond This Horizon—*

Vinge: *Beyond This Horizon* was before I was born, but that was not one of the early Heinleins that I read. The juveniles that he was writing were from 1949 or so onward up until 1961. So those were contemporary to me. It is true that I was originally rather casual about reading *Astounding*, until I realized that the stories that I really loved, the novels, most of them had come out in *Astounding* first. So in my case, your observation about pre-birth influence really goes back to about 1939 or 1940. In other words I did not and essentially never have discovered science fiction before about 1940. There are a few stories from 1939 that I really enjoyed, and there are a few stories from earlier that I discovered much later.

Q: Like Campbell's "Forgetfulness." That's from 1937.

Vinge: It may be that I never read that.

Q: You doubtless read it in *Adventures in Time and Space.*

Vinge: Yes, you're right. I did have access to that. But things like Kipling's A.B.C. stories. I am not aware of running into those until the late '90s and being thoroughly humbled. He actually had discovered the Heinlein "door dilated" principle and exploited it to the hilt, and this was, like, 1907. It's just so remarkable. So, except for the Healy and McComas *Adventures in Time and Space*—and there may be one Conklin book—

Q: *The Big Book of Science Fiction* from 1946, the other major breakthrough anthology.

Vinge: I did have access and did assiduously read those. That does nail it down. But I don't feel as strongly as you do that stuff before 1940 made that much of a difference. Even things like Stapledon's *The Star Maker* I didn't run into until I was late in high school.

Q: I was born in 1952, which makes me eight years younger than you, so if I was reading the same things you were, things like Heinlein's "Universe" and *The Martian Chronicles,* which all predated my lifetime.

Vinge: But I have another attempt to undermine the significance of what you are saying. You've heard the story about why 13 is the golden age of science fiction. The reason this is the science fiction is that, up to that age, you can read great science fiction as fast as you can read. After that, you can only read great science fiction as fast as it can be written. So, in the first thirteen years of your life, you exhaust the corpus of stuff that could influence you from the past. This is me another way of saying what you just said, that you noticed that when you were young you were influenced by things that were older. The reason was, you were reading great science fiction as last as you could lay your hands on it. Well, it's only written at a certain rate, so the chance that the great stuff would be close to when you are currently reading is small.

Q: Consider someone born in 1990. They are 19 years old now. They have a substantially larger body of science fiction to work off of. I can't think they could read it all by the time they're 13. If you hold that great science fiction started with Campbell's Golden Age in 1939, then, yes, maybe around 1950 you could master it all by the time you were 13. I don't think this is true anymore.

Vinge: That's a devastating argument. Do you have knowledge of people born in 1990? Was the stuff that informed their science-fictional life the work that was published four or five years before they were born?

Q: I did have an interesting conversation with that most exotic of creatures, a twenty-year-old, who was an intern for George Scithers for a while. To him, Philip K. Dick and Roger Zelazny were classic writers. Fritz Leiber, James Blish, and Edgar Pangborn, he had never heard of. Interestingly enough, he found Harlan Ellison badly dated and hard to read. Much of the stuff you and I think of as the classic core of science fiction he had never heard of and never read. I am thinking of an article by Judith Berman, called "Science Fiction without a Future." She argued that science fiction was losing the ability to appeal to youth, or to anybody but aging Baby Boomers. So, if the old science fiction could appeal to kids, who had not been born when it was written, and modern science fiction cannot, I wonder what has been lost.

Vinge: It looks to me that if you date the reading experience to the speaker's own birth date, the twenty-year-old you talked to had a profile of influence relative to his birth date similar to yours—or mine. That does undermine my comment. Did you read the introduction I wrote to *The Skylark of Space*?

Q: No.

Vinge: Highly recommended. It tries to explain the difference in quality in science fiction throughout the 20th century. I said some good things about *The Skylark of Space*. I also said some bad things. It is true, I think that the science fiction that so influenced us when we were young really does have a different value structure than the most popular science fiction that was written in the '70s and '80s and '90s. The quality of writing that a Literature person would call good writing has much more weight in those recent stories than it did in the stories that I grew up on. On the other hand, what the earlier authors were shooting for was entirely different, and in many cases they were one of the very first people that were writing about Idea X. If you're the very first person to write about Idea X, it's like the first guy who makes a fire. It doesn't matter that you don't know about chipping flint and making sparks. If you've made the fire at all, you get a lot of credit and you are blessed. And so it's conceivable that if you show your twenty-year-old friend this stuff that you and I liked so much, he would turn his nose up at it. He might say that it was just boringly written and old ideas, which probably is true. Science fiction tends to date sadly. That is my great regret about science fiction.

Q: I point out that the best of Wells hasn't dated at all. I would argue against this idea. Good writing is good writing, regardless of when it was done. It is a shock to read a literate science fiction story from the 1930s, for example, but go find, say, *To Walk the Night* by William Sloane. This is a science fiction novel which was good enough not to be published in the pulp magazines, but as a mainstream novel, by a real book publisher. Sloane could actually write. I think that what you were experiencing with *The Skylark of Space* was that the quality of writing in science fiction went down sharply in the early 20th century and probably bottomed out with Gernsback, so that what we call the Campbell Golden Age is really a period of recovery. Science fiction had at least reached the pulp level again. [Vinge is laughing.] Most of what was in the Gernsback published was sub-pulp. I argue as a critic that we should never excuse bad writing on the grounds that it is old-fashioned. So I think we have to separate out such matters as how literate the writer is—can he use words well—or whether he can describe characters that act like human beings from the science fiction content of the story. It's a different matter.

Vinge: Would you give somebody any gold stars for being the first person to write about a particular idea? Does that excuse them in any way for their not being able to write?

Q: I would say no. It just leaves the idea lying around for someone else to pick up. I note that H.G. Wells wrote about a lot of the major ideas first, but he wrote well, and it was decades before anyone else could even approach that level.

Vinge: I think that is a very persuasive line of reasoning. It saddens me because one of my pet theories has been that in a long-scale term—suppose you move into a new intellectual field. If you're moving into a new intellectual field, it is like wandering onto a beach where there are precious and semi-precious stones. It doesn't take any energy to pick them up. So, on one hand, at the beginning of such a period, you have a lot of brilliant ideas told by people who can't right very well. Then, late in the period, when the ideas have been picked over and picked over, you begin to get elaboration and really good writing, to the point where the ideas are polished up and they shine. That's great. Then very late in the period, you get into another not-so-attractive phase, where the good writing has also been done, the shining up of the emeralds has been done, and all you are doing is elaborating on the footnotes and putting little curlicues on the writing. In a way, that is a terminal phase that is almost as ugly as the initial squanderous grabbing of gems on the sea beach.

Q: Wells didn't squander his gems. At the very beginning, he had it all. Let me suggest, though, that what happened at least in American literature, is that mainstream literature began to equate "serious writing" with realism. Therefore the better writers became very uneasy about producing anything imaginative at all. Before long, fantastic fiction was pretty much relegated to pulp magazines *only.* Back in 1890, any respectable writer could produce a science fiction story, and it could be published in a major magazine. By about 1920, a new science fiction novel was more likely to be a serial in *Argosy,* something like *The Blind Spot* by Hall and Flint, and it was ghastly. But at least the *Argosy* writers still knew what narrative was. Then you get to the Gernsback *Amazing* and even that has been lost, and all that's left is a turgid lecture tour, with footnotes and diagrams, something like *Ralph 124C41+.* Only very slowly did the science fiction field rediscover narrative technique, and only slowly has the mainstream rediscovered imaginative fiction.

Vinge: Embedding this in the technological progress I see around us, I think moving forward we could actually encounter something novel. That is, suppose it is true that the technological singularity is going to happen. That means that in the early years of the post-humans, we will have something that we haven't had in the last 30,000 years, which is the analog of the first short story and the first traveling-salesman joke. So I think that the adventures of the first post-human artists will be very interesting.

I am not disputing the analysis you made of the 20th century, but this does not fit that. Whether my original has any validity or not, it does fit that image. The early post-humans will be like the early humans in that almost anything their artists do will be done for the first time. So that would be a great time to be a post-human, to watch that process.

Q: Would they have any use for human art?

Vinge: This is purely referential within their domain. You'd have to be one of them, presumably, to get the point. It would be new forms of art. It might be written down, but it would very likely not make any sense to us.

Q: Would they still read *Hamlet*?

Vinge: They might read *Hamlet,* but you might find it embedded in something that takes a normal human a hundred years to live.

Q: So if science fiction is reaching this decadent stage you are describing, and the only way out is for us to evolve into something more than human, what is the present-day science fiction writer to do?

Vinge: It is also interesting that this is one of the first art forms that has the possibility of getting itself out of such a box. I think that, although in keeping with the general problems of a transition as big as the Singularity or as profound or as unintelligible a change as the Singularity, it's actually an interesting comment on the future of art—art in a broad sense. I gave a talk at ICFA last year. In the talk I was making this sort of adumbration point—things are getting more and more elaborate—that we have access to probably all the written literature that we're going to have access to from the past, probably all the written literature about humor that we will ever have access to from the past, and so the question of what to do next really needs something like the Singularity. I am sure there are people who think we could continue to trundle forward with all this knowledge and our present level of intelligence and still have great art for the next two or three hundred years. I find this a mind-numbingly depressing thought.

Q: What are you doing in the immediate future, other than planning to evolve into something else?

Vinge: [Laughs.]

Q: Surely for the short-term, you have to write books in the same manner as before.

Vinge: Quite so. I have no transcendental claims to make about my own writing. I am trundling forward with a sequel to *A Fire upon the Deep* entitled *The Children of the Sky.* It's going pretty well. It's about the Tines and set on the Tines' world. It gives me an opportunity to talk indirectly to talk about all sorts of issues about thought. The Tine creatures, these small pack-minds, four or five animals make a person enable me to play out and specifically instantiate all the Freudian things about conscious and subconscious and super-consciousness and so on. I can actually point to the animal and say, "That's the speech center. If we take him out, we will do this to the creature." It's a fun playground for that. It is also, I hope, a story that will appeal to the presently existing readership, since the superhuman readership isn't around yet. I certainly do not qualify as anything except an ordinary human as a writer.

Q: Thanks, Vernor.

PAOLO BACIGALUPI

Paolo Baciaglupi seems to have stormed the science fiction field in the first few years of this century. In 2005 he had a Hugo Award nomination for "The People of Sand and Slag." In 2006. In 2006 he won the Sturgeon Award for "The Calorie Man." His first novel, *The Windup Girl* (2009), collected a jaw-dropping *six* awards: Hugo, Nebula, John W. Campbell Memorial Award, Locus Award, the Compton Crook Award, and the Seiun Award (for best novel translated into Japanese). There were other award nominations before that and there have been some since, including a Nebula Award nomination for Best Novella for *The Alchemist* in 2011, but it was safe to say that with *The Windup Girl* he definitely had the attention of the science fiction field. His career has not gone predictably since. He has published a humorous book for young adults, *Zombie Baseball Beatdown* (2013), a thriller for adults about climate-change denial, *The Doubt Factory* (2014), and two other novels for younger readers, *Ship Breaker* (2010) and *The Drowned Cities* (2012). His first book was a collection *Pump Six and Other Stories* (2008). *The Water Knife* is forthcoming.

For the curious, he informs us, "My last name is pronounced Batch-i-gah-loo-pee."

✦✧✦

Q: Could you give me some idea of who you are, what your background is, your education, etc? What were you doing before you were writing for publication?

Bacigalupi: My background: In college, I majored in East Asian Studies with a focus on Chinese language. I later moved to China to work in business. After that, I turned to internet development, and worked as a web developer for many years. Eventually I ended up as the Online Editor at *High Country News*, a news magazine that focuses on the environment and social dynamics of the American West—public lands, natural resources, communities, and science issues, primarily.

Q: What made you suddenly turn to science fiction? You did indeed seem to come out of nowhere a few years ago and grab center stage in science fiction. Is this a matter of being an overnight success after years of effort?

Bacigalupi: I read science fiction growing up. My father and grandfather were both readers of science fiction, so when I started writing, it seemed natural that those would be the kinds of stories I would try to tell. I had one early success, "Pocketful of Dharma" which was the first short story I ever wrote, but then I spent a long time wandering in the wilderness, writing novels and short stories that didn't sell. By the time I genuinely started to break in, and started selling stories consistently, I think I'd been writing for about ten years and had four failed novels under my belt.

Q: So now you seem an overnight success and at the Cutting Edge of science fiction. Cyberpunk has long since been assimilated. Steampunk seems to be over. So, what is the cutting edge of science fiction and do you feel you're at the edge of it?

Bacigalupi: Cutting edge... I'm not even sure I know what that is. I just want to reach readers and tell stories that feel relevant to me, and I want to make the questions and ideas and worries that engage me feel relevant to others. Science fiction has tools that allow me to do that. But it's not about being cutting edge. It's about telling stories that help us understand our present moment better. Sometimes, it turns out that science fiction isn't even the tool you want, so the most cutting edge thing to do is to not write science fiction at all. When I wanted to write about how our understanding of science is manipulated by corporations, I wrote *The Doubt Factory* as a contemporary novel, because a science-fictional treatment would have blunted the horror of what respected, publicly-traded, companies legally get away with every day. Science fiction is just a tool. It's a powerful tool, and I love it, but it's not the only tool. And the idea that science fiction stories somehow should be ahead of x, or new in way y, or that z is so dead... it just doesn't resonate for me. It's like trying to be the coolest kid in science fiction school. I just want to write stories that start conversations about the world we live in. That's more than hard enough.

Q: What *should* SF writers be writing about, which they haven't been?

Bacigalupi: The problem with telling writers what they *should* write about is that it assumes it's any of my business. I set my own agendas for my stories, whether I'm writing zombie books for kids, or writing public relations caper novels for teens, or writing climate change thrillers for adults. One of the joys of writing is that you get to tell the stories you care about, in whatever way you desire. Some people wish I wouldn't write a book like *Zombie Baseball Beatdown* because they don't see that as serious work. Alas. They get no vote in my dictatorship of the page. People can accept what you choose to write about, or reject it, but they don't get to decide what you type when you sit down to sweat out a story. I worked for a long time to get rid of the nanny voices of what I *should* do as a writer, and I sometimes still have to fight against them, so I'm probably not going to jump up to add my own nanny voice to the chorus. The most I would say is that I hope that writers will write stories they care about, and that they'll also find some joy in the process, because really, writing generally doesn't pay well enough to justify it being a miserable experience. Come to think of it, writing also doesn't generally pay well enough to bother listening to what other people think you should write.

Q: Of course all writers secretly yearn for and fear that Faustian bargain of the publisher with the checkbook, who says, "I will give you a huge pile of money to write another book like ____" or even "Zombie Nazi Surfer Cheerleader novels are all the rage now, so that is what we want from you next." So what happens when a sufficient amount of money is waved at your "dictatorship of the page"?

Bacigalupi: If I was hungry enough, I'd probably write anything. But I think that the goal for a writer is to find win-win scenarios where you get paid *and* get to write stories that you care about. That's been my goal for a while now, and so far it seems to be working. I don't think that being a published author automatically has to be a zero-sum calculation where you're either "selling out" or staying "true" to your art. I think if you're sufficiently skilled and clever, there are options where you get to feed yourself and feed your soul.

Q: A theme I am noticing in some of your fiction seems to be that the human race *will* short-sightedly foul the planet beyond repair, but adapt to the result, as in the story "The People of Sand and Slag" in *Pump Six and Other Stories*, in which the characters seem to thrive on toxic materials and the last real dog in the world (and by implication all natural biological creatures) seems at an evolutionary dead end. I see this in *The Windup Girl* too. People don't learn better, but they learn. Do you think so? Do we face a future of learning to live up to our necks in our own waste?

Bacigalupi: I think Ted Chiang said that almost all science fiction is inherently optimistic simply because of the somewhat unfounded assumption that there will be any people at all left in the future. Science fiction carries that false narrative construct in its DNA, thanks to its need for some sort of protagonist to drive a story along. I mean, you could write a story about a global warming Earth that burns like Venus and where all life has been scoured away, but it probably isn't going to be a novel. For myself, I think that we'll get the future that we invest in today, but I'd also say that just because science fiction needs people to form narrative, the ecosystems that we're currently undermining don't give a damn about whether there's a story to tell or not.

Q: Well there have been novels in which the world ends, everything from James Morrow's *This Is the Way the World Ends*, all the way back to Mary Shelley's *The Last Man* in 1826. The protagonist has to protag, certainly, but he doesn't have to triumph. So if SF seems to be inherently optimistic, is that really the nature of the form or something that is market-driven?

Bacigalupi: It's interesting that you mention the question of markets, because I do think that an author who simply wanted to have a career writing about the world ending again, and again, and again... probably wouldn't have a very long career. I remember speaking with an agent years ago, and one of the comments he made about the difference between being a short story writer versus a novelist was that a novelist ideally wants a reader to want to pick up another book by the author—rather than give up on that novelist and go find other others to read. There's potentially a career limit to how many times you can devastate readers with protagonist-failure and world-ending before you no longer have anything except the most self-flagellating or death-fetishizing readership.

Or maybe that's my bias.

As far as separating SF's literary nature from its market-driven nature... intellectually, sure, we can separate the two and observe that indeed, any kind of novel can be written. But the reality is that we only recognize and talk about those novels that are published and widely read, and it turns out that those stories largely adhere to structural conventions like having living people in them, and having at least a handful of the characters we care about survive. So, even though SF, just like every other genre of literature, can affect any experiment it likes ... if no one wants to read it, does it really matter?

Q: So, is SF supposed to predict possible futures or _prevent_ them? What about its didactic or propagandistic nature?

Bacigalupi: When I'm feeling idealistic, I hope that SF can in some way influence where we're headed. For me, that informs a lot of the reasons that I write, and helps me choose my themes and topics. I think that we're headed for interesting times, so it seems worthwhile to write about those, and try to get a grip on them in some way.

As far as didacticism or propaganda ... is it necessarily bad for a writer to have an opinion, and even to reveal that opinion on the page?

Q: I see what you mean. I met a "retired" writer once who explained that his last couple novels were so gloomy he didn't see the point in adding to the general depression of the world, so he did not publish them. But this does get back to the question of didacticism. _The Windup Girl_ for instance certainly takes place in an undesirable future, but is the point of the book more to warn people about how the future might turn out, or to tell a story in which people adapt to that future?

Bacigalupi: I think I leave that to the reader to decide. There's not much point in my stating my own opinion about what the reader should take away from the story. The story does what it does.

Q: Sure an author has an opinion and it inevitably ends up on the page, but we all know horrible examples of how the author's preachiness or just self-indulgence ruined his fiction. The most obvious examples are the later Wells and the later Heinlein. So how do you strike the right balance?

Bacigalupi: I think that the key probably lies in how deeply rendered the characters and their world is. I think one of the ways you can avoid didacticism in science fiction is to simply make the world define your argument—then the characters can proceed with almost any plot they like, while the world looms in the background, defining their lives. The characters, then, don't need to make moral points of the story. They don't need to preach. They don't need to learn a lesson. They don't need to be on the "right" side or the "wrong" side. I think where authors often get into trouble is where protagonists represent the author's "good" values and the antagonists represent the "bad" values. They become obvious marionettes. Interestingly, I've been flirting with some of those exact problems in *The Doubt Factory*. Sometimes, you just want to wear your values on your sleeve and stop trying to be tricksy about your thinking. Sometimes a good romp over obvious bad guys is just good entertaining fun, and I think if you've got a sympathetic reader, they'll still enjoy the ride.

I think the other place where an author can fail, though, is when you stop thinking about your reader at all. And I think that's very much what happened with later Heinlein. I don't think he was struggling to tell stories for others anymore, not really. I think he was at a point in his life where he'd realized that he didn't need to try very hard. Sometimes, I think that writing is a process of dreaming deeply inside a world. If you aren't immersing yourself in that dream, risking, and testing, you don't get a good story. But the problem is that the dreaming process is hard work. It's more than just setting up the mechanics of a story, or illustrating a concept, there's something emotionally risky about being down deep inside your fiction, and I think when we authors find ways to remove ourselves from that deep dream state, that's when stories start to ring false.

Q: Or is there an opposite of didacticism? Have you had instances where you find that, logically, for story purposes, your characters begin to hold opinions or values that you *don't* share?

Bacigalupi: Again, I think if you let the world make your argument, then the characters can simply exist and do whatever they're inclined to do.

Q: So, what are you working on now?

Bacigalupi: *The Doubt Factory* has just come out. Next spring, *The Water Knife* will launch, it's going to focus on a climate change-driven water war between Phoenix and Las Vegas. After that, I'm working on the third book in the Ship Breaker series. I've also got a few short story projects in the works, including a follow-up fantasy novella to "The Alchemist" in the same shared world that I did a few years ago with Tobias Buckell. After that, I'm not entirely sure. I'm sure something will present itself.

Q: Thanks, Paolo.

PAUL DI FILLIPPO

Not much to say about the when and where of this interview. We did it at a Boskone, sitting in a hotel room in Boston in February. Paul Di Filippo is a regular there, and a celebrity. He is probably best known for a collection of novellas, *The Steampunk Trilogy* (1995) if you have to point to just one thing. He is a hugely prolific author of short fiction. Other collections include *Ribofunk, Strange Paisleys, Strange Trades, Little Doors,* and several more, most recently *Wikiworld* (2013). His novels include *Fuzzy Dice, Cosmocopia, Roadside Bodhisattva,* and *A Princes of the Linear Jungle.* He reviews regularly for *Asimov's SF.* He's one of the very obvious go-to guys if you want to know about the pulse of contemporary SF. So I went.

←*—·—·—*→

Q: Let's start in the middle... I wonder if you have any comments on why we're having a second big wave of Steampunk just now. It's *so* 20th century, something that happened in the late '80s, but now it's happening *again.*

PDF: It's funny, Darrell, that you would bring that up, because that was the topic of a panel, last night, here at Boskone. I think it's an extra-literary phenomenon. There's that aspect of it, where it's become a cultural lifestyle thing that has summoned a whole flock of people. I think it's almost the reverse order. They enter the lifestyle and then start looking for the fiction that originally sparked that lifestyle. So I think that a lot of it is that people feel that there is an audience out there of people who are attracted to the superficial trappings, the costumes and gadgets of Steampunk. Maybe writers feel that they can wean those people off that, or transfer their affections from all those tchotchkes to the literary aspect of it.

But I think the whole genre does answer a certain need that we feel here in the 21st century, where we are distant from our shiny gadgets. They're impenetrable. Nobody knows what goes on inside an I-pod. It's all a mystery. But you know what goes on inside a steam engine or a brass telescope. So I think that's part of the appeal of the genre, that the characters within the Steampunk stories can be very hands-on and proactive with their technology and not just at the mercy of it.

Q: And here I thought it was sort of like Goth, only they dress better.

PDF: Well, there is that. [Laughs.] There is the style element. You don't have to wear so much black eyeliner. It's probably better for the health of your eyes. But, on the panel last night, we had a very neat crowd. We had Lev Grossman, Michael Swanwick, myself and Everett Soares, who has done a Steampunk comic. Michael Swanwick made a very important point about Steampunk, which I think ties in to what may be seen of the malaise of science fiction, which is that Steampunk is generally *fun*. We've heard in recent years that science fiction has concentrated too heavily on dystopias, and there are no more bright and shiny futures to allure readers, and Steampunk offers that, even if it's dystopian Steampunk like *The Difference Engine*. You note that *The Difference Engine* is in a minority in terms of the kind of Steampunk that it is. I think Steampunk offers some of the old allure that Science Fiction in the Golden Age used to have, a future or an alternate reality that you would actually want to live in.

Q: It's more of an alternate past than a future.

PDF: Right, an alternate past. But it's kind of hard to say with some Steampunk. I am thinking of Stephen Hunt, who did two books, *The Kingdom Beneath the Waves*, and there was a sequel out recently. In those books you're not quite sure if it's the past or an alternate continuum or our future. I think, yeah, generally Steampunk seems to be a retro thing, where it takes place in Victorian England or even further back. It's not the future, but it is an alternate timestream that possesses a certain romantic allure that readers find attractive.

Q: What seems to have happened here is an interesting interplay between the culture and the literature, as if the original literature created the culture and now the culture is re-stimulating the literature.

PDF: Exactly. That's what I was trying to say. There's a feedback loop, because it began as a literary movement, and then it was adopted by people who felt they could use it almost in the way the SCA people use medieval times as a weekend recreational thing, or even a 24-7 recreational thing if they incorporate it that fully into their lives. So that built up and then the authors, seeing that phenomenon, realized how they could utilize some of the aspects of it to ramp up their own fiction, or write their own fiction differently. So I think there is a very interesting feedback loop between the people who are the hardcore fans and writers and the people who are on the edges of it as a lifestyle.

Q: We haven't really seen second-wave Cyberpunk. Or have we? The literature had an enormous impact on the culture, but I am not sure it fed back into the literature.

PDF: Right, very accurate. There were generations of cyberpunk writers, as we know. There were people who came after Gibson and Sterling. I am thinking of someone like Simon Ings, a British writer who did some great stuff. He was chronologically younger than us old Baby Boomers, like in his thirties where we were in our forties when we were writing Cyberpunk. So there were writers who came after that Gibson/Sterling wave, but they didn't really expand it or take it in vastly new directions. They amped up bits and pieces of it, but you could see that it was basically a straight line continuation of what the first generation Cyberpunks had done. So, yeah, it hasn't really mutated into anything that is like the mutant off-spring of Cyberpunk. I don't think we've seen that yet.

Q: Maybe the difference was that Cyberpunk was really trying to address the future and even the real world of present, whereas most Steampunk takes place in a never-neverland.

PDF: We talked on the panel about the escapist nature of Steampunk, whether it was good escapism to focus on the Victorian era instead of our current problems, whether that was good, because it gave us a perspective on the roots of our current culture, or whether it was just bad escapism like hiding your head in the sand. Certainly there is that didactic, forward-looking impulse that we found in Cyberpunk is, I think, missing from Steampunk, to a large degree.

Q: Doesn't any writer have to develop beyond these movements anyway? Surely the most superficial of all literary values, not to mention careers strategies, involves getting on someone else's bandwagon. It must wear thin rather quickly.

PDF: I was affiliated with the Cyberpunks, to whatever degree. I wrote The Steampunk Trilogy, so I dipped my toe into that movement. I've even done some stuff which could be classified as New Weird, which of course is a fairly recent phenomenon and quasi-movement, although it is leader-less and diffuse. Personally, I don't like to follow any one pattern of writing or school of writing for very long before lighting out for the territories and looking out for something new; but I think it can hurt a writer's career to be too much identified with one movement. Eventually Steampunk is going to jump the shark and seem passé, and then what do you do if that's all you're known for writing? You can't really conceive of writing anything else.

Q: I noticed that after Gibson and Sterling and so on, there were indeed a lot of little Gibsons and imitation Gibsons, and most of those have faded away, whereas Gibson and Sterling themselves are doing just fine. I will venture a prediction, that you may agree with or not, that fairly soon the New Weird movement is going to crash and burn, but when it's all over Jeff Vandermeer and China Mieville and people like that will be doing as well as ever. It's their imitators who will be in trouble.

PDF: Consider M. John Harrison, a name highly central to the whole New Weird phenomenon. His career is just so vast. He started in the New Wave and he wrote a number of different types of books down the past several decades and his involvement with the New Weird, I think, indicates that he is one of the writers who will persevere beyond this current craze for any kind of surreal, slipstream type literature. So, yeah, I do think those writers you identified, Jeff and China, will have long careers after this whole thing has faded.

Q: Are these really movements, or publicity stunts? I become suspicious when someone declares a "movement." Don't you?

PDF: A think a true literary movement has to have an organic genesis and arise out of a vision, either an individual vision or a shared vision, of what could be in the literature, how the literature could do things differently. I don't think either of us would deny that there have been genuine literary movements. People of like mind found themselves banding together, thinking along the same lines. They work out a certain synergy. You could relate the output of certain writers to each other and against each other. So the history of literature is full of genuine organic movements that have sprung up. Whether some of these that we are seeing today are more factitious, more contrived, I think you have to gauge each one and study the history of it. Use your hype meter too, your bullshit meter and see if it seems to be just dedicated to furthering careers or if it actually represents a genuine response to a deficiency in the literature.

Q: I wonder if charting movements isn't a job for the critics, and the writers should just leave it alone and go on writing.

PDF: I would have to agree. A lot of these things happen in retrospect. People look backwards or they just freeze a moment in time and try to analyze what's happening amongst a variety of writers who might not even be necessarily connected personally or on any kind of actual working level. So, yes, critics obviously play a huge part. Editors also. Look at how instrumental Ellen Datlow and Gardner Dozois were in the Cyberpunk movement. They played as big a role as some of the writers did.

Q: If you were to start a movement now…what in contemporary science fiction dissatisfies you, which you as a writer would like to address?

PDF: I did try to start a movement in a very jokey way, back in the heyday of Cyberpunk. I called it Ribofunk. That word, I invented. I took the *ribo* prefix from ribosomes, from biology, and I took *funk* as the music, as opposed to punk. I jammed them together and created a neologism, and I wrote a little mock manifesto to go along with it, and then, when I was done being satirical, I looked at what I had created and I said, "You know, this actually has some potential," and I wrote a number of stories according to my own imaginary dictates, and they were eventually collected in a volume called *Ribofunk*. Now, if you Google it, you get ten thousand hits for the word I created. A lot of them are duplicates. They're just references to my book on eBay or whatever, but still it's kind of awesome to think that I created that neologism and it's out there. There's another term, "Biopunk."

If you type that into Wikipedia, it says, "Another term for this is ribofunk." So my term has now become a subsidiary to Biopunk, which I think has more actual precedence in the critical terminology.

So at one point I did address what I thought was a defect in the Cyberpunk movement, that it was all about hardware. It was about silicon and turning yourself into software, and I thought that we were neglecting the organic side of our heritage, and the bodily side, and bio-engineering. I felt we should concentrate more on that.

I think that since then there have been any number of responses to that, whether it was in direct response to me or just other people seeing the same perceived defects. So if you go to that Biopunk entry on Wikipedia, you will see a whole list of great books, like maybe Kathleen Goonan's *Queen City Jazz* series. Rudy Rucker has dealt a little with the topic, as has Peter Watts. So that is something I think still needs to be explored. To me the reason that ten thousand years of literature is still intelligible to us is because basically we are the same human organism that we were, with the same mental capacities and physical capacities. We haven't grown four arms or we haven't added extra lobes to our brains. A lot of superficial things have changed, but our brain/body system has remained consistent for that whole period of time, and so we can mentally and emotionally grok Shakespeare and Plato and anybody else as far back as you want to go.

But the prospect of bio-engineering the human organism, that to me is something that needs to be explored more in science fiction. When you change the baseline human, you put an iron curtain down between the new organism and our past, our entire history.

Q: The term "Biopunk" to me suggests outlaw, underground, sleazy uses of biotechnology.

PDF: Yes, exactly.

Q: Rather like Larry Niven's "Organlegger."

PDF: Yes, that's a very good precedent for that type of literature. If you look at something like *Star Trek*. I don't know, canonically, how far in the future *Star Trek* is supposed to happen, how their Star Dates relate to our Christian numbering—

Q: About A.D. 2300, something like that.

PDF: So it's like 300 years in the future, and there have been no changes in the human baseline condition. They haven't amped up their reflexes—

Q: Yes, they have, but it's illegal. There are a couple episodes about that. At one point on *Deep Space 9* there was a big scandal because Dr. Bashir was discovered to be a bio-enhanced person.

PDF: So I am not up on the full canon then and I am deficient in a lot of the spin-off viewing. But when you have a space opera set hundreds of years in the future and you don't acknowledge these changes, it seems unconvincing. Even now, with smart drugs, people are using—what is it?—Provigil, the anti-sleep drug. They're using it to stay awake extra periods and hone their reflexes and so on. There has just got to be more of that depicted in the future. You can't just have these starships populated with regular 21st century people. I just don't think it's going to be a reality.

Q: If you say the word "Singularity" and point a microphone at Vernor Vinge, you're set for the next two hours, but we are approaching that topic. If people are going to be all that much different in the future, how do we write about them comprehensibly?

PDF: You're right. The Singularity is a huge practical and intellectual stumbling block, because if you endorse the notion that there is an iron curtain waiting up ahead of us, beyond which we cannot see, then that effectively limits your story space and your potential for examining the future of mankind. There have been a lot of solutions, each one more or less contrived or awkward. One solution that Vinge himself proposed was different shells within the universe where the Singularity was not permitted to happen within a certain shell of the cosmos. So he could tell stories within that shell because they were within that physical domain, because they were the old, familiar stories that we knew, just within futuristic settings. Then as you moved up his kind of cosmic ladder, things became more and more incomprehensible. So that was one way that he found around it.

I've set stories on an Earth that is more or left deserted, and it's filled with the people who got left behind. The Singularity, as we know, is often called "The Rapture of the Nerds," so this is a kind of post-Rapture story where people are left behind. They weren't subsumed in the Singularity, so you get their story. But once again, as I say, these solutions are kludgy and awkward and they don't really address the problem. It's like showing a human genius, or a human artist of superb talent. When you depict them, you have to depict their stream-of-consciousness or the works they produce. You have to give some sample of it and convince the reader that this really is a genius or an artist of superior powers. How do you do that, because you can only write up to the peak of your own artistry? It's hard to depict a genius on the page. You can show everybody worshipping him, but at some point you have to adduce what he has done to actually be worthy of that. That's the same thing with the Singularity. You've got this entity out there. How do you depict it or make people believe that it's actually superhuman?

Q: I think it's the same way you depict gods or demi-gods or the like. I can't go into great detail here, but one reason I have always been dissatisfied with *Stranger in a Strange Land* is that you have to take everybody's word for it that Valentine Michael Smith is all that special. You can't *feel* it.

PDF: That's the problem I'm talking about.

Q: Now, Gore Vidal in his novel *Messiah* solved this problem very quickly. He wrote about the creation of a new religion, but got his messiah out of the picture quickly, then wrote about all the quarrelling disciples. So what you do is write about the other people reacting to the genius, rather than about the genius.

PDF: The thing about the Singularity is not to say that it is the only feature of the future universe. Say it comes into being locally, on a planet or in space, or whatever. There is still the rest of the universe to write about. The Singularity can be something like a black hole. It can be something that every other character, the rest of the universe has not ramped up to yet, so they are viewing the Singularity from the outside. Plotwise it can figure either negligibly or to a large degree, depending on your needs. So the Singularity can almost function like an astronomical black hole. It's there. You can't get at it. It has an effect if you get too close, but you can tell stories around it, at a distance.

Q: To bring up *Star Trek* again for a second, aren't the Borg the people who have passed the Singularity?

PDF: There you go. [Laughs.] The Borg are probably not the model we want for ourselves. Or you could always deny it. The Singularity is just a theory. It's not a law of the universe. It's a theory with some justification behind it, or some line of logic behind it, so you could always deny the Singularity and say it's not possible and that human consciousness or machine consciousness will never reach these dimensions so that they become unfathomable.

Q: Or it may that once it happens everyone will take it for granted. One of the great science fiction stories on this subject is "The Shape of Things That Came" by Richard Deming. Have you ever read it?

PDF: No.

Q: Most of us when we were kids got a two-volume Groff Conklin set from the Book Club, *A Treasury of Great Science Fiction.*

PDF: Yeah, of course.

Q: In that there is a quite short story, first published in 1951, about a man from Victorian times who invents the "time-nightshirt" and goes to see the future, then returns to his own time and writes about 1950, where they have cars and airplanes and telephones, and so on. His editor back in 1890 says, "This is very imaginative and wonderful extrapolation, but what I can't believe is that anyone would ever take these things *for granted.*"

PDF: That's wonderful. We are living, as a lot of people have noticed, in a science fiction world. It has crept up on us. It hasn't assumed the full dimensions of jet packs and food pills and so on that was present in a lot of Golden Age SF, but like the frog in boiling water, we have succumbed to this future without quite realizing that it is a science-fictional future. Try explaining much of what we take for granted to someone from, even, 1960.

I think they would just look at you as if you were insane. It's an ongoing process. We are inventing the future day-by-day, and assimilating it almost as quickly, I think.

Q: You ask a sixteen-year-old to explain to someone who is fifty what that little thing they're operating with their thumbs is.

PDF: This brings up another whole point, which Charles Stross has brought up on his blog. He did a post about the impossibility or near-impossibility of writing short-term future SF. That is what he is currently working on. He is working on a sequel to his novel *Halting State*. That was near-future SF. It took place like, whenever—five, seven, twelve years into the future, and involved theft of virtual currency. That was the McGuffin at the heart of it. There was this gaming world like Second Life and someone broke into the virtual bank and stole the virtual money. The straight cops who had no idea what this was all about and were just baffled. Is this a real crime? Can we prosecute? How do we go about solving it? So within months of the publication of *Halting State,* that actually happened. There have been several robberies of virtual banks. So Charles Stross said, "Well, my novel was outmoded six months after it came out. Now I've got to write the sequel, and I am just stumped, because two weeks later I am still in the middle of the novel and the thing put in chapter one has come true." So he had an interesting post about this, which you can easily find if you go to his blog, claiming that the pace of change is accelerating so fast that it makes it very hard for the SF writer who wants to deal realistically with current trends. It is impossible to stay abreast of it, given the year-long cycle of manuscript to published book.

Q: This is not a new thing. Some books just ride past that sort of problem without any difficulty. The example that comes to my mind is Tom Disch's *Camp Concentration* which is set in 1975. It was published first serially in 1967, but certainly by the time most people had read the book it was "obsolete." I don't think this slowed it down much.

PDF: Well great art will hold up, for sheer narrative value. That is why we still can read with pleasure the Golden Age SF which *has* been superseded. We read about some hypothetical Moon-landing, and we know it doesn't match reality, but we still enjoy the story for the sake of story. Think of the Hal Clement story, "Dust," in which the moondust sticks to the visor. We know that didn't happen, but it's still a suspenseful and intriguing puzzle story.

So, yeah, great works of art still give us pleasure on many levels even if their predictive elements have fallen short. Charlie may be *angst*ing a little too much, because, as you say, it has always been an issue. I always remember that great anecdote about the Asimov story, in which the reason that mankind could never get to the top of Mt. Everest is that there was an alien base on top. The story saw print in a magazine the same month that Hilary reached the summit of Mt. Everest, so Isaac said that he was very disappointed that his timing had been off on that one.

Q: It could have been worse. It could have been printed a month later. But today we'd say it was all part of a conspiracy cover-up. But we approach a serious subject here. All this stuff about the Singularity and the inability to cope with the near future is turning into a consensus in science fiction, and if we have a consensus about what the future is going to be like, it might be science fiction that comes grinding to a halt. So maybe the task of the writer is to subvert the whole thing.

PDF: That's a very important point, Darrell. Any consensus should be distrusted. It's like that bumper-sticker, SUBVERT THE DOMINANT PARADIGM. What was that French critic, who back in the '60s and '70s argued that science fiction was wasting its energies writing all these separate futures and we needed to get together and establish a consensus future? It was Jacques Sadoul…?

Q: Someone brought up that idea in American fandom in the 1940s and it was very sensibly laughed down.

PDF: Yeah, so that notion that science fiction could be made much stronger and do a better job if it narrowed its options seems to me insane. What you want is to let a thousand flowers bloom. That's the whole point of science fiction, that the alternatives that it can propose are endless and boundless, so you get that hybrid vigor as the different scenarios interfertilize. If you narrow it down to where, yes, the Singularity *must* occur and I have to acknowledge it in my fiction, you're right. It's a lack of diversity of possibility.

Q: Given the infinite number of possibilities, why do so many science fiction writers of late seem to be shying away from the future? Some have suggested that the whole alternate history thing is simply a way to avoid writing about the future.

PDF: That is a major defect in the current marketplace, or the marketplace of ideas, maybe. The old style—let's use Heinlein as the main exponent of it—that old Heinlein style of SF has disappeared. I think writers succumb to despair and they are absorbing the cultural malaise that we're in, and that should not be their job, I think that especially in science fiction we need to be a counterforce to counterbalance the gloom and doom and cultural malaise that's out there. But you know what it is…. There is probably a term for this in philosophy, or in physics for all I know. This has always struck me. The universe has a very narrow set of conditions for most things to go right, whereas the conditions for things to go wrong are almost infinite. If you have a teacup, there is basically only one way to keep it safe on the shelf. There are a million ways for it to get broken. That unfortunately is the way the universe is set up. I often think about the multiplier effect of this too. You take that fellow who violated airport terminal security in New York. It was the young Asian man who wanted to say goodbye to his girlfriend, and so he ducked under the security rope. Now his little action of ducking under that security rope shut down the terminal. It has a multi-million-dollar consequence, and it impacted the lives of literally thousands of people. What simple action could you or I take which would have a *beneficial* effect of that nature? How could we duck under a rope and instantly add millions of dollars to the Gross National Product and benefit the lives of thousands of people? It's just not possible. The universe is a perverse entity where simple actions can cause tremendous damage, but the same simple actions generally cannot cause tremendous benefit.

This is a long, round-about way of saying that it is always easier to envision the gloom-and-doom scenario when you are sitting down to write the story than it is to envision the positive one. I think that is a natural human failing which explains why dystopias are easier to write.

Q: If you could figure out, even satirically, what that beneficial action would be, you'd have a great story.

PDF: There's one little story that I think about. It's a Mack Reynolds story called "Depression or Bust." [Published in *Analog* August 1967—DS]. I think of it in the current economic conditions too, because it's very relevant. We follow Joe Q. Public. He's coming home from his job. He looks at a display of televisions in the store, and he says, "My television is on the way out. I'd like to buy a new one, but I didn't get that raise, so I'm not going to buy the television." Then it cuts from him to the store owner, who says, "Gee, I didn't sell twelve televisions this month. I only sold eight. I've got to lay off a worker." Then Mack Reynolds builds this cascade where, by the time it is done, the economy is in shambles. There's a world-wide depression. So all the scientists and politicians get together and say, "What the hell caused this depression? We were humming along great." That track it back to the man who didn't buy the TV. They go to his house. They give him $200 and say, "Go buy yourself a new TV." Then it cascades in the reverse direction and all of the sudden the global economy is humming again. So, yeah, you wonder, are there hidden *tai chi* pressure points in the world. You're right, it would be a wonderful story, and it might be more fantasy than science fiction, though you could put a science-fictional spin on it, where someone discovers psychohistory only it's not psychohistory. You'd have to come up with some great scientific term for it. But someone discovers the pressure points of the universe. It you can touch it just right, something great happens.

Q: You write it.

PDF: I think I will. You've inspired me.

Q: I guess we should talk about what you are writing now or about to publish.

PDF: I have two books coming out from PS Publishing, Pete Crowther's wonderful UK small press. They're coming out this year. The first one is called *Roadside Bodhisattva,* and it's a totally mimetic, naturalistic novel. I am very proud to have him publish it. He's done a little straight crime stuff with Ed Gorman's books, but he doesn't do mimetic novels, so I have a feeling that he liked this one and thought it was worth doing. I've written a couple of previous novels which have contemporary settings, but the events are so absurd and surrealistic that even though there's nothing supernatural of fantastical, to me they always read like fantasies. This earlier books are *Joe's Liver* and *Spondulix.* The events were over-the-top and outrageous and postmodern. But I wanted to sit down and see if I could actually meet the goal that everybody tells us is so great, and write a literary novel. It's not super-literary, Thomas Pynchon or anything. But I wanted to try to write a strictly naturalistic novel, and I think I did a pretty good job. But it did feel like having one hand continuously tied behind my back. Every time I had an impulse to put something fantastical on the page, I had to stop myself.

So that's coming out, and the second book from Pete's firm is my sequel to *A Year in the Linear City.* That's one of my best-received books. It got onto a couple award ballots and people have been asking me for a sequel for a long time. I kind of resisted, because I don't do sequels, in general. But I finally got a way to wrap my mind around doing a sequel. So this one is called *A Princess of the Linear Jungle.* It's kind of Burroughsian, which I think might appeal to a lot of readers, but at the same time it's a kind of New Weird, science-fictional mishmash that I hope will take off.

Those two are coming out, and I've a picked up a novel that I'd put aside called *Up Around the Bend.* It's named after that great Creedance Clearwater Revival song. It's kind of a post-apocalyptic thing, but with a lot of surreal, timeslip elements in it. That's pretty much my major project right now.

Q: Thanks very much, Paul.

TANITH LEE

It's very hard to sum up the career of Tanith Lee so far. There's just so much of it. She first came to the attention of most readers with *The Birthgrave* (1975) which clearly announced the arrival of a major talent. She is perhaps best-known for her Flat Earth novels, and tends to focus on exotic, fantastic adventure in exotic settings, but she has written science fiction, straight horror (such as *Dark Dance* and its sequels), historical novels, detective fiction, screenplays (including a couple episodes of *Blake's 7*) and quite a bit more. *Two* special issues of *Weird Tales* have been devoted to her, which is only appropriate since it seemed to me when I was co-editor of that magazine that her work expressed the *Weird Tales* aesthetic more perfectly than that of any other living writer. Among her awards are two World Fantasy Awards for best short fiction (1983, 1984) plus eight more nominations; and a British Fantasy Award for Best Novel in 1980 for *Death's Master* plus five more nominations. She has published over eighty books.

Note: Tanith Lee died in 2015.

⊷⊷⊷

Q: I notice that a lot of your recent books have been for Young Adults. I mean *Piratica*, etc. Your first novel, at least the first I am aware of, *The Dragon Hoard*, was also for younger readers. Is this a return to an early ambition for you? It is of course obvious that J.K. Rowling has made this sort of book more profitable, but I cannot imagine you chasing anyone's coattails. So why this change, now?

Lee: No, I'm not returning to a previous interest at all. I've been writing YA books alongside adult work for most of my (mad) career. In fact, my very first published work was a short adult horror story, written when I was about 18. ("Eustace"). By the time *The Dragon Hoard*, *Princess Hynchatti* and *Animal Castle* were published in the early 1970's, I'd already written *Don't Bite the Sun* and the first draught (the first of only two novels of mine ever to have two draughts—the second was *The Gods Are Thirsty* in the 1980's) of *The Storm Lord*, I just hadn't found a publisher. While working with DAW books, between 1974-1988, I also published six YA/childrens' novels, and later on seven others (see the Unicorn series, and the *Claidi Diaries* (or *Journals*, as they are in the USA). The *Piratica* books are just part of an on-going commitment to this kind of writing.

Q: How is writing for younger readers different for you than writing for adults?

Lee: To me there's no major difference. Some ideas that come to me seem to fit the adult bill, others prefer the YA medium. Two exceptions I can quote—*Volkhavaar* was originally thought of by me as being for the YA range—but before starting it, it seemed to me I could move more freely among some very adult themes if I began with an older viewpoint. The other is a recent proposal turned down by my YA publishers over here, which I have frankly now seen might work much better as a very dark adult novel. (Incidentally they had already rejected the idea of a fourth *Piratica*. Nor did the American firm of Dutton wish to print the 3rd already published Piratica, though all these books seem to have done well in both Britain and the USA, not to mention in translation—Russia, Spain, Japan etc: I still get endless worldwide letters asking for another book in the series.

The only criteria I keep in mind when working on YA is that violence should not be gross, and certain more awful things, though spoken of, stay 'off-stage' as it were. And the same with the sexual act. Though there are of course sexual reactions evidenced if not adultly described, and things left unsaid that the older, or more experienced reader will pick up on.

As for so called 'Bad Language' I don't use it, save in 'invented' form. Examples of Lee-invented really Vile language exist in both the *Claidi*s and the *Piratica*s. Have a look, say at the noun 'tronker,' maybe, and see what you think it might be…! (*Claidi*) or many of the terms in the *Piratica* novels…

Q: Isn't all fantastic fiction to some degree aimed at youth? After all, it's about newness and wonder, the discovery of things we (or the characters) did not previously know to exist, and that is very much the condition of youth.

Lee: This presupposes any writer aims at anyone or thing. Some writers, of course, simply write, as they feel they are driven to do, by outer/inner inspirations. If, after the work is written and, hopefully, published, others respond—that is the Champagne. But we, or some of us, don't write for the champagne. We write because we write. However, to address the premise that Fantasy and all Fantastic literature is 'aimed' at youth, well, perhaps then at the youth of the heart and mind, that is if we apply the criterion of 'newness and wonder.' Not everyone who grows older loses this ability (yes, ability, skill, not failing). C.S. Lewis had a glorious and most aware comment in his Narnia novels, to the effect that nothing was worse than a child who was too childish, and an adult who was too grown-up. We all know these awful kids, but thankfully they may (ha!) grow out of it. I suppose the dire aged may also grow out of the over-adultness.

Your question equates the wonder and surprise, the delight of finding, with all we "didn't know previously existed." OK. In the 1500's grown-ups thought the world was flat. But apparently it isn't. (Or IS it? Another new thing to find out, maybe…) What I mean is, new facts are always coming to light, and I don't just mean in the cosmos, or the outer environ. In ourselves. That is, if we stay, at least on some level, pliable enough to listen, to see, to feel. The 'condition of youth' is a state we should, and must, internally, hang on to, and try to preserve (a juxtaposition of notions—preserving—pickled youth!) Basically that trite phrase the 'inner child'—trite phrase, yet intelligent thought. The 'fantastic' therefore may be a key component in arousing the sleeping spirit in our physical souls. If I ever get to 100, I'd want to be filled with wonder and wild, adolescent, wide-eyed interest in newness. So let's keep the flame burning. Let's stop thinking everyone over 29, or 49, has to be reinforced by concrete.

Q: When did you start reading and writing fantasy?

Lee: I couldn't read anything until I was almost 8—dyslexia. (Unrecognised at the time, in the early 1950's.) The first book I read, Hans Christian Anderson's *Fairy Tales*, was, of course, Fantasy, like all fiction (and indeed, some non-fiction.) To clarify, my mother was a great aficionado of all SF and fantasy, the early *Galaxy* and later *Weird Tales*, and early novels by Asimov and Clarke—*Childhood's End* and *The City and the Stars* being two favorites—were well known in our various homes. The first Fantasy story I am conscious of having read as such was "The Silken Swift" by the amazing Theodore Sturgeon. I suppose I read that in my early teens, just as I read Mary Renault's *The King Must Die* when I was 11-ish. These wonders were like finding a major truth of books, (just as first hearing Shostakovich, Prokofiev and Rachmaninov was like finding music I had always known, but somehow mislaid—or been robbed of.) When I read Jane Gaskell's *The Serpent* (at about 18) however, I suddenly realized the scope of what one might be 'allowed' to write. By which I mean, breaking-all-rules of sticking to the so-called Real World, might be allowed into print. Pathfinding genius that Gaskell was/is, she lit a special light for me along the road. Not long after, I embarked on my first draught (only one of the two—the other was my French Revolution novel *The Gods Are Thirsty*—books I ever did 2 draughts on) of *The Storm Lord*. But I must add I'd already written a fantasy novel, set in a parallel ancient Mediterranean, when I was 16. It came naturally. As writing should.

Q: Most writers report, as you do, that writing is just what they *do*, rather than something they decided would make them a lot of money. That being the case, when you discovered you were a natural writer, and had written an entire novel by the time you were 16, how much deliberation did you then apply? Did you read books on writing technique? Did you find that the way you read other people's fiction changed? Did you start reading critically, to see how stories were put together?

Lee: I have *never* read *anything* to see what I should be doing, or how to plot, construct, voice a particular story. I read to enjoy myself, to be transported elsewhere, and yes, to learn—but for its own sake, not in a self-conscious or precise way. I read what entices, terrifies, amuses, enlightens me—as a human thing. Meanwhile, I must suppose that reading wonderful writers may, inadvertently, teach an avid reader a great deal—not only about life and other matters, but about how to write. Therefore doubtless I have benefited from frequent immersions in the glowing genius of others. It would be nice to think so. (I do actually think so). But to improve my skills will never be the prompting force of my reading—that's just literary lust.

Q: Did you have the worry, as many people do in such a situation, "This is what I want to do with my life, but what if I don't make it professionally?" and then have a back-up plan, or did you just plunge into writing?

Lee: In the beginning I had no idea I would ever be 'allowed' to make my profession that of a writer. And in this sad mind-set I was encouraged to stay by a great many persons, for a great while. So, if I had a plan then, it was only for a wretched sort of survival, doing other work at which I was largely incompetent, and where my unhappiness was matched only by my confusion. When I was about 21, this condition almost drove me mad—I do mean that. Through it all, however, I kept on writing, since to me that was the only sanity and bedrock in my life. It was the only Real place to go. (I wrote *The Birthgrave* during this period). When finally I was rescued from my false 'working life' by Don Wollheim and DAW Books, I had no sense of wildness or charging off any rails. I had none of the often reported fear of being unable to cope with my new situation. It was the former situation I had been utterly unable to cope with. Now, writing every day, and being paid for it and encouraged to do it, it was as if, in the midst of the clichéd dark and stormy night, I found the magical inn, its windows golden lit, and Summer was due to start tomorrow. I can only work at one thing well. Deprive me of that, and my 'back-up plan,' even now, will be the empty, stormy, darkened heath—where, incidentally, even unpublished, somehow I'll still be writing.

Q: Let's talk a little more about the Jane Gaskell influence. What most inspired you in her work? Was it entirely the work, or the fact that she published her first novel at 14? That I should think would inspire many teenaged novelists.

Lee: When I was a child I found children largely uninteresting—not as people but to read about. As a young adult I was a little less elitist, but not much. (Only David Copperfield and Pip in *Great Expectations* got past this barrier. But then, that's Dickens for you.) The fact therefore that Gaskell had published a couple of (fascinating) novels when very young would have held little allure for me, let alone been any sort of encouragement. (I read *Strange Evil* and *King's Daughter* after.) Of course, anyway, they are about adults, so even my intolerant child-persona would have liked them. But Gaskell had written with sensibilities far beyond her years. *King's Daughter*, precursor of the glorious path-breaking *The Serpent*, is an astonishing work for one that young (14, 15 I seem to remember). Who writes an ending like that, when so 'immature'?

What I first read by her was *Attic Summer*, a then contemporary novel. I loved/love her humor and her cynicism, (apparent in all her work) her play with color and every one of the senses, her take on—not only sexual romance—but sexual and romantic psychology, indeed all forms of psychology, for a 'Romantic Novelist' is definitely *not* what Gaskell is. Also, I valued the fact that she wrote inside at least two very separate forms—what I now know had been labeled Fantasy, and what is straight 'reality,' and mixed the two in the most cunning, witty and apt of ways.

So what inspired me most? As with any writer I love, all of it—*all*.

Q: CS Lewis said he started writing fantasy because the books he wanted to read were not on the shelves? Did you have some of the same feeling? When you started to write, after all, fantasy was not nearly as widely-published as it is today.

Lee: I only read the Narnia books (typically) when I was 50. (I'd tried as a child, but the child heroes, as explained, didn't interest me much). At fifty, though, I did get a lot from the work. The books are intensely spiritual for me, though not religious in perhaps the sense Lewis might have wished to convey. His use of the Dionysian aspects of Jesus Christ charmed me, (I agree with them) and some of the sequences are wonderfully beautiful and profound. What a curious combination, adventure and laughter—and cutting-edge visionary reports from the edge of the afterlife…

But to return to your actual question: I did and still do, in some way, wrote and write what I want to read. Perhaps that is true of many writers. Meanwhile there are hordes of authors whose work thrills me, so I got and get plenty of nourishment without scribbling it personally. On the other hand, too, when I started to find what was by then classed as Fantasy, I was shown that alter-worlds and otherwheres were completely possible—by which I mean capable-of-being-recognized (and published.) And while, still, I had very little hope of that myself, I grasped that I need not shy away from something that had been internally beckoning me for quite some time. In retrospect I am both surprised and dismayed to see in this that I must have taken some (inadvertent) notice of all those who tried to wean me from my proper path. How odd. Thank God I found it anyway.

Q: You have written some non-fantastic fiction, such as your French Revolution novel. Is the craft of non-fantasy any different for you? Would you ever want to write a purely realistic, contemporary novel, or is the whole appeal of writing for you to get away from that?

Lee: The writing of my French Revolution novel, *The Gods Are Thirsty*, was in one way different for me, but not in any creative or artistic sense. Except I preferred to do two draughts. I was obsessed with it (as I always am with what I write), and wrote it in floods (also usual), having to pause only to do research. (This can happen even when dealing in fantasy or SF, or any type of other genre book/story. For example, if I have to describe a copper mine or glass foundry, I do some research on them first.) The main and very pertinent difference for me with *The Gods Are Thirsty* was not, either, to do with the fact that the people in it had historically lived—were 'real.' My own invented characters seldom feel invented, to me. They're equally actual, and so are their stories and otherwheres. So, the one salient difference with *The Gods Are Thirsty* was that I had available to me from the start almost all the known facts and events. And—I knew the *ending*. It was established, revealed, and unalterable. Sometimes pre-knowledge of many facts and scenes does happen when I use an 'invented' plot. But it's rare, and always subject to great/slight change—the work tends to meta-morphose. While 19 times out of twenty I don't know my book's ending, until it evolves or simply displays itself, occasionally shocking me.

On writing 'purely realistic contemporary' novels—well, I've done so. The problem was, and remains, getting publishers to look at them, let alone publish. They seem to have trouble accepting the books as valid, and might entertain others. Seemingly, someone writing outside their genre-ghetto is not normally encouraged to do so.

I have written as Esther Garber, a character not a pseudonym, (though such a unique voice her books were published as 'Tanith Lee writing as Esther Garber'). These volumes—*Thirty Four* and *Fatal Women* are Lesbian fiction, set in our world, but inside a kind of floating historic vista, (ranging approximately between the late 1800's and the present day) and often also in France.

The novel *L'Amber* (written only by me!) is placed in 1980's-ish London and environs. *Grayglass* has a slightly earlier and later timeframe, and uses London generally, with a brief excursion to New York. Otherwise this book does operate within an underplayed yet intense supernatural twister. *Death of the Day* is a detective novel, influenced by and therefore in the tradition of Ruth Rendell. It resides in 1990's Kent and Sussex, England. There are two other novels—*To Indigo* and *God's Dogs*. *To Indigo* stays firmly in London during the 2000's, but contains a strange alter-motif concerning a Prague-like alchemical city around the late 1700's. Be warned though: the last is because the book's main character is a writer, and the alternate location represents his single (closet) fantasy novel! *God's Dogs* is set in 1934, mostly in England, but with flashbacks to a slightly earlier time in mainland Europe. *L'Amber* and *Death of the Day* were published, too, by the same small press (P.O.D.) that brought out the Garber books. None of these books is now available, however, as the firm packed up. *Greyglass* did nearly make it into print but had the door slammed in its face by the same outfit a couple of days before release. Meanwhile, both the Garber books got very good reviews in *Locus*, and so did *Death of the* Day over here, in the *Guardian.*

Frankly though, when I first started to write novels, (about 16 years of age, circa 1963-64) I did opt for parallel historical, and finally out-and-out Fantasy and SF venues, indeed in order to escape 'ordinary' fiction—even though I still continued to enjoy, along with fantastical material, reading about the so-called everyday. With impressive geniuses like Graham Greene, Jane Austen (historical, yes, but still this world and the everyday for then), Jane Gaskell, J.B. Priestly and Richard Llewellyn, working in that area, my interest isn't surprising. But by now I find for myself no discrepancy that way when I write 'ordinary world' novels. For me they're all part of a carpet I keep on weaving, in company, in a curious manner, with all dedicated writers, artists and composers, as with all I do of whatever leaning. I relish my contemporary books, cherish them, am obsessed by them. They flow or sometimes stick—just as the fantasy ones can. It's all fiction, after all. And all real to me, or more real, than the world (beautiful or horribly cruel) that we physically inhabit.

Q: I know you've written a few teleplays, including a couple installments of *Blake's 7.* Have you wanted to write more for the screen, big or little, or do you prefer writing for the printed page?

Lee: When I first started to write at any sustained length, (about age 12) I wrote plays almost exclusively. (Though I confess to writing a Priestly-inspired novel at 10/11—it was called *Forsythia Square*, a contemporary work (1950's) of curious type!) I loved/love live theatre, and radio drama—which then was far more omnipresent than now—though BBC Radio generally maintains a stunning standard in both acting and production. I immensely liked writing the two *Blake's 7* scripts. I'd watched the show from the beginning and was fascinated by all the characters. (My original hope, had the series continued, was to write an 'in-depth' script for each of them. At least I got to tackle Cally, Avon somewhat, and Servalann.)

I can imagine, now, writing other radio plays.(I did actually write one years back, which I never submitted, finding it too dark—it was called *Darkness*—a consideration that I'm afraid wouldn't stop me today— But my radio contacts are mostly gone. As for TV—it's changed such a lot I'm not sure. While a movie, knowing as I do something of the paraphernalia and muddle that seems to attend all script-writes, (see F. Scott Fitzgerald if in doubt, and that was back then!) might not be a challenge I'd choose to take on. Luckily I'm spared that choice so far: no one has asked. Incidentally anyway, when

I write for the 'printed page' I personally see it as a movie, (aside from how the characters relay their inner thoughts and mental attributes). All within my head. It's all, for me, happened, or is happening. All on film.

Q: And, what are you working on now? What might we expect to see from you in the near future?

Lee: The Flat Earth books are due, all of them, to start being reissued in 2009, from Norilana Books, the established five to be followed by at least one more. And there are loads of my short stories and novellas either recently out or about to be, in anthologies and magazines such as *Realms of Fantasy, Asimov's* and *Weird Tales*—see my website: (Also your own anthology on *Werewolves*.) [Note: She is referring to *Full Moon City* ed. Darrell Schweitzer and Martin H. Greenberg, 2010.]

Meanwhile, my two main UK publishers, Hodder and MacMillan, have between them rejected three proposals from me for new work. These were the detailed proposals everyone now seems to need, and both firms rather oddly kept the two (Hodder) and one (MacMillan) packages—and myself—hanging on for six months in either case. (I had been publishing YA books with Hodder, incidentally, for 10 years. 5 for adult work with MacMillan.) That then was my main income gone, if nothing else. Neither company gave any encouragement that I should offer anything else, rather the reverse. Not, frankly, that I felt inclined to.

The small UK press as well, Egerton House, which was publishing other work of mine, such as contemporary novels, a detective novel, and Lesbian fiction, had already folded, leaving many accounts unsettled.

I have since attempted to interest a number of other houses. Reaction here has been mixed, the smaller presses indeed seeming the least inclined, and—in a couple of cases—very cavalier. Other possibilities do exist, but unfortunately due as they say to circumstances beyond my control, at present, I have not been able to discuss any new commitments—hopefully the new year will resolve this situation. Also there has been, as ever, a constant flow of openings for short fiction, which has been a real joy to do. Alas, it doesn't pay the bills. Altogether, that financial way, I am now in a nightmare scenario.

But, as said before, while able, I will always write. It's like breathing to me. My current project is a weird contemporary novel called *Ivorian*, which veers between a detective story and a supernatural—or is it—take on sibling hatred. Also, I have two completed contemporary novels and one collection of mixed Lesbian, gay and heterosexual short stories, all sitting in the cupboard. Oh, and the rejected ventures? What they were to have been, and still may be, were: 1) *The Firesmith*—a violently and erotically bronze-iron age adult epic, whose priest-mage-metalsmith-protagonist must survive in a dark age savaged by fire-blasting dragons. And for Young Adults: 2) a 4th pirate novel in the *Piratica* series—*War and Pieces of Eight*, the final saga of Art and her handsome husband Felix—he now consort of the Queen of Scotland, and featuring a more than guest appearance by Apolleon, the Napoleon of their history. Plus 3) *Glitterash*, or *King of Ghosts*. That being the story of a one-handed pianist gang-warrior, in an SF worldscape of blazingly ruinous cities and oil-slicked, wasp-infested seas, where the written word has been dumbed right out of existence, and reinvented 'modern' Tarot cards have become the credo of Law, religion and power.

Sound a bit flat, don't they? Far too unoriginal and slow for any publishers to take a risk on.

I must admit, I never thought, after all the years of working as a professional writer in and out of the genres, I would end up at 61, back where I was at 20: unknown, unpaid, unincluded, uncertain.

Q: Thank you, Tanith.

PATRICIA McKILLIP

Patricia McKillip has written the expected large shelf of books, including the classic *The Forgotten Beasts of Eld*, which was the first novel ever to win a World Fantasy Award in 1975, and the *Riddle-Master of Hed* trilogy. She wrote fantasy for adults when this was still rare. Despite the increased competition in recent years, she is still one of the world's leading practitioners of the art.

Recorded at the World Fantasy Convention, 2010.

Q: Let's go right to the heart of things. Why fantasy? Why do you write fantasy? Everybody has a different answer to that.

McKillip: I started writing when I was very young and they tell you to write what you know, and what I knew was fantasy, I suppose. When I was seventeen I stayed up until three in the morning reading Tolkien and was *so* astonished by it, I think, because I am a post-Baby Boom child and was brought up very rigidly Catholic. So, as a Catholic your mythological world has a wall around it, and Tolkien just tipped that wall right over. He demolished it. He made you feel like the imagination was something you could keep on going through and go through and never find an end to.

So I started doing research. I literally tried to find his worlds. I didn't know what they were, whether they were real or not. I looked in history and then I got the idea of looking in mythology, poetry, and legends and got into really finding his sources. Things grew from there, and I had to write the trilogy.

Q: American culture seems to have been very much cut off from the fantastic and from myth. I think the reason that Tolkien took everybody by storm is that, before that, what was there for most people except Disney versions of fairy tales? So, were you aware that there was an actual fantasy literature, as opposed to just Tolkien?

McKillip: Well, there wasn't very much. When I was growing up there was Andre Norton. There was Fritz Leiber. I grew up partly overseas, so I had to read what was in the library there, because my dad was in the Air Force, and I would read whatever was on the air bases, which is where I ran into Fritz Leiber. I loved his stories of Fafhrd and the Gray Mouser, and Andre Norton was also very interesting to me, but that was about all there was until I got into college and I read Ursula Le Guin. I thought her science fiction was wonderful. I can't remember anybody else. I was going for a master's in literature at that point and was reading anything but fantasy, and that's about all the fantasy I can remember.

Q: Like most of us Baby Boomers, I'm a child of the Ballantine Adult Fantasy Series. Were you much influenced by those books that Lin Carter did?

McKillip: That was after I'd gotten started, after I got published, that they came out. But, no, I did not read a lot of those books.

Q: So you may be one of the last fantasy writers who began writing without any sense of being part of a generic tradition. What Carter did was assemble a canon, so subsequent writers would see themselves as being part of that canon. But you would have started writing before there was a canon. Is this so?

Killip: At least as an English major I didn't look in the part of the library where they might have put a fantasy canon. Literally in the book-stores there was one small shelf of fantasy and one small shelf of science fiction. Tiny. two feet long. That was it.

Q: When I was in college there were still professors who had been programmed to despise James Branch Cabell. Lord Dunsany was okay because of his association with Yeats, but otherwise the impression you got from the educational system is that fantasy is acceptable literature up to about Mark Twain, and only if it is satire.

McKillip: Even the very few writing teachers I had did not know what to make of my fantasy. I took about three writing courses. I went to San Jose State, which did not have a writing program then. It was encompassed within the English Literature department. Nobody knew what to do with fantasy. I tried writing some modern stuff, but the teachers weren't happy with that either. So I just did what I wanted.

Q: Your first couple of books were juveniles. Did you encounter the assumption from publishers that fantasy is for kids?

McKillip: Well the first book was more of a ghost story than a fantasy, and it had a lot of English history in it. It's about the (delete: old 14th century) *four hundred year old house* that I lived in as a kid over in England, and the priest-hole *in the basement*, and I imagined ghosts down there. So it had a lot of history and not really a lot of fantasy. But I published that when I was in college, getting my master's degree. I was really, really embarrassed. I'd been reading Henry James and Faulkner and God knows who all, and here I came out with this little YA novel, and was published, and all the teachers were going, "Whoa!" I was going, "Oh, sorry!" [Laughs.]

Q: But you had a published novel and they didn't.

McKillip: I think they were impressed.

Q: Are you then an entirely self-taught writer? It sounds like you didn't get much from the educational system.

McKillip: I was taught by the books I read. I learned early that reading was just as important as writing. You read everything you could get your hands on. You wrote everything you could think of. Those are my two basic rules. Other than that I did not really have writing courses, and the one really good teacher I had was a poetry teacher, oddly enough. So he never saw my fantasy, though he liked it once he got hold of a couple of my books.

Q: As I remember it, from the perception of the fantasy field, you came on the map very suddenly in 1975 with *Forgotten Beasts of Eld,* which won the first World Fantasy Award for novel, and everybody wondered, "Who is she? What else has she written?" I've never seen your first two books, the ones that came before that point, but I've heard about them as a result.

McKillip: The second one was *The Throme of the Erril of Sherill,* which is a very short story. It is only about 50 pages long and is definitely a fairy tale, nicely illustrated and bound. But it is not one that you would really find unless you were looking for it. The third one was *The Forgotten Beasts of Eld* which won the World Fantasy Award. That I wrote as an adult novel, but after it got rejected by the adult department at Atheneum, my children's editor, Jean Karl, took it. She wanted cross-over novels for teen-aged girls, which was kind of rare in those days.

Q: Did your career suddenly turn around as soon as that novel crossed over in paperback into the adult fantasy category?

McKillip: Pretty much. When my editor called me and told me what the financial offer was for the paperback of *Forgotten Beasts,* I told her I nearly fell off my chair, and she said, "So did I." It wasn't that big by modern standards, but by those earlier standards it certainly was. The next novel that came out was a basic YA with no fantasy, and after that came the trilogy, and that launched my fantasy writing career.

Q: The rest is history, coin a phrase. But to speak of history, the generation before us doesn't seem to have had much use for fantasy. I think people who grew up in the Depression were too caught up in daily life, and the ideology of the time was certain one which equated "serious literature" with realism. Then things changed. Do you have any sense of why fantasy came back?

McKillip: I think that it was just what I said before. A whole generation grew up and was able to go to college. I was certainly one of the first in either one of my families to go to college. So we had a lot of different influences that our parents didn't have. Tolkien just opened the doors to imagination. I think our generation was ready for it, because when we were growing up we didn't have the immediate concerns that our parents had, you know, in terms of paying the mortgage and stuff like that, so we could let our minds sort of wander—and boy, they wandered!

Q: We're talking about a literature which is often called escapist, but I think it was C.S. Lewis who said that the only people opposed to escape are jailers. You must have gotten into these discussions when somebody asked you, "Why don't you write anything serious?" Fantasy writers have to explain that it is about something real. So how do you explain to people who ask questions like that, what fantasy is about?

McKillip: I try to avoid explaining as much as possible. To me it is a very profound thing. It is literally the quest to find the correlative stories that will make you look at them and say, "Oh yes, I need to do this," or "I need this particular symbol." You respond to these things. That's the heroic quest. I don't know. I keep thinking of some kind of video game where images light up if you hit the right button. I think it's very true as I was growing up that what I needed I found in literature. Those symbols—my response to them—made me realize that this is what fantasy was about, the quest for unification and peace within yourself. This was the way you went about it. You fought your way through these various tales that you needed, that you responded to.

Q: Joseph Campbell, for example, worked out a very elaborate model of what the quest fantasy is about. I wonder: should fantasy writers be thinking theoretically at all, or should they just do it?

McKillip: I think just doing it is important, because you know what you need to do as you do it. But I have thought about it. You can't help thinking about it. I've read some Jung and read Campbell and Robert Graves, gained enough from them to realize that I wasn't the first person to be thinking about all this. It is a legitimate way of looking at fantasy, but I don't have hard and fast rules about what you should do in fantasy. It's what you *need* to do that's important.

Q: Do you feel any conflict between what you need to do and what the marketplace demands? Is there any sense from the editors and publishers that a fantasy is expected to have certain expected tropes or ingredients?

McKillip: Only in the sense that if I need to pay my mortgage, then I would write something that would be sellable. I have done that. But I don't really think that it compromised anything I needed to do. I still drag my feet at the idea of writing about vampires or zombies. I don't think I could do it well.

Q: I think the appropriate response to a really tight formula is to get silly. You could probably write a funny zombie story.

McKillip: [Laughs.] *You* could write a funny zombie story.

Q: After your Riddle Master trilogy you shifted to science fiction, with *Moon-Flash, Fool's Run,* etc. for a few years. Why did this happen just then?

McKillip: After I finished the Riddle Master trilogy, I swore I would never write another fantasy. That's how difficult the 12-year process of writing it was. A friend who loved both music and s/f encouraged me to try a science fiction novel, so I put him into it as my keyboard playing musician. It took me eight years to write that novel, partly because I was very much aware of the critical faculties of s/f readers, and knew that I'd hear about it if I wrote it poorly. The YA novels *Moon-Flash* and *The Moon and the Face* I wrote before I finished *Fool's Run*, as a kind of respite from the difficulties of writing adult s/f.

I enjoy reading s/f, and some of the best of what I read is written by people with degrees in science. I found that intimidating, back then.

Q: The Clute-Nichols *Encyclopedia of Science Fiction* goes so far as to suggest that you are more at home with fantasy than with SF. Would you agree?

McKillip: I knew my way around fantasy; I had to flounder my way around in s/f. So, yes, I think the Clute-Nichols *Encyclopedia of SF* is correct: I am more comfortable writing fantasy. I could use a much broader vocabulary in *Fool's Run*, than I had writing the Trilogy. I could envision aliens and strange planets in *The Moon and the Face*. All this is quite wonderful, and I enjoyed doing it very much.

But I don't think easily in terms of s/f. I did try other s/f ideas but they didn't get off the ground. So I went back to what I knew best. In the late 80's everyone seemed to be writing series. I envisioned writing a line of novels that had nothing in common except that they were fantasy. So I started to work on that. And now, after a couple of decades and many fantasy novels, I'd like a change.

Q: What are your writing methods like? Do you outline a novel? Do you discover it as you write it?

McKillip: I try to write about four hours a day, because that is the limit to the amount of time I can do absolutely nothing. If you do absolutely nothing long enough, you get bored and start working. So that helps a bit. I don't outline. I tried that once many years ago, and realized that once you have outlined the entire story, it's just gone. There's no reason to write it. I'm trying to think if there is any one way to do a novel. I don't know.... Some of them come easily. Some you have to really research. Just flail about until you find whatever it is that makes you pause and look at it and think there is a story in this somewhere. Then you start finding the story.

Q: Do you write the first chapter without knowing what's in the second?

McKillip: No. I like to know. I like to think I know, but usually I don't.

Q: Some writers report that when they're writing a book, sometimes something very odd happens and they wonder, "Where did *that* come from?" Has this ever happened to you?

McKillip: When I was writing *Fool's Run,* I had written half of it and then a character popped up and I thought, "I need this character in the whole book." So I had to go back and rewrite it. *The Forgotten Beasts of Eld* is one that I just sat down and wrote. It took **me** five weeks to write that thing, and I had no idea what was going to happen, and that is very rare. Usually you have to work harder at it than that, or I do. But I have to go back a little bit. My father was born during the Depression and was one of those people who was rigidly Catholic and probably never used what imagination he had. But he sat down with *The Forgotten Beasts of Eld* before I published it. He was an Air Force captain by then—six kids, thoroughly military— and he turned page after page. He told me later that he had to keep reading it to find out what was going to happen. I thought that was just wonderful. Actually he was out of the military by then. He was working for Lockheed. **He** was very proud of that novel.

Q: Isn't this the essence of any storytelling, that it compels the reader to turn the page to find out what will happen next?

McKillip: Yes, but my own father? Who would have thought?

Q: Obviously you had the power to captivate and convert people.... So, do you have any sense of what you'd like to do in a novel that you haven't done yet?

McKillip: I'd like to bring the world in more. I'm feeling a little over-extended in fantasy these days and I would like to change the way I look at writing and change what details I put in and see if there can be a different way of mingling fantasy and reality and history and geology…you know, the various things we encounter every single day. How do you put all that into a novel and call it fantasy? That is what I am really curious about.

Q: Are you a fan of T.H. White? He was a writer who seemed to just pour everything he knew and read and felt all into one book, *The Once and Future King.*

McKillip: That was one I read six times while I was in high school, even before I read Tolkien. I should have remembered how much I loved that book. Yeah, but his tone was such that he didn't tell us *how* to do things so much as show us what kind of voice he had. I don't know. That novel is so complex that I cannot imagine even trying to imitate it.

Q: I don't think imitation is what you want. Tolkien has been imitated many times, but whenever somebody writes an imitation of Tolkien they merely prove that he is inimitable.... So, what are you working on now?

McKillip: I am working on a novel to pay the mortgage and I am also trying to work out a way of being happy with it, despite all its beginning flaws. I am just trying to figure out what's wrong with it.

Q: I assume you'll wait until you're happy with it before you publish it, so this is just part of the discovery process.

McKillip: It occurred to me that it's something I could sell. Maybe it's YA, maybe it's adult. I don't know yet. I've been wanting to give up on it fifty times since I started on it several months ago, but there is something about it that intrigues me, and that part of it that intrigues me is what keeps me going, because I don't know what it is that I want out of this yet.

Q: Presumably you are your own first reader, and you write to please yourself first.

McKillip: Yes, and I am my own first critic. I really try and criticize everything. I read like a critic and like a reader who is trying to love what she's reading. Then my agent gets a hold of it and tells me where I have gone wrong, or my husband reads it and he tells me it's boring. These things help.

Q: Most of your fantasies have been ones in which you immerse the story in another world, as Tolkien does. But there's another approach, in which the fantasy intrudes into our world. Have you felt any inclination to do this sort of fantasy?

McKillip. Only in the sense that I'd like to write more about the real world because had lots of words that I don't get to use in fantasy. I don't know, like coffee urn and deodorant and stuff like that. You can't say those things in an epic fantasy. Yeah, I would like to put fantasy in the real world. I just don't quite know in what fashion yet. I would love it to somehow… I don't know. That's tough for me. I'm still thinking about it. I haven't thought of it before.

Q: You *could* write a fantasy in which you mention coffee urns and deodorant. It would be a very different kind of fantasy.

McKillip: You can mention things like that in *The War for the Oaks* or something like that.

Q: We have a standard post-Tolkien fantasy now, in which the setting is pre-industrial and rural, and that's why they don't have coffee urns in them. But why does this have to be so? Is there something inherent in a pre-industrial setting that makes epic fantasy happen? Why couldn't they have a steam engine in there?

McKillip: They do these days. They have steampunk all over the place. To me that's fantasy too, and it's wonderful. [We are in the green room at the World Fantasy Convention. Voice from behind us: "Coffee to your left and teapot to your right."] That's something you can't hear in one of my fantasies, isn't it? I've forgotten the question.…

Q: Can we break out of the rules? Is our idea of what a fantasy is itself restrictive?

McKillip: It is for me a little bit, because I have been writing this way for years and years, but not for other people. Charles de Lint has his modern cities, and Nalo Hopkinson's *The Salt Roads* was an incredible fantasy. I am not sure what exactly it was, but it was amazing, and she ranged from Caribbean history to French history to modern times. People do anything they want in fantasy nowadays. They can use any language they want.

Q: Presumably you could do anything you wanted.

McKillip: Presumably. One would hope that I could change at my age.

Q: Why not? I am reminded of something Picasso said when he was about 80. He was asked by an interviewer, "What are you doing now?" and he said, "I'm looking for a new style."

McKillip: So am I.

Q: Thank you, Patricia McKillip.

ROBERT SILVERBERG

Robert Silverberg was one of the first people I ever interviewed, back in 1974. Now after many years and many miles, we have a go at it again. Then he was in the midst of his highly productive "middle period" in which he produced such classics as *Nightwings, Downward to the Earth, The Tower of Glass, Dying Inside*, and many others with astonishing rapidity and regularity. A pause, or brief retirement followed, after which he returned to the field as a somewhat different writer and made himself more popular than ever with *Lord Valentine's Castle* and its successors. These days he has probably given up long fiction, but still maintains a column in every issue of *Asimov's SF.*

⭤⭤⭤

Q: Let me start with what is doubtless on your fans' minds these days. Have you really retired from writing fiction? If so, why? Maybe it's because I haven't been at it as long or with such intensity, but I find it hard to understand why someone would stop writing when they still could.

RS: The only thing I've retired from is writing novels. After I wrote *The Longest Way Home*, somewhere around 2002, I said I would not write any more novels, and I haven't, despite several offers from publishers. I just don't want to make the big commitment of time and stamina that a novel would require. But I've continued to do short stories and even the occasional novella, like the recent *Last Song of Orpheus*, and in fact I finished a new short story this very month. And I still do essays for *Asimov's SF* and introductions for other people's books. I won't deny, though, that I'm far less active as a writer than I once was. I'm 76, after all; writing takes time and energy; there are still a lot of things I want to do in the time that is remaining to me, other than writing more science fiction. And it isn't as though my existing bibliography is a skimpy one.

Q: Is fiction writing for you a job or a compulsion?

RS: Probably both. The fact that I've written so much over the years, even after economic pressures ceased to be a driving factor, very likely indicates that something within me keeps pushing me to move words around on paper. I've been doing it, after all, for seventy years or so, if you count the little stories I was writing in the third grade. And I don't seem to stop.

Q: Has this changed for you over time?

RS: I write more slowly than I once did, and I spend much less of my time each year doing it. I don't think there's anything unusual about that. Some writers stay prolific to the end, like Frederick Faust (Max Brand), but Faust died when he was in his fifties. I wonder if he'd still have been knocking them out at the old rate if he had lived another twenty years. Another of my prolific heroes, Georges Simenon, was 68 or so when he wrote his last novel. (Though he did go on compulsively writing autobiographical works to the end of his days.)

Q: Do you find yourself, after all this time, comparing your career with those of other writers? (Here you are citing Frederick Faust and Georges Simenon.) I suppose we must all look with envy on the career of Jack Williamson, or on Gene Wolfe, who seems to be at the top of his game and turning out novels at great speed at 80.

RS: Envy is not much of a psychological issue for me, and never has been. I've been able to sell everything I write and have it appear in the places where I want it to appear, and the success of other writers is something I cheer, not bemoan. Sure, I'd like to have Stephen King's income or Neil Gaiman's popularity with huge crowds of readers, but my work is not much like theirs, is not likely to appeal to great multitudes of readers outside the central s-f audience, and so be it.

The only writers I ever compared myself with were Philip K. Dick and Robert Sheckley, back at the beginning of my career nearly sixty years ago. They were quick, clever, prolific writers, and I wanted to have the same sort of careers they had. I kept count of the number of stories they had published, studied their work carefully to see how they did it, watched their progress with immense admiration that I guess could be seen as a kind of envy. In time I became as prolific and widely published as they were, they both became my friends, and I stopped keeping count of their published stories. (And I hardly envied the courses of their lives as they unfolded, with Dick dying young and Sheckley going through all manner of career and financial problems. I could never have imagined, back there in 1952, that they would finish so badly).

Simenon and Faust also were writers I admired rather than envied. I saw them as gifted predecessors whose productivity over an extended period I hoped to emulate. But emulating Jack Williamson would be a fool's game: Jack was a unique figure in our field, endowed with extraordinary longevity and remarkable lucidity of mind right to the end of his long life, and I applaud him without any expectation of doing what he did. Staking any emotional capital on the notion of following his path and winning Hugos and Nebulas in my nineties would be just plain silly. As for Gene Wolfe, yes, he's doing great things at an advanced age, but I regard Gene as a late starter: I began publishing in my teens and have been a full-time writer for nearly six decades, whereas he entered the field ten or twelve years after me and continued to hold down his day job until he was in his fifties or sixties. Writing is something he does for the love of it; to some degree that's true of me, of course, but it has also been my only job for all these years. I've done an enormous amount of hard work over those six decades and it should surprise no one that I want to cut back on my output now.

Q: In any case, any retirement you declare for yourself now must be on a very different basis than the last time, circa 1977. Then the backlash against the New Wave was in full blast, and the publishing world's idea of SF seemed to be Laser Books or *Star Wars* knockoffs. It must have been a very grim time to be a science fiction writer with any serious ambition. Was it?

RS: It certainly was. A bunch of us tried to remake the field in the 1967-72 period with a burst of original and creative science fiction, and we were greeted with vast indifference and even overt hostility by most of the readers. It became very difficult for the best people of that group—Joanna Russ, Chip Delany, Tom Disch, Norman Spinrad, John Brunner, Barry Malzberg, to name just some of them—to earn any kind of livelihood writing s-f, and most of them turned to other fields of endeavor. Because I had built up more economic security than most by virtue of my prolificacy, I shrugged an angry shrug and walked away from writing altogether, and stayed away for nearly five years. This time around, as I slide gradually into retirement, I'm still not happy with the course that commercial s-f publishing in the States has taken since the collapse of the New Wave a generation ago, but I'm not angry—just interested in slowing down, relaxing, living the sort of life that most people my age do.

Q: The story goes that when he was very old, Picasso was asked by a reporter, "What are you doing now?" and he said, "I'm looking for a new style." Are there always, likewise, new horizons for the writer?

RS: I suppose. Not for this one. I've had my turn as a revolutionary. Any writing I do from here on in is going to be very much like the sort of writing I did in the past.

Q: If you've been writing for seventy years and are now seventy-six, that means you must have started writing when you were six? That does suggest it's inborn, doesn't it? How long before you knew that this was to be your life's work?

RS: My earliest published work was done for my elementary-school newspaper when I was, as I said, in the third grade. I also began writing little stories about the same time. (I continued to do school-newspaper work all the way; I was the editor of my junior-high paper and my high-school paper, and when I was at Columbia I was the drama reviewer for the university paper.) I was fairly late discovering science fiction—I was about ten—and didn't write my first s-f story until I was nearly thirteen. But I made up for that slow start later on.

Somewhere along the way—probably in junior high school—it occurred to me that being a writer was probably what I was going to do when I grew up. By the time I was in my late teens, it was clear to me and everybody around me that a writer was what I was, and I never deviated from that path after that.

Q: Let's talk a minute about being a "revolutionary." During the New Wave era you weren't particularly given to rewriting *Finnegans Wake* as science fiction or constructing a story entirely out of typographical tricks (the way Donald Barthelme has done on occasion), much less any of the extreme oddities of J.G. Ballard. It seems to me that when you were writing things like *Nightwings* or *Downward to the Earth* or *Dying Inside*, you were writing what was recognizably science fiction, only better, with more emotional depth and maturity. So what exactly didn't the readers want?

RS: I was never as radical an experimenter as some of the *New Worlds* crowd in the Moorcock period, say, or as downbeat as Ballard, or as radical in my world-view as Delany, but *Son of Man*, which I wrote in 1969, was far-out plotless stuff, some of my short stories of the period had a distinct Barthelmian absurdist flavor, one ("Many Mansions") was a pastiche of a Robert Coover piece, *Dying Inside* was mainstream in tone though built around a science-fictional concept, and *Book of Skulls* was or was not science fiction, depending on how you interpreted the ambiguous information about the immortals in the Arizona desert. So, all in all, I had moved quite a distance from the standard pulp tropes and what I was writing, though I regarded all of it as recognizably science fiction as I understood the term, was very far from what Asimov and Heinlein and Clarke had done. (It was not that far from Sturgeon or Bradbury or Leiber.) *Nightwings* was still straight s-f and won a Hugo, but I wrote that in 1968. By the time of *Skulls* and *Dying Inside*, a few years later, the majority of the readers had turned hostile to my work, or so it seemed to me, and that was when I decided to give up writing.

Q: In any case, when you do something innovative, isn't it inherent in the nature of such an enterprise that you are going to leave some of the duller or lazier readers behind? Surely when Bester wrote *The Stars My Destination* he left Captain Future fans behind him in the dust. Is this a problem?

RS: It was a long way from Captain Future to *The Stars My Destination*, sure. But for all its verbal and conceptual brilliance, *Stars* still followed the pulp conventions, sturdy hero triumphing over his adversaries. In a lot of my work of the period the hero wasn't all that sturdy and he didn't always triumph.

Q: Or was it more of an economic issue, that, say, *Son of Man* or *The Book of Skulls* did not sell as well as the latest post-Tolkien knockoff trilogy, and publishers were beginning to notice?

RS: Nobody ever expected those two books to outsell the standard kind of s-f. (The trilogy boom had not yet really begun.) My publishers were still willing to buy from me. But I had lost heart. I was very tired, having done something like 15 novels in just a few years and most of them very exhausting things to write. I just wanted to go away and rest. And I did.

Q: Would you say then that *Lord Valentine's Castle* and sequels were a successful compromise, then, i.e. something which fit the current taste but which you could still write with integrity?

RS: Yes. It's a cheerful, positive book full of interesting ideas, and the protagonist comes out okay at the end, but it is recognizably Silverbergian in style. Nothing experimental about it, but nothing that was written down for a slow-witted audience, either.

Q: An aside, now that I've mentioned the title. I have seen a reissue of The Book of Skulls that says "soon to be a major motion picture" or something like that. But no movie. What has happened to it?

RS: It went right to the edge of production—a director had been chosen, even. (William Friedkin.) Then the head of the studio, who was Friedkin's wife, lost her job and all her projects were canceled. You grow used to this sort of thing when you deal with Hollywood; you cash the check and hope for the best, and it's foolish to expect anything good to happen beyond that, though sometimes it does.

Q: You've seen movements come and go in SF by now. The early '50s seems to have been a fairly revolutionary period. The New Wave is surely assimilated by now, to the extent that writers who grew up on the New Wave are now influencing younger writers. One might argue that Slipstream is the New Wave all over again, only with fewer science fiction tropes. So, what do you make of this? Are we going to be looking at revolution and reaction followed by complacency followed by revolution over and over, forever?

RS: That's what I would expect. This sort of cycle has been going on since Gernsback days. The Sloane *Amazing,* in 1933, began running astonishing semi-abstract covers by an artist named Sigmond. Like nothing s-f mags had ever seen before. (Or pretty much since.) The readers rose up in fury and the magazine reverted, in 1934 and 1935, to some of the dreariest illustrative covers ever seen in the field. I know, this is illustration, not fiction, but it indicates that any attempt to change the formulas brings, usually, a reaction, and often an overreaction.

Q: I've seen those covers and know what you mean. Then again, Gernsback experimented with abstract covers on *Wonder Stories* about the same time. There was one that was little more than a field of dots. It must not have gone over very well with the readers, because it was soon stopped.

But maybe you're basically right. Robert E. Howard remarked in the middle '30s that he didn't want to write SF, because it was far *more* formulaic than other forms of pulp fiction such as westerns or sport stories, and the readers would howl if there was the slightest departure from formula. But is this *still* the case? Do you think that SF is inherently conservative? If so, isn't it an odd paradox that this literature which is supposedly about the future and limitless horizons rejects new approaches?

RS: I do. What a lot of us tend to forget from time to time is that s-f in the United States is a branch of popular entertainment, not a kind of avant-garde literature. There's a certain core of readers looking for sophisticated visionary experiences, sure, but most of the audience is just interested in finding an hour's light entertainment. When that substantial portion of the audience runs up against fiction that is difficult to read (Aldiss's *Barefoot in the Head*, for example) or difficult to understand (a lot of the modern high-tech stuff) or heavily downbeat (Ballard, let's say) it goes off in search of something more to its taste. I guess it's paradoxical that so many readers of a kind of fiction that deals in infinite horizons of time and space want the same old thing every time, but that's the way it is, and so be it.

Q: If so, then what makes it worthwhile for a writer to struggle *against* what he knows the readers actually want?

RS: We don't always realize that we're doing that. Even as sharp-eyed an observer of trends and tastes as, ah, Robert Silverberg failed to notice that he was swimming upstream all through 1969 and 1970 and 1971. Then, too, some of us write just for the pleasure of it, and don't give a damn about commercial requirements. To a certain degree that's what I was doing during my big creative period in the late sixties. And some of us are very obstinate.

Q: Do you read enough contemporary SF to have any sense of the state of the field today?

RS: No. I read hardly any, these days.

Q: Do you have any sense that anybody is standing on your shoulders?

RS: I'd like to think so. When Elizabeth Bear complained that the older writers don't read the newer ones, I made a point of reading some stories by three of the writers she cited and saw distinct signs of my influence on all three. It may have been at second or third remove, but I do believe the fiction I wrote in the 1967-73 period, and some of the later work, had a lasting impact.

Q: As for what the readers allegedly did not like in your work in the early '70s, I can't help but notice that books like *Dying Inside* and *The Book of Skulls* have shown real staying power. Particularly *Dying Inside* is now regarded as a classic. So, what happened? Might it not be that the conventional book will be easily replaced by another conventional book, but that the unique one, even if it sells fewer copies at first, can't be and therefore stays in print?

RS: They don't stay in print. They have to be brought back, again and again. Each time they find a new (small) audience, and eventually they slip out of sight again, and then some adventurous new publisher takes a chance on them, with the same result. I've been assiduous in finding new publishers for my books, but, then, I'm alive to do it. Sturgeon and Blish and Kornbluth aren't, and but for the work of some dedicated small presses they'd be forgotten today.

Q: Isn't it some cause for optimism that publishers keep trying? After all, in today's market very little stays continuously in print. I can cite an example. I found a letter in a 1972 fanzine in which James Blish is bemoaning the fact that one of his short story collections published in mass-market paperback by Ballantine (he doesn't give the title but is probably talking about *So Close to Home*, 1961) has "died the death" and gone out of print *after eleven years*. You know better than I do how that just does not compute in modern publishing terms. Story collection by a midlist writer? In mass-market paperback? In print for 11 years? Who could imagine it today?

RS: Publishing has changed quite a bit since then. Books like the Blish collection, and *Son of Man* and a lot of other off-beat things, were published by Ballantine before it morphed into Del Rey. Betty Ballantine loved her authors and coddled them, and was willing to publish things that could be seen a priori not to have big commercial futures; she would stand behind those books for years. She ran the company as an expression of her personal tastes and counted on big sellers like her Clarke books to carry the rest along. Eventually the Ballantines had to sell their company. There may be a connection there.

Q: I'd like to posit something to you about *Dying Inside*. Is this the last major psi novel? Of course you were working in the field when psi was everywhere and John Campbell seemed to think it was an "essential science" on which science fiction had to be based, just like physics or astronomy. But while there have been novels since which have had psi as one component among many, I cannot think of a later one (within the SF category, not counting something like Stephen King's *Firestarter*) in which psi is the primary subject. So, were you in any sense consciously bidding farewell to this old and tired SF trope? I can well imagine that John W. Campbell would *not* have approved.

RS: I wouldn't know. Probably there have been psi novels since mine, but I haven't been aware of them. Campbell, of course, would not have cared much for *Dying Inside*, because of its near-contemporary setting, the sex, the mainstream tone. There was some irony in the book's getting a special award from the Campbell Award people (not the worldcon award, the other Campbell award.) And the same year Barry Malzberg won that Campbell award for as unCampbellian a book as could be imagined this side of Samuel Beckett.

Q: While I've brought his name up, could you describe your working relationship with John Campbell? Is it true that you and Randall Garrett used to race each other to see who could sell Campbell a story based on one of his editorials? Or is this just fannish legend?

RS: No, not true. John wanted his writers to pay attention to his editorials, but he didn't want them simply to feed his own ideas back to him, and he rejected stories that were of that sort. What he wanted was to establish a sort of Socratic dialog, the writers working with the concepts in the editorials but adding their own spin. Poul Anderson was better at this than anyone, though Garrett did it well. There was a distinct Campbell "slant" and we all knew what it was—he disliked stories in which aliens get the upper hand over humans, for example—but selling stories to him was not the simple button-pushing business fans think it was.

I did try to push buttons, now and then. Garrett and I used a Scottish protagonist, Duncan MacLeod, for an early story, and sold it to John. John was always partial to Scots. I wrote some stories for Horace Gold in which people were confined in close quarters, as Horace was, and he bought them. But when Garrett and I concocted a story for Tony Boucher, who was Catholic, a notorious opera-lover and cat-lover, and an expert on detective stories, about an opera-loving priest whose cat solved a murder mystery, Tony rejected it with a grin of appreciation for the stunt—but rejected it all the same. (Bob Lowndes, who was an Anglican but otherwise shared Tony's interests, bought it.)

Q: Surely the trick is to not let the editor know his buttons are being pushed. Besides, that kind of stunt writing is something you do when you're younger, isn't it? Do you find as you get older that you're less interested in writing stories which are contrivances aimed at a market?

RS: I certainly don't aim at markets, these days. Everything I write is sold before I write it, so why twist myself out of shape to meet someone else's slant? But stunt writing—well, yes, I still enjoy doing that, writing a story in the voice Jack Vance used in *The Dying Earth*, or doing a novella interwoven with "Vintage Season" to tell the other side of the story, or playing around with themes out of Conrad.

Q: So, what are you writing these days?

RS: Not much. I did two Majipoor stories this winter to round out a collection I'm assembling, and a Time Patrol story for a Poul Anderson memorial anthology. But I've got nothing on my schedule now except a lot of introductions to reissues of old work of mine. For the time being I want to take a break from writing fiction, and I don't know how long that break is going to last—six months, a year, forever, maybe. I can't say. And won't. Lord knows I've written quite a few stories for one human being in one lifetime, and I don't feel enormous inner pressure to add to the list.

Q: Thanks, Bob.

ALLEN STEELE

INTRODUCTION

Allen M. Steele is one of those science fiction writers whose fiction is more often than not set in outer space or on other planets. His first published novel was *Orbital Decay* (1989), which is the beginning of his Near Space or Rude Astronauts series. He is best known for *Coyote: a Novel of Interstellar Exploration* (2002) and its various sequels and companion volumes. He has won the Hugo Award three times, twice for novella, for "The Death of Captain Future" (1996) and "Where Angels Fear" (1998) and for novelette, for "The Emperor of Mars" (2011). He is originally from Nashville, Tennessee, but presently lives with his wife Linda in Massachusetts.

⊷✻⊶

Q: You could give our readers some idea of your background, where you're from, where you were educated, what you thought you would do with your life before it was taken over by science fiction?

Steele: I was born and raised in Nashville, where I spent the first couple of decades of my life. My education was public-school until the seventh grade, when I went to the first of the two private schools I'd eventually get kicked out of. Nashville was a very conservative town in the 60's and early 70's, so if you were an upper middle-class kid in that place and time, it pretty much meant one of two things; either you'd get with the program and make good grades, go to church every Sunday, vote Republican, keep your hair short and your lip buttoned up, and go on to marry a cheerleader and get a job at a bank or an insurance company and otherwise have a comfortable but dull life … or you'd rebel.

I think I began to rebel as early as the fourth grade, but by the time I was in junior high school it had become pretty serious. If you can name some kind of trouble I'd either cause or get myself into, chances are I did it. I managed to make it all the way to the ninth grade in one school before they had enough of me and invited me not to return for my sophomore year, so my folks shipped me off to the Webb School, a boarding school in west Tennessee, where I lasted for only six weeks before I was thrown out. I spent the rest of that school year in a public school before my father managed to get me reinstated at Webb, this time letting me know that, if I didn't knock off the Patrick McGoohan act, military academy was going to be my next stop.

There's a couple of bits of irony there. First, I later compared notes with guys like me who'd been sent to military academy, and they told me that, once they got past having to wear a uniform, they had a blast; it was like being given a license to raise hell, so long as you didn't actually blow up the place. So I might have been happy there. Second, John Scalzi went to Webb's sister school in California, where he had a great time. But the Webb School in California was a far more progressive place than the Webb School in Tennessee, and I had to throttle down quite a bit.

Anyway, I decided to put up with things I didn't like, telling myself that, if I could just get through high school, I could leave all this behind and go do what I really wanted to do with my life … which, by then, was become a science fiction writer.

Q: Related to that, when *did* you realize that your life was going to be taken over by science fiction?

Steele: My life was taken over by science fiction as soon as I began reading the stuff, and that was around the time I started visiting the principal's office on a daily basis. I'm not going to blame SF for being the root cause of all my bad behavior, but it certainly was a contributing factor. One of the subtle yet omnipresent themes of SF is nonconformity, of questioning the beliefs and attitudes of the world around you and acting upon it. SF can be quite subversive, really, although it's seldom recognized as such. Anyone who believes that Robert Heinlein was a conservative writer hasn't read much Heinlein, or very deeply … and just wait until you graduate from Heinlein juveniles to Harlan Ellison!

One of the best things I got from SF, though, was an interest and respect for science. Tennessee schools in the 60's and 70's were particularly lousy when it came to science, and that went for the private schools as well as the public education system. There was even a biology teacher at Webb who was teaching creationism … I spent a weekend raking leaves after I challenged him on his views of evolution. And one of my best moments was walking out of a Sunday school class when the teacher tried to tell us that the Book of Genesis was literal truth. I learned about science from reading Isaac Asimov's column in *Fantasy & Science Fiction*, Jerry Pournelle's column in *Galaxy*, and every issue of *Analog* from cover to cover. I really didn't have a formal science education worth speaking of until I got to college, but in many ways I got a better understanding of science from the magazines and novels I was reading late at night than the classes I was dozing through during the day.

And in the meantime, I decided to become a writer … very specifically, a science fiction writer.

Q: So, when you were in school, was reading science fiction itself a form of rebellion? I can't imagine that creationist biology teacher would have had much use for it. Indeed, the two chief messages of science fiction are inherently subversive: that the future might have different values and not everything about the universe and our place in it is known yet. If you believe in a literal interpretation of Genesis, all has been revealed and there is nothing to speculate about.

Steele: I kind of think so, yes ...although in that place and time, reading anything for pleasure was uncool, unless it was *Playboy* or *Sports Illustrated*. Very few teenagers I knew read SF or fantasy, and those who did had better sense than me and left their books at home or in their dorm rooms. I carried my paperbacks and magazines at all times, so I could read them between classes (and sometimes during class, in the time-honored tradition of hiding them within my textbooks). I got a lot of crap for this which I remember to this day, although I got over it a long time ago. It helped to learn, around the time my first novel was published and I was making a name for myself as an up-and-coming new writer, that the big-jock-on-campus who'd call me "Dr. Spock" and ask me how things were on Mars was pumping gas in a one-stoplight town in Louisiana.

But you're right ... there's a certain mindset behind pious acceptance of creationism and the like which says that the universe is unchanging, and it often manifests itself in an inability to step outside what are considered the accepted community standards of behavior. SF stands in opposition to this. Sometimes, though, even kids I knew who were trapped in those roles would find ways to get out. One guy I knew back then had a fundamentalist mother who wouldn't allow any books in her house besides the Bible and his school books. He was a SF reader, though, so he got around it by keeping his paperbacks hidden beneath his mattress and getting rid of them as soon as he was finished. We'd talk about the stuff we were reading when we were sure no one else was around. I understand he grew up to be a preacher, just as his mother intended, and I've also been told that he's one of my biggest fans. Rebellion can be a quiet thing. I was just a little more up-front and in-your-face about it than most.

Q: I've read your famous (and Hugo-winning) "The Death of Captain Future" and this raises two questions, one geeky and silly, the other more serious. The silly one is why this future nerd/obsessive did not have his precious 20th century pulp magazines de-acidified. You can do that now with a spray from the Gaylord Company, for about $35 a magazine. It renders the paper PH-neutral and stops the decay. I am sure this will be even easier to do in the future. His copies should not be crumbling.

Steele: Well, if you really want to be persnickety about it, you can also ask why Bo even bothered to collect pulps in the first place, but instead simply download them as ebooks the way we can now. The fact that my story was written in 1995 before this sort of digitalization became widespread isn't an excuse ... obviously I failed to predict the future! So that's a reason why "The Death of Captain Future" is no longer worth reading, isn't it?

I think the tendency of fans to nitpick the stories they read for real or perceived errors is one of the things which have hampered science fiction. It doesn't really accomplish anything of practical value, because authors seldom have a chance to make revisions to published work beyond changing or scratching out a few words here or there, and it adds to the public perception that SF is the sort of stuff only read by people who still live in their parents' basement. And more often than not, the nitpicking is either flat-out wrong—like an online reader-review for my new book, *V-S Day*, which claimed that I didn't have any of the 1940's scientists in that novel using slide-rulers, when you see them doing exactly that in the very first chapter—or carried to absurd lengths. Bob Eggleton told me that he once overheard a couple of fans at a convention discussing a painting he'd done of a dragon and criticizing it on the basis that the musculature of its wings wasn't sufficient to allow it to become airborne. It's a dragon...*they don't exist!*

Fans will say that they're keeping writers on their toes, but I think this is only self-justification for petty behavior. Really, it discourages writers from being specific in their details. If you know you going to get hammered for not telling the reader the exact atmospheric pressure of the planet your characters are visiting, then why bother with trying to be realistic? Call the place Oz, let them get there in a hot-air balloon, and shrug if anyone complains that the flying monkeys aren't aerodynamic.

Q: The serious question has to do with the story itself. This is what some critics would call a Late Science Fiction story. It is almost a metafiction. The characters even discuss science fiction. The story is written with a great awareness of the past of the field, which was very different than it was for the actual pioneers like Edmond Hamilton or Jack Williamson, who had very little behind them. I like the way the characters apply science fiction to their actual lives, i.e. using it to create a myth of heroism when space travel has become as dull as truck driving. But isn't this inherently self-limiting, sort of the way late classical Latin poetry got when it became mostly a matter of references to earlier works? How do you feel about the inevitable self-awareness of the form that comes with writing science fiction these days?

Steele: The major theme of "The Death of Captain Future" is how real heroism is much different from fictional heroism. Bo is someone who believes that heroism means recklessly running into a dangerous situation without thought of the possible consequences of his actions. Rohr, the narrator, is a pragmatist who knows that the universe is a dangerous place that can kill you if you're careless. Bo thinks being a hero means emulating Captain Future, and in the end this dissonance leads to him to his death. Rohr survives because he knows better … and in the end, he becomes the hero who saves the day and gets the girl, although it's Bo who gets the credit.

So, yes, the story is commentary on SF itself. One of the things I find odd about science fiction—although there's a lot less of this lately—is the notion that, in the future, people will have forgotten that there's ever been any SF. You'll see first-contact stories, for instance, where no one ever stops and says, "Yknow, wasn't there a *Star Trek* episode that dealt with something like this?" In the real world, you can barely get through the day without someone remarking that such-and-such "looks like science fiction, but it isn't." As many people have noted, we live in an SFnal world, but SF itself often exists in a cultural vacuum …except perhaps for references to Shakespeare, which everyone seems to have read and is able to quote at the drop of a hat.

That's been changing in recent years, though. I'm seeing more SF stories where SF itself becomes a cultural reference. I don't think this is a limitation any more than it would be, say, for a character in a horror story to mention in passing that they've read *Dracula* and how Stoker said that using a wooden stake is the proper way to dispatch a vampire. Mentioning a previously published story doesn't necessarily mean that a writer has to limit himself or herself to what was done before. It's just an acknowledgement that the past does indeed exist, and someone back then was thinking about the future before it actually happened.

Q: Well I suppose Bo wants the original *Captain Future* pulps because they are sacred artifacts to him. He wants them for the look and feel and even the smell … which may be why he didn't get them chemically treated to prevent their decay. They must have cost him a fortune, particularly if you factor in the cost of getting them up off the Earth into space.

Steele: The problem with discussing a story published 19 years ago is that someone who read it just recently is probably more familiar with the details than the author. I imagine that Bo wanted the originals because they're valuable, as you suggest. I have an extensive collection of pulps myself, and although I can read their stories in the anthologies I have in my library, I prefer the original versions. It's sort of the poor man's answer to collecting antique cars. Bo is probably the same way …but again, that's something you'd have to infer from the benefit of hindsight. If digitalization had been commonplace when I wrote "The Death of Captain Future" in 1995, I might have used that technology instead.

Q: I think you're right that any future we are likely to face from now on, unless it is a post-holocaust, barbarian one, will have science fiction in it as a cultural reference. I am reminded of that astronaut they had at the Nebulas who said, "We went into space because you guys told us to." So what do we say to the people who say that science fiction is done? There are those who insist it's run its course. I don't believe this is so, and I doubt you do either. The last time someone explained to me at length why science fiction was finished and could no longer be written was in 1983, and Cyberpunk happened the following year.

Steele: People have been saying that science fiction is dying or dead for as long as I've been actively involved in the SF field. I remember when people were claiming that the field was being destroyed by the Perry Rhodan paperbacks Ace was publishing in the '70s. When my first novel came out in 1989, *Star Trek* novels were the killer asteroid which was about to wipe out the genre. Now it's vampire books and steampunk and military space-opera and whatever other fad that comes through and sucks all the air out of the room for a while.

Science fiction survives. It outlasts fashions and trends and gluts because there are always readers who prefer the real thing over the stuff that gets churned out for a quick buck. One of the reasons why I'm something of a traditionalist and have been careful to avoid band-wagons is that longevity belongs to those writers who don't just go where the money is. Cyberpunk was the rage when I entered the field in the late 80's, and many of the new writers who came in the same time that I did were doing the c-punk thing. Most of them have vanished, while those of us who've survived did so because we wrote SF and fantasy of a more durable variety. Our books may not be bestsellers, but I prefer to have written a novel like *Coyote*, which is still in print after 12 years and is now being taught in college SF classes, to a book that hit the bestseller list for two or three weeks but can now be found providing insulation for the walls of a used book store.

Q: At the same time, how do we avoid SF getting too in-groupish and self-referential? Do you see a split into two streams, science fiction for the mainstream and science fiction for the science fiction audience?

Steele: As coincidence would have it, I'm currently reading the second volume of William Patterson's excellent biography of Robert A. Heinlein—Tor was kind enough to send me an advance copy before publication—and there's account of correspondence that passed between Heinlein and Forrest J. Ackerman. Forry objected to the stories Heinlein was publishing in the *Saturday Evening Post*, saying that they were watered-down SF that weren't like the material Heinlein had previously written for *Astounding*, to which Heinlein responded that the readership of the slicks was much larger than that of the pulps, and his objective with stories like "The Green Hills of Earth" was to interest general readers in space travel, not to get them to read more science fiction.

I think history has proven Heinlein right. There are times when SF has been very in-groupish and insular, and you see that in those periods when the average SF novel or story can't be understood by anyone who hasn't already read everything from Aldiss to Zelazny or isn't conversant in singularity theory or quantum entanglement. Up until a few years ago, that was my chief criticism of the field. That's changed lately, although not for the best reasons. Fads and trends are currently dominating what's being published, and I sometimes think that if I see another novel about an alien invasion of Earth or a dystopian society where teenagers are having fire-fights with soldiers in power armor, I'm going to hurl my lunch.

It's great when a SF novel hits the literary mainstream and becomes a bestseller. The genre can't remain the sole province of geeks and fans and still have a healthy future. The problem is that, because such books are often produced by writers who have little prior knowledge of the genre, they often deal with subjects that previous generations of SF authors took on years ago, without much visible improvement. So the SF bestseller lists are being swamped with retreads of retreads. The literary frontier is still deep within the genre, with the print and online magazines—as always—providing the unexplored forest beyond the sunny and well-populated beach.

Q: What intrigues me about your more recent "The Emperor of Mars" (2010) is that I think you've hit on an interesting, albeit narrow vein here: science fiction about how science fiction effects the culture of the future. A difficult trick to pull off, is it not? I don't think anyone else has put any particular emphasis on this.

Steele: When I learned that the Planetary Society had persuaded NASA to place a disk containing a library of Mars stories and artwork aboard the Phoenix lander, I was so happy that I didn't mind the fact that they hadn't asked my permission to also include my story "Live from the Mars Hotel" on the commercial release of that same disk. I was just pleased that my first widely-published story was finding its way to Mars. I'll probably never walk on another world, but my work will be there, and that's good enough for me.

When I saw the list of stories on the disk, one of the things that jumped out at me was the fact that most of them came from the pre-space flight era of science fiction. Along with Bear and Benford and Varley and Steele, there was also Wells and Burroughs and Weinbaum and Bradbury. And it occurred to me that, if a future Mars colonist were to ever recover the disk and successfully download its contents, he or she would probably enjoy Brackett more than Clarke, or Zelazny more than Robinson, because their stories represented a Mars that didn't look very much like the place where they were now living. That Mars—the so called "old Mars" to use term recently coined by George R.R. Martin and Gardner Dozois for the anthology for which "The Emperor or Mars" was originally written—is the one that's more appealing in many ways, the one which prompted everyone from Robert H. Goddard onward to want to go there. If I was a morbidly depressed Mars colonist who was stuck there with no immediate way home, this might become a fantasy world in which I'd gladly retreat.

So this story is about two things. The obvious one, of course, is how we often use fiction as a means of dealing with reality, particularly the scary or tragic events that sometimes happen to us. Anyone who's ever latched onto a book as a way of dealing with this sort of thing knows exactly what I mean. But the other and more subtle context of the story is something which intrigues me about science fiction itself, how it occasionally helps form a creative feedback-loop in which writers look over the shoulders of scientists to get ideas for stories, and then scientists in turn gain inspiration from the SF stories they read for their own real-world efforts.

I've seen this in action lately during the recent 100-Year Starship and Starship Century conferences, where SF writers and scientists have gathered to discuss the prospects for building interstellar spaceships within the next hundred years. At these things, there's been very little division between these two different kinds of visionaries. The series of stories I'm currently writing comes straight from my notes of presentations delivered by Freeman Dyson and Jim Benford, and the scientists who spoke there often alluded to SF stories they'd read.

If no one else has written a story about this sort of thing, then I guess I'm a bit surprised. It seems like such an obvious insight.

Q: The point about "mainstream SF" is that there are lots of books, like *The Postmortal* by Drew McGary or *Never Let Me Go* by Kazuo Ishiguro which are science fiction by any definition but are not published as science fiction and may well reach an audience that doesn't ordinarily read science fiction. Is there still a real difference in technique, or how language is used in such a book? You wouldn't start a story for a mainstream audience with "The jumpship dropped out of warp half a parsec from Rigel IV." That would be gibberish to them. But it would pass without notice in *Analog*.

Steele: This is one of those questions where there is no answer that can't be argued by counter-example. If "mainstream SF" is distinguished by the lack of technical jargon, then where does that leave, say, Michael Crichton's novels? If we decide to call it "literary SF" instead and use the same definition, then what do we do with novels like Gregory Benford's *Against Infinity* or Gene Wolfe's *The Shadow of the Torturer* or Samuel Delany's *Nova*, which are clearly "literary" in intent but also use genre techniques? If "mainstream" or "literary" SF doesn't concern itself with traditional SF subjects like space exploration, then what do we make of a novel like Mary Doria Russell's *The Sparrow* or much of Doris Lessing's work? And if we decide that it's simply a matter of publisher labels—i.e. "mainstream SF is the stuff that isn't being called science fiction"—then what happens when we point to books like, on one hand, *Fahrenheit 451*, which was originally published as a genre paperback from a genre publisher but has since become accepted as part of the mainstream canon, or, on the other hand, *1984*, which never was presented as SF but clearly is?

Because there's no clear answer to this, it's one of those things that drives SF writers, editors, and serious readers completely crazy, and I believe the reason it does so is the genre's long-standing inferiority complex. Those of us who live and work in this so-called ghetto have a tendency to look over at the clean streets and well-manicured lawns of contemporary fiction (aka the "mainstream") and become jealous of its perceived wealth and success, and get just a little pissed off when something is published that explores ideas first developed in genre SF but gets reviewed by *The New York Times Sunday Book Review* instead of *Analog*. But I know quite a few mainstream writers, and their books are usually ignored just as much as SF novels are. Indeed, the average SF novel is often more successful than the average mainstream novel.

I had a chance to become a mainstream writer. My writing teacher was Russell Banks, and the first novel I produced, *Play Dirty*, was a contemporary novel that I wrote under his tutelage but went unsold and unpublished. Russ was very disappointed that I returned to science fiction, a genre he despises, to write my second novel, *Orbital Decay* (which, of course, is regarded as my "first" novel), but I think that, if I'd stuck it out in the mainstream, my career would have lasted only a few years and eventually I would've become just another writer who'd published a couple of now-forgotten books before getting a job teaching creative writing at some community college. Or worse, a middle-aged journalist who'd now be out of work because the slow death of the newspaper industry.

Yeah, it's probably a difference of technique. Probably also subject, approach, depth of characterization, marketing and any of a number of different factors. Ultimately, though, it comes down to one thing: are readers going to enjoy your work? If they do, and continue buying and reading over the years, then does it really matter that you'll never get a MacArthur fellowship?

Q: So let's talk more about *Coyote*. Is this going to be your *Dune*?

Steele: I'm reluctant to have my best-known work compared to one of the acknowledged classics of the genre. The book has been in print for almost twelve years, yes, and now it's being taught in college SF classes, but it may be a bit presumptuous to claim that it's entered the canon. On the other hand, I'm very complimented by the fact that a number of people have lately been describing it as "the new *Dune*."

The thing that's most satisfying about *Coyote*'s success is that, because the book takes an unconventional form, it was initially rejected by quite a few genre readers. There were some bad fan reviews for this novel when it first came out. It's not a linear novel, but instead told as a linked series of stories, with different narrators, viewpoints, and tenses, sometimes even divergent reiterations of the same events. Halfway through the novel, I kill off a character who'd been presented as the main protagonist. All of this was intentional, but it disturbed readers who are more accustomed to straight-forward narratives with an obvious hero as the central character. This untraditional approach rattled some people and they reacted negatively, but in the long run its unconventional nature has given *Coyote* some staying power.

Q: Taught on college classes? Do you hear from the students? How does it feel to be a classic, just like Herman Melville?

Steele: It would be even more presumptuous to compare *Coyote* to *Moby Dick*, although I believe that, if Melville were alive and well today, he'd probably be writing science fiction. I know this sounds weird, but when I was taking a college class in American transcendentalist literature, it occurred to me that what Melville wrote about was very similar to what SF writers would later be doing: using a voyage into the unknown to the dark side of human nature. And when my class visited the historic New Bedford seaport and went to the customs house where Melville worked, I saw it as an early 19th century analogue to Cape Canaveral. Bradbury perceived much the same thing, I think, when he wrote "Leviathan '99 "—an overlooked later work which made me jealous because I didn't do it first.

I've heard from students who've read *Coyote* as part of their curricula, and a couple of times I've done guest appearances at schools in the area where the kids have been reading the book. Interestingly, they often understand the novel better than some fans have. Maybe it's because they've come to it without a lot of preconceived notions about what a SF novel ought to be. I don't know. But it was a strange thing to once visit the off-campus college bookstore that supplies UMass students with their course reading and find stacks of *Coyote* on the inventory shelves alongside text-books.

Q: About that feedback loop between science and science fiction, do you usually get your story idea from science (or a scientific presentation), or do you start with an image or a situation and then start looking around for scientific stuff to rationalize it?

Steele: It seems to come all at once as a brainstorm. I'll read something in the scientific literature, hear a lecture, or watch a documentary, and something just clicks: a story begins to form in my mind, and with it the major character or characters. If I've remembered to carry my pocket notebook that day, I'll jot down a few story notes, and if I'm still playing with the idea after a week or two, I figure that I may have something there and start doing serious research.

Very often, I'll bounce the story off my wife to see what she thinks of it. Since Linda doesn't read SF besides mine, her feedback can be a good thing since I'm trying to appeal to readers who aren't necessarily SF fans. And because she's pretty good at telling me whether it's a dumb idea or something worth pursuing, she's saved me from embarrassing myself with stories that shouldn't be written. But early in my career, Harlan Ellison gave me some advice: a bad idea can occasionally lead to a good one if you work with it long enough. I once had an urge to write a sequel to *Voyage to the Bottom of the Sea* until Linda talked me out of. I still wanted to do an undersea novel, though, because that was what I was really trying to get at, so the story eventually evolved into *Oceanspace*.

Overall, the genesis phase is organic process that I try not to analyze too deeply. It's the research and development phase that takes a very long time, sometimes longer than the actual writing itself. The novella I wrote last fall—"The Legion of Tomorrow," which will be in the July issue of *Asimov's*—took about a decade to move from notes to published form. *Coyote* had a couple of false-starts before I got it right. Very seldom do I have a story that comes to me in such a hot flash that I begin writing it immediately, and I've seldom been happy with those that have.

Q: I think you're right about Melville. *Moby Dick* is one of those non-science fiction books which has had an enormous influence in science fiction, because it is, thematically, very close to SF. We've had at least two science fiction sequels, John Kessel's "Another Orphan" and Philip José Farmer's *The Wind-Whales of Ishmael*. Did bit have a science-fictional feel to you when you first read it?

Steele: The first time I tried to read *Moby Dick*, I didn't finish it. On the other hand, I don't think is a book that should be assigned to kids as school reading. The second time, though, yes, I had that sort of feeling you can get from a SF novel ... but that wasn't until after I visited New Bedford and had that revelation I mentioned earlier.

A contemporary, non-fiction book about a similar subject had an even more profound influence on me than *Moby Dick* is *Sea of Glory* by Nathaniel Philbrick, which is about the U.S. Exploratory Expedition of 1820. This was a real-life science fiction story of sorts: a five-year global sea expedition which, among other things, resulted in the first landfall on the Antarctic continent, the first mapping of mthe Fiji islands, and a collection of rare plants that would later form the basis of the National Botanical Garden in Washington D.C. The most interesting part of the story, though, is its commanding officer, a young U.S. Navy lieutenant who was put in charge of the expedition despite the fact that he didn't have command rank and was unqualified for the role, but who got the job because his wife's father was a senator with considerable political clout. His ineptitude cost the expedition one of its ships and the lives of many crewmen, caused several scientists to jump ship and make their own way home, and very nearly resulted in mutiny. It was only the actions of his first officer, a more experienced seaman who should have been made captain, which saved the expedition from complete failure.

Sea of Glory inspired me to write about much the same sort of situation in *Spindrift*, and the book received an incredulous reaction from quite a few readers and fan reviewers. They couldn't believe that a ship's captain would be so stupid. In hindsight, I've come to believe that many SF fans have been thoroughly indoctrinated in the *Star Trek* notion that captains are always right, the crew is always loyal, and no one ever makes mistakes. I call this this sort of thing "the perfect people future." But when you study the history of exploration, matters are seldom so clear-cut and simple. Exploration has often been messy, gut-wrenching, and very dangerous, and I have little doubt that it'll be the same as we go out into space.

Q: Other than getting one of your stories placed on Mars, are you aware of any other impact your fiction has had on real science? Isaac Asimov could see roboticists following his ideas, but I am not sure how many other SF writers get to enjoy that experience.

Steele: Another favorite moment of my career was when I had a friend, a fan I'd met when he was an engineering student at UMass and who'd since gone on to work for NASA at the Johnson Space Center, tell me that he'd decided to pursue a career in the space industry because he'd read *Orbital Decay*. I've also received a few letters from other people actively involved with space exploration tell me that my books have encouraged them to keep at it despite the frustration they've often felt. This sort of praise makes it all worthwhile. It's told me that I'm working for a higher purpose than selling books or getting awards.

Q: I suppose what I mean about the Coyote series becoming your *Dune* is that it could take over your career. I mean, we all should have this problem, but the publishers could just keep on saying, "Here's half a million bucks, write me a book just like the last one," and this goes on and on until they won't let you do anything else. Do you think you could get to the point where this is all anybody knows about you, that you're the *Coyote* guy?

Steele: Hah! If my publisher were to offer me a half-million dollars to write anything, let alone a new Coyote novel, I'd gladly do so. People tend to overestimate by a considerable factor how much writers earn, though. There's only a small-and-getting-smaller handful of full-time SF writers who earn more than a middle-class income, and I'm not one of them.

Aside from that, though ... yes, the success of the Coyote series has threatened to overshadow everything I've done since then. That includes the three spin-off novels—*Spindrift*, *Galaxy Blues*, and *Hex*—which are set in the same universe, but only have brief scenes on Coyote itself. Unfortunately, I've learned that, unless the word "Coyote" appears in the title, the readers who loved the five novels in the main sequence aren't as interested in them. This has been a disappointment, particularly since I worked as hard on building Hex—the Dyson sphere that's the title world of the novel—as I did Coyote.

After I finished *Coyote Frontier*, the third novel of the original trilogy, and was about to move on with *Spindrift*, the first of the spin-offs, Ginjer Buchanan, my editor at Ace, warned me that I might not be able to leave Coyote as easily as I thought. She told me that Frank Herbert had felt trapped by his own creation; he was proud of what he'd written since then, but his readers only wanted more Dune books. Ginjer was right. I'm getting the same thing now. I put a cap on the Coyote series a few years ago with *Coyote Destiny*, the fifth novel, but when I've published an unrelated novel like *Apollo's Outcasts* or *V-S Day*, I get letters or comments to the effect of, "Well, that's nice, but when are you going to write a new Coyote book?"

I've got some ideas for a sixth Coyote novel and have written down a few notes, and one day I may bite the bullet and get on with it. But those books were hellishly difficult to write. They all have an eight-part structure which have two or three concurrent plots involving large casts of characters, and this octagonal narrative approach sometimes switches viewpoints and voices. So I refuse to do a new Coyote book simply for the money. If I find a better reason than that to write a sixth Coyote novel, I will. But if I don't, then I won't.

Q: I gather you are a "talker," i.e. a writer who can talk about an idea before writing it. Larry Niven seems to think that if the idea can't start an argument first, or at least a lively discussion, it is not worth writing. But there are other writers for whom *any* talking about the story beforehand will remove the impulse to write it. I am much closer to that camp myself.

Steele: It all depends with whom I'm talking. I generally refrain from discussing works-in-progress in public, such as convention panels, except in the most general terms. Ditto with readers and most other writers. On the other hand, I've discovered that it's helpful to be table to talk these things through with people who are on the same wavelength. The kind of stuff I write is fairly complex on several levels, and it helps to have someone who can listen to a story that's being developed and offer advice. Besides Linda,

I have a number of close friends—writers, scientists, fans—whom I can turn to while I'm in the research and development phase and discuss things. And in recent years I've begun enlisting first readers, something I didn't do for a very long time. I had a great first-reader in my late friend Ace March-ant, who helped me with the later Coyote novels and the spin-offs, and after he passed away a couple of years ago I replaced him with Rob Caswell, who also supplied the frontispiece illustrations for *Galaxy Blues*, *Hex*, and *Apollo's Outcasts*.

But talking through stories isn't something everyone can or should do. If you don't think you can discuss a work in progress without losing the urge to put it on paper, then by all means, keep it to yourself. I know writers who wouldn't tell you the first thing about what they're working on even if you tortured them on the rack. And I think you need to be careful that you're not boring the person you're talking to. Before I met Linda, I lost a girlfriend that way. She'd actually get pissed off when I'd start discussing the great idea I just had for a story. That's when I found out that listening to a writer talk about his work can be just about as dull as listening to a golfer talk about his last game.

Q: So, what ideas are intriguing you now? What most excites your science fictional imagination?

Steele: For quite a while now, I've been fascinated by the discovery of exoplanets. This began about fifteen years ago when Marcy and Butler announced their finding the first handful, including 47 Ursae Majoris-B, the setting of the Coyote series, and its continued ever since. What's really amazing about this is that, in a very short period of time, nearly everything we'd assumed to be true about solar systems in general and planetary formation in particular has been thrown in question, if not out the window. Indeed, much of what I learned in my college astronomy classes—which I took along with about a handful of other science courses to make up for a lousy high-school science education—has become obsolete. The universe seems to be a much stranger place than we believed, and even science fiction writers had no idea just how weird. Well, most of us, anyway… Hal Clement and Larry Niven were way ahead of the curve.

Q: And what are you working on now and what have you just finished?

Steele: I'm currently working on a story arc I'm calling the Arkwright series, which is about the first starship from Earth. Although that may sound like a rewrite of *Coyote*, it's a stand-alone novel and something else entirely, a reconsideration of the effort it will take to build and launch a ship to another star. Like *Coyote*, I'm writing this as a series of novellas for *Asimov's*. I've already mentioned the first story, "The Legion of Tomor-row." The second story, "The Prodigal Son," will be published sometime later in the year, I've just finished the third story, "The Long Wait," and after that will be a forth story. Eventually I'll rewrite interstitial material to bind everything together as a novel, but for now I'm treating it as a series of stories, which is my way of tricking myself into writing a complex work.

Q: Thanks, Allen.

Steele: And thank you, Darrell.

JOHN CLUTE

Introduction: John Clute has written science fiction, most notably the novel *Appleseed* (1999), but he is best known as the field's pre-eminent critic. His work as co-editor of *The Encyclopedia of Science Fiction* (with Peter Nichols) and *The Encyclopedia of Fantasy* (with John Grant) has been particularly influential in influencing how we think about and describe fantastic literature. He has coined a good deal of what is now becoming the standard critical vocabulary. Books of his reviews and essays include *Strokes, Look at the Evidence, Scores, Canary Fever* and *Pardon This Intrusion: Fantastika in the World Storm*, the latter containing essays He is currently working on a revision of *The Encyclopedia of Science Fiction*, a deliberately incomplete beta version of which was launched in early October in conjunction with Orion/Gollancz.**Q:** Let's start with your general background, how you got into the science fiction field and how you became a professional critic.

Clute: By accident. It is a very slow process, becoming a professional critic, certainly if such a career descriptor did not actually exist before you started becoming one. In 1960 or so I began reviewing semi-professionally, and in the '60s when I was reviewing amateurishly and professionally—both at the same time—I do not think one have then pointed to any career track for someone who hoped to "move up" in the sf world from doing occasional reviews to doing reviews and review-essays in a venue that recognised this as a role not a succession of accidents. So there was no beginning point for me. And it never became a day job, even though it took all day....

Q: So what were you doing before that?

Clute: I was too young to be doing anything of interest to anybody except myself. I was nineteen when I wrote my first review, early twenties when I wrote my first sf review. I did the usual various odd jobs that most people did back in the '50s and '60s. I worked for six months on a coast freighter. I was a fork-truck driver, supply teacher, research associate for Professor Taduesz Grygier, whom I disappointed grievously I think... things of that sort. *Really* fascinating to recount. [He speaks with obvious irony.]

Q: Was it always your ambition to be a critic, or were you one of those people who started out writing stories and then found yourself writing more and more *about* fiction?

Clute: Yes, I was first a short-story writer and an *exceedingly* bad poet. Writing reviews was not for quite a while anything I really felt I could get my teeth into and actually make me proud of doing. I wrote a few stories that were published here and there. Not very many of them. I am not a fiction writer by instinct or compulsive drive. I did publish two stories, or three, in *New Worlds* in the mid-'60s. A few others since. And I wrote a very inevitable first novel that was completed in 1964 and which Michael Moorcock purchased in 1965 for Compact Books. It was an astonishingly fortunate fall for me that Compact Books went immediately bankrupt, because it was not a good novel, and might have locked me into the hetero-naturalistic pretentiousness that I have so *obviously* avoided in my later career. Michael was doing was doing what Mike always did, but he didn't say what he was doing then and I didn't quite catch on. Mike's publishing policy embodied, as it were, the dictate "Do what thou wilt. And pay for it." Later on this became extremely useful as I began to write seriously explorative non-fiction pieces for *New Worlds*, which any traditional editor would have blue-penciled into oblivion. (Maybe rightly.) But the only other novels I've written are *The Disinheriting Party,* which was published in 1977, although it had been finished quite a while earlier, and *Appleseed* which was published in 2001, a genuine sf novel. That's basically it. So in reality I've been a non-fiction writer from the beginning. **Q:** It is a complete different talent, isn't it? In non-fiction you're writing about ideas, and in fiction you are writing about experiences. There is a kind of narrative in non-fiction, but it's not the same, is it?

Clute: No, the narratives are different but I find they're closer together and less distinguishably mixed for me than for a lot of people. I think, to be honest, there is a *lot* of moat-defensive nonsense talked about the distinction between creative and non-creative writing. I do think there are obvious, significant differences, hey, but novelists, who do not like to be understood (being understood is not exactly the same as being praised, hey), and who use the argument that only a creative writer can *get* what creative writing is to defend their moat; critics, in this view, especially critics like me who try to hijack the guts out of the page read and make it right, are those who can't *do,* and therefore *teach.* (I doubt anyone who ever actually had to teach would *ever* suggest afterwards that teaching was the soft option, or that in any way successful teaching could not be accomplished without creative fire.)

Q: Then again, I heard from any number of professors when I was in college that the essay is a creative form too. They felt they were just as creative as the fiction writers.

Clute: Frankly I think that writing a novel at the peak of one's skill, which is certainly what *Appleseed* took, which is every jot and tittle of my skill, and writing a book like *The Darkening Garden,* which is subtitled *A Short Lexicon of Horror,* which came out in 2006, are both books that required very similar intensity from me. It felt to me like a creative intensity. I have published three or four times a comparison between the two different kinds of writing. I can repeat it very quickly if you like. It's based on the works of Georges Simenon. In very, very short compass, what I argued at longer compass, is that he Simenons which do *not* feature Inspector Maigret are the pure novels, *Romans purr,* I think he called them. They start off with a situation which seems more or less stable. They usually have only one protagonist and one point of view, and something happens to knock that person off the existential perch of his or her life. By the end of the novel, you have reached the cold gaze of the abyss, as it were. Somebody has been murdered, somebody has gone to ground and can't find the exit, somebody has committed suicide. Some desolation has occurred. That's a form of novel that can be called pure, creative writing, pushing to the edge of chaos, and then ending at some resolution that feels like an aesthetic resolution: an icy formality that is the next thing to chaos exploding. The other side of Simenon's oeuvre is the Maigret. The Maigret novels begin where the pure novels end, where some devastation has already occurred—almost always in the Maigrets, this will have been a murder. Maigret arrives on the scene (the chaos of a world frozen shut by the artifice of an art that knows how to stop at the brink) and creatively intuits the broken lives, reweaves them, allows them solace and forgiveness, solves the murder, and by the end the world has become an operative thing again. That's the act of criticism. In a piece I wrote about this at length, I called criticism "a surgery of the Fall." *There.* **Q:** When you wrote *Appleseed* after so many years of writing criticism, did this give you a different perspective on writing fiction? Surely you have *thought* more about what fiction is and how it works than most regular practitioners of fiction.

Clute: Maybe thought, maybe mused in a corner: but certainly *listened.* I think *Appleseed* if it shows the non-fiction writer, the writer about sf, shows us not so much cognitions about the field, although obviously I have thought about things, as it shows a sensitized ear to the sound of sf being told, what other stories underlie it, what kind of echoes can be heard in the aisles of the story. It is in *that* way that *Appleseed* is multiplex, multilayered. It is full of echoes. This isle is full of noises, and it is, at my own level, which is at a moderate, but *hugely* less significant level than the man I am doing to mention, it is how William Shakespeare wrote. He in his high maturity could somehow create a passage of verse that meant three or four things with the same words, because different corridors of narrative passed differently through the same words; there were different connections back and forth, sometimes way more than we can be hear and be *conscious* of hearing, but always so that we are enriched by what we hear or read. We know something is happening, and at its deeply epigonal level, *Appleseed* is a novel where you should feel more comfortable with things not clear at a glance than you can quite work out why.

Q: I should think this would give you a great sense of deliberation. You've thought so much about theory that nothing would happen in that book by accident.

Clute: That is the case if the theory itself is what you might call a house of taxonomy. But if it is the kind of theory that I generate, and it works right, it is usually comes as a series of apertures, of strobes, of incompletions. I don't think I've ever had a theory or a big think that was not more or less open-ended and subject to change. When you are writing a novel, you are changing the meaning of every word you lay down, so there is a lack of ordinary, denotative closure to the presentation of ideas; certainly this conviction, or hope, is visible both in my non-fiction and my fiction. In my non-fiction, there is a deliberate refusal of monadic theme criticism, and in a fiction that refusal is inherent to the way fiction should be written. You close as many doors as you can, or you can never start. But then you start and those closed doors or those half-opened doors turn out to be your material. They're not the locks. They're your material. They are the lock, you are the key. They're how you begin to tell, as Stravinsky said in the early 20th century that, within limits, every constraint is a freedom. He was most free to do exactly what he wanted to when he was following rules.**Q:** In a sense that there is more freedom in a sonnet than in free verse?

Clute: Yes.

Q: But the sonnet requires a higher level of expertise.

Clute: It may take a higher level of expertise, but it has a higher rate of return, too. Anyway I'm not very Tea Party about knowledge being an interference in every American's constitutional right to embody Higher Truth in whatever he says (because he says it). Terrible sonnets are not that usual, because the form hoists your pants up, though I suppose the only really popular American sonnet writer was Edna St Vincent Millay, who used the form to pull her pants down. And there are also great sonnets. But it is *radically* easy to write bad free verse. At the same time, I think it would be presumptuous of us in 2011 to say that what T.S. Eliot was beginning to create in terms of his scansion in 1911 with "Prufrock" was free in the sense of undisciplined, free in the sense of eschewing difficulty, eschewing the hard course to the most economical utterance possible.

Q: I suppose this is more true in poetry, but it may be so in other forms of writing too. What looks completely free in one generation—tennis with the net down—looks classical to the next. Would you agree?

Clute: Yeah, the perception thing, reader perception issues. But if you define free verse technically as verse without a fixed scansion, verse without a rhyme scheme, verse without stanzaic form, then there are certain things that can be called free verse, as opposed to more constrained poetic form. That doesn't change that much, but our perception, our understanding of that which makes something which is uttered in free verse meaningful may well deepen over the years, because we begin to learn. It becomes part of our language of understanding. Certainly T.S. Eliot became *quotable*. **Q:** Concerning literary theories generally, do you think literary theory is description of what has been done or what can (or should) be done? Which way in time do they point?

Clute: I think, as I suspect you know, it is a question that is answered "Yes and yes" or "No and no." Or, as one might put it, "It's immiscible, old son." Though a lot of scholars attempt to understand what has occurred and perhaps with them the element of prescription is less foregrounded. Attempting to properly define the Elizabethan sonnet in terms of rules they obeyed and we have to relearn is probably not going to be as world-shattering in terms of intent as the work of someone like Northrop Frye, who was trying to create a four-part model of the various forms of prose fiction, a model that encompasses and predicts and shapes everything it touches. That's a huge difference. I'm way on the Northrop Frye side. Probably most people who try to analyze sf at all are so. We are prescriptive all the way through. We have to be in part because sf is difficult to describe taxonomically—and the taxonomies of sf or fantasy are fantastic as a whole, I find relatively boring. I find it much more interesting to try to give verbal, narrative understandings. Which are the only way to touch the tale. To touch is to inform. Narrative understandings always move into the future.

Q: If you are saying how science fiction should be written according to your theory, then surely some creative type will come along and ignore you completely.

Clute: Oh, yeah, if it were the case that I was in a position of saying that I think sf *should* be written in a particular way, rather than saying that particular kinds of sf look to me as though they are doing a particular kind of thing and the particular kind of thing is best done this way. I don't think I have ever suggested in any of this stuff I've done that X is the way to do Y, as though any formal description of sf were a haiku that would cover the whole of the reality of the thing examined. I have certainly made suggestions, of course, like anyone. We had a panel today on urban fantasy, and my way of understanding of urban fantasy proved quite different than that of most relatively young writers. But when I said urban fantasy was a way of narrating a modal understanding of how we live immersed in the world cities of our time, I wasn't suggesting that the only way to write it was in conscious adherence to that diktat. Urban fantasy in the hands of 2011 is a narrative vaguer and *far more profound* [Clute speaks in an ironic tone] than that.**Q:** What I have in mind is the relationship between the definition and the actual creative act. If you set out to write sword & sorcery, for example, writing to the definition, then you are probably defining the story form by its clichés. It's defined as having these elements, and if you take them away it's not sword & sorcery. I should think that the thing for the writer to do is ignore theory and ignore the prescribed model, and just write.**Clute:**

You sound like a fish that has managed to escape the aquarium and thinks it can continue to breathe without some really good advice about oxygen. I don't see anybody can write—certainly in the 21st century, equipoisally thrusting your way through that genre and shrugging aside this one and wallowing in them all—I really don't see how anybody can write anything as an idiot savant, as someone who doesn't know or pays no attention to any of the rules. I think we are always paying attention to the rules. I think this does not mean that we are rigidly adhering to a written down set of maxims. But we're paying attention to the rules all the time, especially in the fields that we work in.

Q: Do you think that there are simply certain universal traits of narrative which *work* and really don't change? I think so myself. If you read, say, Apuleius's *The Golden Ass,* which is almost two thousand years old, it reads remarkably like a modern fantasy novel, a Terry Pratchett novel, at least until the last chapter.

Clute: This seems to be absolutely clear, when you see it at that level and *hugely* difficult to put into words. I keep on trying, myself, to work out ways to lay down a few things. I lay them down, and I forget most of them, thought they seemed good in context. I have certainly laid down for my own satisfaction a variety of ways of trying to get at—to use a term that apparently I invented, though I was not aware of inventing it because it just seemed to be a word—what makes material storyable. To discover what is storyable and how it becomes storyable out of discourse and what is the particular, intense, magical affinity between a story and the way the human psyche works, that's sort of like, beyond me to capture, but I don't know if it isn't beyond a lot of people. Though it may be. All we know is that it's there. And as we get older and older in our culture—this may almost be a paradox, but it's not really, I don't think—we begin to intuit that the more purely visible the story is when you're telling it, the more story is like magic. The more story is like magic, in a sense paradoxically, the more we live in it like fish in an aquarium, without being able to say what is we are breathing. It may be a species anosognosia not to be able to see the story within us. But this we do know. We are story creatures. We live in story-shaped worlds. We tell story-shaped stories. "And then, and then, and then." *Then* is miraculous. One could imagine some species not being able to hear the gap between *then* and *next,* in terms of words, in terms of narrative. How could we ever arrange to meet?**Q:** What do you make of various writers who attempt to dispense with narrative? How far can you cut away narrative forms and still have something of interest?

Clute: For me, not very far. I am very glad to know that certain extremisms do exist. It's like knowing that there is a lighthouse warning you not to go in a particular direction. The light shines brightly. It's a benefice, but it's also a warning. But I find most forms of that kind of experimental writing—and in music too, experimental music that has pushed the various acoustic and mathematical non-narrative potentials to the uttermost—seem to be a kind of cultural moment: not a discovery that is the road forward but a marker of our extremity and confession of nearly fatal self-consciousness; but also a clearing of the communal throat. The adventurers of the twentieth century didn't like to think of themselves as clearing the throat, but although we write now with greater knowledge of all of the discoveries made, we do not adhere to those discoveries. I don't think there are very many successful *anti-roman* science fiction novels. I don't think Robbe-Grillet's science fiction novels are very widely read at the moment.

Q: Or Aldiss's *A Report on Probability A* for that matter.

Clute: As you say.

Q: This suggests an idea which has caused some controversy at times, which is that experimental fiction is actually a very familiar path. That is, once in a generation someone says, "We will get rid of all that narrative stuff." Then they try, and the audience goes away, and the writers who survive are the ones who learn to write narrative. Then another twenty years or so goes by, and it happens again.

Clute: I don't think that's an eternal law. I think it's historically grounded. I think this had been legitimately been going on since the end of the 19th century, in waves, but not exactly repetitive. Testing the mould in 1920 was to uncover a world that more and more sophisticatedly writers were understanding as perhaps not amenable to narrative forms, or perhaps requiring far more difficult forms of writing which verged on non-narrative, or else we were all insane: in 1920 (and now) we would be insane if we believed a word of the official Story, the story that still tells us that our Terminal Badlands is progress. The twentieth century required, I think, that we recognise that to describe things had become suddenly more difficult. Our world *is* difficult, and that difficulty of the world, that problematicness of the world, is a body English of the pure ontology of the epistemological unlikelihood that we will ever get it: ever get it right. So therefore there are all sorts of modernist redoubts, fictional redoubts, like *Finnegans Wake,* or many other difficult books which are *meant* to be difficult, because difficulty is the nature of the Thing Itself, once exposed. That I find interesting, but obviously sf (this is another topic) is anything but modernist. It took us readers decades to suss a mildly disruptive test like *Gormenghast."* I do think that the greater texts of fantastika, from Franz Kafta to Gene Wolfe, are intrinsicate with a modernist understanding that the world is shite, and the world cannot be understood, and that we lack a matter and we lack a history and that we are in the badlands. But the difficulty they force upon us is making us see.

Q: I think we can safely say that any serious story comes out of the writer's vision and the writer's life, not a matter of being self-consciously experimental, but more of "I'm going to write this story and this is what this particular story requires. To hell with the rules."

Clute: Yeah. OK. I did think for a second you were moving toward a critical fallacy, conspicuous over the past 100 years or so, which states basically that the writer cannot write about what the writer does not know or has not experienced. This weird presumption drives most of the idiot theories about Shakespeare not being Shakespeare, and is enable through a deep misapprehension of what it is a writer does: because although a writer *can* theoretically reflect in some direct way direct knowledge, most writers never really try to climb that asymptote: the closer you get to a recovered truth, the more abyssal the gap between you and telling it. Shakespeare did not have to see the seacoast of Bohemia to write about the seacoast of Bohemia, where we live more fully than in Brighton.

Q: I always want to know how they can prove that the Earl of Oxford didn't write the works of Thomas Dekker. That is, if you apply the same level of scrutiny to the reality of any other Elizabethan author, you will get the result. We know less about most of them than we do about Shakespeare. So how do we know that *all* the works of Elizabethan dramatists were not ghostwritten by noblemen?

Clute: Because someone would have confessed to the cops: much of Elizabethan/Jacobean drama risked being treated as seditious. What kind of fool would let the Early of Oxford get away with anonymity, if the wrack threatened? There are, of course, other reasons. Whatever, it didn't take very long for historians and critics to start getting the Elizabethan world wrong. So we get *all* of this stuff about *Doesn't it seem unlikely that some- body like Shakespeare was supposed (by us) to be would have given the second-best bed to his wife?* Or, *why does his will not mention his library, which he must have had?* The first being of course a convention that had nothing to do with the value to the widow of a certain object. The second— Shakespeare's not having a library in Stratford—is another misprision: Elizabethan or Jacobean wills didn't list things like that. They were listed in separate codicils which were physically handed over to the probate court and destroyed. Certainly, after we get rid of all this crap, there is actually so much known about Shakespeare. He was the most popular playwright in Elizabethan and Jacobean times. More Shakespearean plays were pirated than anybody else's, more than two or three other authors's work put together. It is extraordinary how much there actually is about him, now that it's possible to study the record for what it contains, not for what it doesn't.

Q: I get deeply cynical about this and suspect that the reason the nutcases go after Shakespeare is the same reason the science cranks go after Einstein. They always pick the biggest target. If you debunk an obscure figure, no one will care.

Clute: It reminds you of people with recovered memories. Always Cleopatra or Caesar.

Q: Yes, it is never the kitchen maid. Well…so, how do you think they'll misunderstand science fiction in a couple of centuries?

Clute: I think sf will be misunderstood, certainly American science fiction of the pomp years from '25 to '75 will be misunderstood if it is understood to be a fair representation of—how to put it politely?—if it is thought that somehow or other that the people who wrote engineering science fiction in the 20th century were doing so in entire good faith. I think almost all of them are denying something. I think their works whiff of denial. I think they know damn well that the futures they were advocating were not only pretty monstrous, but also impossible to achieve. In the real world, engineering solutions are drowned by side effects. You can't create utopia by pre-planning. You can't prophesy the field of the future very well if you're an engineering mind, because engineers solve problems. They don't anticipate side effects, which is to say they don't *get the world*. That's not their job.

I think sf will be properly understood in its great years as the most astonishingly *incompetent* attempt to understand its subject-matter that any self-articulated genre has ever managed to present. Science fiction writers did an *astonishing* bad job of prophesying the field of the future. I brought this up in a talk I gave a few weeks ago in Norway about Clifford D. Simak. The "City" stories that were published in the mid-'40s in *Astounding,* in which it was made clear that Simak thought and that Campbell thought and that his readers thought and that the episteme thought that it was a fair cop to say cars would start dwindling away about 1960 because they were no longer necessary and people became *bored* with them; that human beings would begin to abandon the great cities of the world—the "huddling places," which is what Simak had the effrontery to call them from—into what seem to later readers to be nothing more than McMansions with trout streams, decorously spread across rural regions, dislocating the farmers who aren't needed anymore because we had yummy hydroponics now, that loyal robots would replace the nine tenths of the world population who still (2011) starve that our golf course be irrigated; and that this was not only a plausible representation of the changing world from 1944 on, but one that any rational American properly longed for. In 1944, which is to say, Americans in particular were demented. They thought that their future was going to work without side-effects. They thought, most of them thought—now I am interrupting myself, but remember that survey I did on Fictionmags asking whether there was a single sf story from before 1960 or 1965, or any illustration for any such story, which depicted a traffic jam or anything like the catalytic transformation of America , which one can cartoon as solely because of the Interstate Highway System, but which was more widely caused of course? We didn't find any. We found nothing. Science fiction, the genre that was going to shape our dreams so that we could shape the future *did not notice the interstate system.* It did not notice Walmart, did not notice the catalysis of America into eviscerated patches of "wilderness" eaten into daily by viral tracts with Progress billboards hiding the dead fauna. It didn't notice. Didn't notice.

Q: It didn't notice the internet either. Not even ten years out. Did anybody write about the internet in 1980?

Clute: By then they were beginning to write about something like it, but they should have been writing about information in terms of miniaturization, through the transistor long before that. John Brunner did a little bit, but having a John Brunner around is a bit like Chinese civilization. How many times do you have to invent gunpowder before gunpowder actually starts to actually blow up the enemy's forts? It takes several times in Chinese civilization. It doesn't matter if there's an occasional example, touted by a contrarian. What never happened was that Brunner etc made any real difference to the way stories were being written. You may get hints of an information explosion, but pretty tentative. To return to my own *idee fixe*: there is no hint of the transportation explosion, the catalytic explosion that occurred between 1900 and 2000 that we are still busy normalizing ourselves to, just in time for the oil to run out.

Q: I must have missed most of this on Fictionmags, because the most bizarre example I would have brought up would have been David H. Keller's "The Revolt of the Pedestrians," which, if you read it very carefully, comes off as a Gernsbackian technological story as written by Poppy Z. Brite. Do you know it?

Clute: I don't know the story.

Q: It's one of those great ex-classics. It used to be regarded as a major story in the field. It was published in 1928, and is set in a future in which the automobile has totally revolutionized everything, so that no one ever gets out of their cars. They spend their entire lives in little personal go-carts.

Cities are transformed. There are no stairs anymore, only ramps. It's as if everybody was in handicapped carts, all the time. Their legs whither away. But there is one tribe of Pedestrians in the Ozarks somewhere, and they are the last walking people on Earth. It also turns out that all this civilization runs on broadcast power from one source. There are no backups. No one has any batteries. As the Pedestrians feel threatened, they ultimately shut off all the power and leave everyone to starve to death in the dark. It's one of those feel-good-about-genocide stories that you get in the early pulps. But it's even more bizarre that that. There is a young man of the Pedestrians who infiltrates the Automobilists. How he gets into one of those carts and hides his legs is difficult to imagine. How he goes to the bathroom, we won't ask.

Clute: Perhaps he would have told us if his editors had allowed him to. Keller was a piece of work.

Q: He would. The young man goes and gets a job. He becomes a secretary. Of course women's roles have not changed, so he has to pretend to be a woman. Then the secretary next to him starts to find herself attracted to him, without understanding why.

Clute: How long is this story?

Q: A longish short story. But the really bizarre part—this is the Poppy Brite part—is that when the lights go out and about 99% of the human race is doomed to die—that's seen as okay—the other secretary's erotic passion bursts out. The spy reveals himself to be male. That she could be a lesbian is not thinkable. Before she dies, she wants one last romantic embrace, which she gets, whereupon she ecstatically rips out his jugular with her teeth and wallows in his blood. This is a Gernsback story. I don't think anybody read it carefully at the time or understood it, but it *is* all about the transformative power of mass transportation.

Clute: No. I doubt that story was really well understood at the time. I am hearing it in retrospect clearly as a transportation story, but within the context of 1928 it is also very much a rather imaginative dystopian story, because a lot of the imagery seems to dramatise how you become robotic in a dystopia, with one power source, one voice telling you what to do, et cetera, et cetera, and rigid role divisions. So it looks to me, in listening to it, what you're saying, is that David Keller—who was a bad writer most of the time, but actually a very interesting writer—did some really interesting things there. But it would not have at that time been read as a transportation story—all the transportation things would be seen as exemplifications of totalitarian dystopianism, in a pulp way. He might have meant both, but he would not have been read as having much to do with transportation.

Q: Why do you think science fiction does such a bad job of understanding its own subject matter, or understanding the future? It can't be because the writers are lazy. Some of them are, but many are not.Clute: No, as I said, I think it's because a lot of them are deniers. I think that over the last fifty years a lot of professional science fiction has been written by people who knew better in terms of the simplicities of outcome, in terms of the ability for technological fixes to work, in terms of the understanding of the forms of sf as actually useful and clever ways of not only entertaining folk—which is not a lie to do—but of telling the truth. I think a lot of them knew and know better. That doesn't cover the whole of the genre though history, because a lot of people believe what they say, and a lot of people don't write that kind of stuff anyway. As regards earlier decades, it's simplistic just to say we were all demented in 1940, but it's not simplistic to say that some sf writers, for historical or accidental reasons, in the States, got hitched to the engineering wheel. The central creator in so many ways of American science fiction, as you know very well—

Q: John W. Campbell. Jr.?

Clute: I would say Robert Heinlein.

Q: John Campbell created Robert Heinlein.

Clute: It doesn't look that way. Have you read the bio? [Clute refers to *Robert Heinlein, In Dialogue with His Century*, Vol 1, *The Learning Curve* by William H. Patterson, Jr.—D.S.]

Q: No. Not yet.

Clute: Read the bio. I found it very elucidating. We always knew that Robert Heinlein was actually older than Campbell, and hugely more experienced in the world than Campbell by 1939, but there's more. In his fervent effort, over five years, to become a naval officer despite his health, he did become a qualified engineer. A few years later he got involved in a lot of very, very hands-on, very, very, as it were non-Asperger street-stumping for Upton Sinclair's Social Credit movement. He was married twice in the 1930s. By the end of his first adult decade, he become a very experienced and highly proficient man of the Californian world, and it is this figure, as we can now see from that utopia he wrote at the end of 1938, which was his first real piece of fiction, who gives birth to everything else. *For Us, the Living* permeates his Future History. *For Us, the Living* is an engineer's utopia, a utopia in the traditional lines, in which the visitor/protagonist is brought into the future because he makes a few stupid mistakes back now—Heinlein was really good about male sexual possessiveness and jealousy—and gets whipped around a bit for that; but basically what he does is begin to fix things. They've already been fixed pretty well, but he's an engineer and there's nothing that can't be fixed. Heinlein was *hugely* influential at the end of the '30s and in the '40s. If you read the bio you get the sense that this man was actually (or in terms of experience) older than everybody else in the field except L. Sprague de Camp and L. Sprague de Camp had already been ringed by some kind of…you know…wood-destroying thing. He was a stick even then. And Heinlein seemed to know everybody. Everybody else was influenced very deeply. It was a very small field. Did you listen to the Katherine MacLean interview this morning?

Q: Alas, no.

Clute: She was talking about the sensation they had in the mid-'40s, when she would have been twenty or twenty-one, very young and very mentally active—she's still mentally very active—that the whole of the science fiction cohort of active writers would sit around sometimes—I guess it was in New York, so it wasn't obviously all of them—and talk all night the ideas that were going to change the world. This kind of small kind of cohort was not only a good way of brainstorming, but actually very influenceable. And of course Campbell was very much involved in the kind of story that *had* successful outcomes, that domesticated, that made visibly possible, all sorts of transformations in the world. So therefore science fiction in the States was predisposed to think along certain kinds of lines. With all the exceptions and the people like William Tenn and Sheckley and Dick a few years later, that particular kind of serious/non-serious, predictive/prophetic writing was set off on the wrong track from the get-go.

Q: Was it that these writers were deniers, or that they were not allowed to tell the truth for marketing reasons? That is, if they told the truth, no one would buy their stories.

Clute: One needs to be kinder than that. That was an *inflammatory* thing to say.

Q: I mean that they were not allowed to be honest with their material, for marketing reasons.

Clute: I don't know, and I don't know whether they're deniers as we've come to know the term, but I do think that a lot of people over the last fifty years were persuaded to write stories they knew better than to believe in. Maybe they *wanted* to believe. It is like this gambler's refusal to give up on some scheme, even though the house always wins. Sf gambled against the house in those years of its pomp, gambling that planning could fix things, at certain kinds of utopian thinking actually worked well enough to be followed, even though it kept on not working in reality (even though the cars did not dwindle away), and even though you had to ignore the world transforming under your feet like snakes and becoming more and more irreducibly complex *to the perception*. These stories, *Analog* still publishes them, these stories are still happening. There are still writers who do them. But they are shadow people. They are at the end of a particular era.

Q: In the tone of what you're saying, you're describing science fiction in the past tense, as if its glory years are over.

Clute: It has been addressed to me before that I have called sf dead. I don't think the real literature of the fantastic that is premised on arguable worlds is dead. I think sf as a genre has been, as it were, colonized, overgrown, made irrelevant, made smaller, bigger, and become so complex and diffuse as a series of texts, not as a series of release-points, that in the 21st century, I have felt, while doing *The Encyclopedia of Science Fiction*, that basically there are two encyclopedias. There is the one I am focusing on very hard right now to finish off, which is the intention to anatomize and deeply to honor the American SF, in particular, of the 20th century and to maintain and to rehabilitate where necessary not only the entries on the authors, but also the theme entries that attempt to map that twentieth century enterprise. The second Encyclopedia of SF is the encyclopedia that attempts to create a series of models of theme entries and author entries and entry structures in general that will serve as a series of lattice-works over the complexities of the badlands that we inhabit now. Though the new pattern of entries will meld imperceptibly, I hope, into the old, it is the new which will try to give openings into the kind of sf someone like China Mieville or Elizabeth Hand writes. For you cannot really retrofit them comfortably into the twentieth century. Not that sf was ever exactly fixed.—Do you know the five-finger exploding palm device in *Kill Bill*?

Q: No.

Clute: You don't know the five-finger exploding palm device in *Kill Bill*!? Ah. It's this ultimate move in martial arts. You go…like that— [*makes a motion*] —in a particular way and your assailant does not know what has happened, but after five full steps, he or she drops dead. I think science fiction as a coherent enterprise suffered that particular move in 1957 with Sputnik.

Q: It doesn't know it's dead yet?

Clute: It is hard to define what a step is in the genre, but maybe the five steps have already been walked through and that particular thing is dead, and maybe we have another step to go, but basically the dragging of the space race, the dragging of the engineering dream of linear expansion back into the real world and dirtying it up with laundry, with all sorts of debris and real-life politics well, meant that that was the point where the blow had been struck. That was when it was killed.

Q: What does a young science fiction writer today—someone who is about twenty and just starting out—have to face? Do they try to reanimate a corpse?

Clute: If they are trying to write YA novels based on Heinlein, they are trying to revive corpses, yes. They may be great young adult novels, and Heinlein had elements of greatness as a writer, but I think there is something zombie about Heinlein YA Redivivus, sure. But if you are a young writer and you are actually trying to write a serious story, you should just think of yourself as going out into the world and trying real hard to recognize something, and if we recognize something really well, some tiny evanescent flash of now we can make work as a meme, we'll be writing sf, as we understand it now, which no longer focuses on the particular half-century of pomp we love and mourn and bury.

Q: Thanks, John.

ELIZABETH HAND

Elizabeth Hand is the author of the novels *Winterlong, Aestival Tide, Icarus Descending, Waking the Moon, Glimmering, Black Light, Generation Loss,* and *Mortal Love.* Her short story collections are *Last Summer At Mars Hill, Bibliomancy, Saffron and Brimstone, Errantry, Chip Crockett's Christmas Carol, Available Dark,* and *Radiant Days.* She has won the World Fantasy Award, the Tiptree Award, the Mythopoeic Fantasy Award, the International Horror Guild Award, and the Shirley Jackson Award. She has also written movie tie-ins and for comics. She lives in Maine.

◄─*─··─*─►

Q: When did you decide you wanted to be a writer?

Hand: I had the usual writer's origin story: I wanted to write from a very early age, even before I could read. My mother gave me a toy typewriter when I was small—I was always using her old Underwood—but it broke because I was actually trying to write on it. She then got me a proper Royal Upright.

Q: Was this your first plan for a career? I note that you did not publish your first story (if the dates on Wikipedia are to be trusted) until you were about 31. So how long had you been trying before you succeeded?

Hand: I never had any kind of plan for any kind of career. As a kid I loved zoology, paleontology, science stuff like that, but I always assumed I'd be a writer. This would happen by magic, as I had no clue as to how the business worked, other than sending manuscripts out then having them returned to me. I never went to a convention or knew any writers or editors. And I didn't study creative writing at university—when I finally got a degree (after ten years) it was a BS in anthropology. I fell into my job at the National Air & Space Museum by chance and stayed there for a number of years because I loved the people and I loved working at the Smithsonian and having behind-the-scenes access to all the museums, something you'd never see today.

But I knew I'd never have a career at the Smithsonian without an advanced degree, and I grew increasingly panicky in my late 20s because I'd never been published, or even written much that I'd actually completed. The thought of *not* being a writer—literally the only thing I ever wanted to be—terrified me. I had no backup plan, no career track, no money. I was very, very fortunate to get my first sale when I was thirty, and see the story in print a year later. I honestly don't know what would have become of me if I hadn't. I'd either be a miserable burnout like Cass Neary, or a miserable low-level government employee. Not sure which would be worse.

Q: Making a first sale is one thing, but we all know how you could sell five stories a year (5000 words x 6 cents a word = $300 x 5 = $1500) and maybe sell a novel for a $4000 advance, at which point you have an annual income that will qualify you for living in a cardboard box. Wasn't it a scary leap to become a full-time writer, or have you still had some kind of safety net?

Hand: No, no safety net, really, except for that offered by the state. And I was extremely fortunate to have a fabulous and supportive literary agent. I moved to Maine with Richard Grant in October 1988; we both had modest book advances (mine for *Winterlong* was $10,000, minus commission) and lived on that. I got occasional part time work as a proofreader for National Fisherman Magazine down in Rockland, and also worked a few hours a week at a local organic farmstand, which paid $5 an hour and gave us some food to eat. I was also reviewing for the Washington Post, selling the occasional short story, and wrote some lucrative articles for Hot Talk, a spinoff from Penthouse Magazine. So we got by, but barely. Eighteen months later I bought Tooley Cottage with the down payment for the UK edition of *Winterlong*, which was about $6,000. I was eight months pregnant; the cottage was actually what Mainers call a camp, a tiny lakefront structure for fishing and hunting. It was 300 square feet, with no indoor plumbing or running water, just an outhouse tucked beneath some evergreens. The only source of heat was a tiny woodstove called a parlor stove, which leaked smoke and would only burn wood for a few hours.

My parents gave me a few thousand dollars to hire someone to build a tiny addition, another hundred square feet, so there'd be a room for the baby, a future bathroom, and a tiny sleeping loft. There was enough money to build it and frame it in, but not to insulate it all, so the only room that was insulated in the whole place was the baby's room. In those days, there weren't as many people from away in that part of rural Maine, so people knew who we were: the crazy writers who'd moved into a fishing camp with a newborn baby. A California photographer studying at the Maine Photographic Workshop in Rockport somehow heard about us, and came and did a feature when Callie was a few weeks old, with some nice photos of me painting the baby's room and sitting with her out by the lake. I have no idea if or where it was published, but I still have the pictures. I was writing a review for the Post two days after Callie was born, holding her as I typed.

It sounds romantic and exciting now, but it was a very difficult time.

We were both writers, and we were very poor. There were holes in the floor, no insulation, and of course no internet to connect us to the rest of the world. We'd take showers at a friend's house in Camden and haul in gallon jugs of water. In the summer and fall, I'd haul water from the lake for washing up. You had to heat it on the stove for hot water, so I learned how little water you need to keep dishes clean (not as much as you think). When winter came, Callie's room was warm but it would be 27 degrees in the rest of the cottage. I'd climb down from the loft to feed the woodstove and check on her obsessively in her crib—she was bundled up like a little Eskimo. For a while there was a porcupine living under the cottage, and in the middle of the night I'd hear him gnawing at the floorboards. They can be very destructive, and all I could think was, "I'm living in this falling-down place and a freaking *porcupine* is going to bring it all down unless *I kill it now*." So I'd throw on my LL Bean boots and a parka and grab a baseball bat (I don't remember where that came from) and tromp outside in the snow and bang on the side of the cottage until I scared him off. I did that for about a week and he finally gave up and left for good.

I'd go to work at Fresh off the Farm, the organic food store, with Callie in a basket behind the register, and people would exclaim "There's a *baby* back there!" In the fall I bagged apples for them and weighed out granola, things like that. The owners were very kind, and sometimes the owner paid me in food. I applied to the Maine heating assistance program to get some firewood, and two very nice men came out to deliver it. They must have gone back and reported how cold the place was, and how we had a baby, because a few days later a brand-new, very efficient woodstove was delivered and installed. We were very fortunate that the state's assistance programs were better-funded then—it infuriates me now when social programs are cut. I was working poor, but I was working my ass off. By the time my son was born in 1992 things were a bit easier, but definitely more crowded. We'd made a lot of friends, and were learning how to live in Maine, prepare for the winter and get by. I learned how to stack firewood, light a fire, can food (not well), haunt the corners of the grocery store where they sold reduced produce and dinged-up cans. I went to tag sales and the local dump, which has a swap shop where I found furniture, clothes, toys, even a cookstove. Most of Tooley Cottage is furnished from tag sales or the dump. As an artist friend told me back then, "Maine is a good state to be poor." Because a lot of people struggled to get by, but they did. There was a great newsletter called The Tightwad Gazette written by a woman in Maine, which taught you how to do things like make your own baby wipes and granola and clothing. When Y-2K came down the pike, I was ready.

Q: So, tell me about your transition from short-story writer to novelist. Do you find the long form more attractive?

Hand: I was never really conscious of any transition—I'd start out writing a story, and it would either be a short story, or a novella, or in the case of Winterlong, a novel. The latter started as a novella, "The Boy in the Tree." I knew that if I wanted to have a career as a writer, I'd have to write novels, so at some point I decided to create a second storyline and attempt to write a novel. *Winterlong* doesn't actually function very well as a novel—it's more of a picaresque, or a long fever dream. But it was my first book, so I was learning as I went along.

My real preference is for the novella. I love writing them, and I tend to be able to immerse myself in the process and create a novella in about three weeks. I think the novella's the best form for supernatural fiction: long enough to create intricate characters and background, but short enough so that you can create and sustain an atmosphere of unease. Ideally one should read a novella all at once, so that the mood isn't broken.

That's one reason why I think that long supernatural novels are less successful than shorter works—at some point you have to book the book down.

Q: You've certainly written books which more or less approximate supernatural horror novels. So, how do you deal with the problem of maintaining the mood over length? Of course we get back to the question of what a supernatural horror novel is, anyway, other than a book that can be marketed as one.

Hand: Well, I do it—or did it—but it's more difficult than with something that's novella length. I haven't actually written a book-length supernatural novel since *Black Light*. *Generation Loss* and *Available Dark* have flickers of the supernatural, and they share some of the elements of a horror story, but they're both much shorter (I think *Available Dark* is about 80,000 words). My favorite supernatural novel is Richard Adams' *The Girl in a Swing*. It builds the mood very slowly—I think the first 100 pages are devoted to back story, and then it progresses into a love story, and while the first section establishes the supernatural element, genuine horror isn't introduced until pretty far along. That novel was a bestseller when it came out, but I suspect it would have trouble finding an audience today—it's a long novel, and from the outset the narrator tells us he's some kind of clairvoyant, but it's not obviously a horror novel. On the other hand, the rise of various e-reading devices seem to have created a market for shorter fiction, so maybe this will result in a boom for novellas.

Q: When you write science fiction, do you decide that this one will be science fiction, or does it just come out that way? I mean in the sense of, "okay, the fantastic element in this one will be rationalized."

Hand: I never really think about it beforehand. I generally don't like rationalizing the fantastic elements in my stories. I look at it more as reportage: I try to write down a particular experience in as much concrete and emotional detail as possible, then let the reader decide what's going on. What exactly happens in "Near Zennor" or "The Maiden Flight of McCauley's 'Bellerophon'"? You tell me.

Q: Indeed, what *does* happen in "McCauley's 'Bellerophon'"? Before asking that, I stopped and reread the story. A lovely piece of work, but is this fantasy? The only unexplained fantastic thing is the green light that zaps the flying model. Is it a kind of alternate history or secret history, because your characters discovery (but destroy the evidence for) a pre-Wright Brothers flight? It's as if you turned the "fantasy" dial down as far as it can go without turning it off, to a low whisper. But it _feels_ like fantasy, and it won the World Fantasy Award. So is the fantastic more a matter of feeling, an emotional resonance of a specific sort, or is it a matter of content?

Hand: Well, as I said, I really don't like to over-explain (or even explain) the events in my stories. I wanted "Bellerophon" to balance on a knife-edge between fantasy and science fiction, and there are elements of both in there. I don't see it as an alternate history, but I'm happy it can be read that way. And you're absolutely right—I do like to turn the fantasy dial all the way down. I want to create a world that's recognizably our own, but with that one tiny element of strangeness that throws everything off balance. A single inexplicable thing like the emerald foliot in "Hungerford Bridge"—it completely recalibrates the known world, as much as a larger discovery would. I think I'm just more interested in the small picture than the bigger one. Uccello's "The Hunt in the Forest," the painting used for the cover of *Errantry*—it's not a particularly large painting), but it holds an entire world that expands the longer you look at it. I saw the original at the Ashmolean Museum, and you can just fall into it, without ever quite understanding why it's so mesmerizing. That's a sensation I'd love to capture in writing.

Q: I can see how this sort of writing could have trouble in commercial terms. Do you experience any sort of generic pressure (in the sense of expectation from the publishers) in the sense of "If this is going to be published as fantasy it had better have fantasy elements in it!" or are you safely into the realm of the Brand Name (Stephen King's term) where anything you do is just published as an Elizabeth Hand book?

Hand: I've pretty much ignored any good advice I've been given insofar as conforming to market expectations. So yes, I think I've become a brand, though definitely an acquired taste. I have a low boredom threshold, and I write what I want to write. I've made no bones about it when I've done hack work like novelizations. I really enjoyed writing the Boba Fett juveniles, but I paid back a substantial advance for an adult Star Wars novel—the most money I've ever been offered—when I realized I wouldn't enjoy writing it, and wouldn't do a good job.

It's not that I disdain commercial success—I don't know a single writer who does, and I know a lot of writers. But you can go crazy trying to write a quote-unquote commercial novel. The hard truth is that no one can predict what the reading public wants. I've reviewed hundreds of novels over the last twenty-five years, and I've probably seen thousands of publicity packages for new books. Sometimes the muscle that publishers put behind a title pays off, but often it doesn't. Sometimes a well written, plot-driven novel takes off, but usually it doesn't. If you get a great review on the front page of the *NYTBR*, you've probably got a bestseller on your hands, but who's cracked the code as to how that happens? Not me, that's for sure.

At the end of the day, you have to enjoy the process more than the final result. It's that old cliche about the journey not the destination—that really is what matters. That and not being a finalist for the Bad Sex Writing Award.

Q: I wonder if "Bellerophon" might be a rare instance where the term "American Magic Realism" actually means something (other than a marketing strategy which translates as "the fantastic which is trying to distance itself from genre fantasy). A story like this isn't so much built out of a "What if?" premise, but a way of looking at the world slightly askew, and using small unreal details which the characters see as part of their daily lives. So, Liz Hand, American Magic Realist? What do you think?

Hand: I think the American Magic Realist label works as well as any, though it doesn't really encompass the Cass Neary books (although those have a subtle underlying supernatural element). I guess if I had to choose a term to describe the work, it would be 'fabulist,' which covers more literary territory. Winterlong is really a supernatural novel set in wthe future. Graham Sleight made a persuasive argument to me for Glimmering being read as alternate history, though it was written as a near-future SF novel with supernatural elements. Radiant Days is a mostly mainstream historical novel but with timeslip. "Near Zennor" is a straightforward homage to Robert Aickman.

So really, the stories are all over the map. Though the truth is, I'm working without a map. Because if you just let yourself go with the experience, there's nothing wrong with being lost.

Q: What are you working on now?

Hand: I'm working on the third Cass Neary novel, *Flash Burn*, and after that will wrap up *Wylding Hall*, a neo-gothic YA novel. When those are in the can, I hope to get back to some short fiction. I haven't had the chance to write any shorter work for sometime, and I'm craving it.

Q: Thanks, Liz.

MAURICE BROADDUS

Introduction: Maurice Broaddus made his first professional sale with "Family Business," published in *Weird Tales* IN 2006. The story won the World Horror Convention story contest the year before, the judge being none other than Darrell Schweitzer. Broaddus's short fiction has since appeared in *Apex, Doorways, Space and Time, Black Static, Asimov's Science Fiction,* and numerous anthologies. He branched out into novels with *King Maker, King's Justice,* and *King's War*, published by Angry Robot, 2010-11 and recently reprinted in an omnibus *The Knights of Breton Court.* He has edited two anthologies with Jerry Gordon, *Dark Faith* (2010) and *Dark Faith: Invocations* (2012).

＋＊⋯＊＋

Q: Tell us something of your background, who you are, where you're from, your education, what you did (or still do) as a real job other than writing? Are you full-time these days?

Broaddus: I was born in London, England, but moved to the states when I was a wee lad. Immediately lost my British accent with the flawed idea that I needed to fit in. I would kill for that accent now. My mother is from Jamaica and my dad from the States. But I've lived most of my life in Indianapolis, Indiana and when I can, I set my stories there.

I am married (interacially) going on 15 years no. Raising two biracial teenage boys. As a part of how we do life, we're very intentional about living in a diverse neighborhood, going to a diverse school, and attending multi-cultural events.

I have a B.S. in biology which I used for 20 years as an environmental toxicologist. Then I went full time freelance writing for a while before getting involved in a homeless/re-entry housing ministry. But writing is my part-time job and first love.

Q: What attracted you to the fantastic, as opposed to other types of literature?

Broaddus: Honestly, I think my fourth grade Sunday School teacher had a lot to do with it. He was teaching on Noah's Ark and the flood one day. I put a bunch of floating bodies on the flannel-graph next to the boat because I figured a world-wide flood meant lots of bodies. He and I immediately bonded. We had a mutual love of comic books and he introduced me to Dr. Who and later Stephen King. This also may explain why issues of faith so often enter my stories.

Q: Your remark that you'd kill for that accent now is intriguing. Do you think that a writer has an advantage if he can present himself as exotic, i.e. the Prince from Another Land (Norman Spinrad's phrase) rather than Joe from Down the Block?

Broaddus: Well, I was originally thinking in terms of my accent aiding me in picking up women during my college days. But, frankly, also it'd be a great asset when I'm speaking on panels. I'm prone to spouting whatever gibberish pops into my head in that instant. Everything seems so much more erudite with a British accent, even gibberish.

As for your actual question, I think there are two phases to that, as there are in general to the life of a writer: the writing and the marketing. As for the writing, it's about finding your voice. Whatever helps define your voice as unique is what you bring to the literary canon. British culture is a part of who I am. Jamaican culture is a part of who I am. Being African American is a part of who I am. Being a man of faith is a part of who I am. Those all go into forming my writing voice.

As for marketing myself, heck yes, I'll take any advantage I can to stand out in a crowd. An accent would be awesome, anything to help folks remember you.

Coming up, I *was* the diversity at most conventions I went to, and very much felt like a Prince from Another Land. A very lonely prince. Now things are starting to get better. While I'm in no danger of becoming "Joe down the block" just yet, hopefully, in terms of diversity I will be soon. Thus I'll have to rely on being charming and witty.

Q: So, how long were you writing before you sold anything?

Broaddus: That depends on if I mark my writing life with the first short story I wrote. "The Big Mac Attacker," the sordid tale of a Big Mac being devoured from the point of view of the Big Mac. I was in fifth grade, although, to be fair, I also won an essay contest that year.

In college, 1993 I began writing short stories, even received an honorable mention for the Isaac Asimov Award for Undergraduate Writing. I also started my first novel. It took me seven years to write that beast, but I finally reach The End. That was in 2000. That's when I typically mark the beginning of my writing career. One of my professors told me that "writers finish things" so I never considered myself a writer until I finished it. I sold my first story, "Soul Food," to the small press *Hoodz* magazine in 2001.

For the record, that novel is still unsold. As is the second novel I wrote. And the third. Someone once said that you have to write 250,000 (or was it a million) words before you start getting the hang of it. These were all words to make that threshold.

Q: We would qualify this by saying that an upper class British accent sounds more erudite. A Cockney, much less so. You will notice how American snobs (particularly in the East) try to sound veddy veddy British. You must have certain insights from being both an insider and an outsider at the same time, which informs the perspective of your fiction.

Broaddus: Outsider. To truly get that, and how it informs nearly ALL of my work, I probably ought to give you some perspective. I mentioned that my mother is Jamaican and my dad African American. I can't begin to tell you how many discussions around the dinner table began "The problem with you people is…" I never knew which side of the "you" I was supposed to be on. This was compounded by the fact that other than my home, I was raised in a mostly white environment: special school program and the church my parents sent me to which formed the bulk of my social life. I was over being the "token" in any given social situation pretty early on. That being said, it left me with a sense of always being the outsider in any given circumstance. Even if I were among my own people.

Case in point: my first professional sale was the story "Family Business" to Weird Tales Magazine. In it, you have a son raised by a Jamaican mother who goes back to Jamaica on his own for the first time to experience the culture for himself, as himself. It's a story that partly reflects on identity (as a lot of my stories do) and cultural exploration. Even then, there's the sense of me writing, and the reader experiencing the story, as an invited outsider.

Plus side, the outsider perspective is also a relational cheat. Everyone at one point or another has been the outsider, so they can always relate to that perspective.

Q: This may be a politically sensitive question (everything is these days), but given that an editor is dealing with a name on a manuscript and can't even tell if the writer is African American, and therefore couldn't exercise prejudice even if he were so inclined, why *do* you think that African American writers have not (at least until recently) been entering SF/fantasy in proportion to their numbers? I admit I can't think of any at all before the 1970s other than Samuel R. Delany.

Broaddus: I can only speak to my experience. To grow up black and geek meant swimming against the tide (not so much these days). I felt alone, as if I was the only one out there. I didn't discover Samuel R. Delany or Chester Himes or Charles Saunders until I well well into genre stuff. So I came up reading stories that I couldn't identify with. Stephen King, Neil Gaiman, Clive Barker, were who I came up reading. Still great stories, but part of me couldn't identify with some of the work. When I read Octavia Butler, I discovered a missing part of myself. Just like reading Stephen King encouraged me to incorporate my faith more into my work (Desperation was a real turning point for me), Octavia Butler challenged me to explore my culture more in my work. To truly find my own voice.

Editors can be more proactive though. I co-edited the Dark Faith anthology series and the upcoming Streets of Shadows anthology. Every time I sit down to put together an anthology, I put together a list of writers I'd love to work with. I don't consciously count people of color to make sure I have a good mix, but I know that diversity is important to me and I actively reached out to as diverse a group as I could. So I don't let editors entirely off the hook.

Q: I think it was Bradbury, who said you had to write a million words, and he was thinking more in terms of a story a week for a year. You must be brave or at least stubborn to work your way all the way through those novels that did not sell. Didn't it occur to you to try short stories first, until you started selling, and only then attempt a novel.

Broaddus: I *love* short stories. I fell in love with Stephen King, Neil Gaiman, and Clive Barker through their short work first. Eventually I read some of their novels. My first short stories, way back in high school, were all shades of Poe. In college, all I wrote were short stories. Short stories are my first love. And short stories kept me sane.

So my first novel attempt, *Strange Fruit,* took seven years to write. Like most writers, I live on the rush of being able to type "The End" when I've completed a work. But, seriously, seven years? I can only take so much delayed gratification. So I would take breaks and write short stories just to be able to complete something.

Plus, short stories are my little private laboratory. I can always experiment with style and voice and teach myself new literary "tricks" that I can then bring to any novels that I write.

Q: But now you're a big-time novelist. They were giving away copies of you're the *The Knights of Breton Court* at the World Fantasy Con at the World Fantasy Con in Brighton, and I thought, "Hey, I know that guy!" and carried it back across the Atlantic. I was very pleased to see how far you had progressed in your career. So, what is this about an Arthurian Mythos set in Indianapolis?

Broaddus: I don't know about big-time, but I do have my own Wikipedia page!

The Knights of Breton Court was such an interesting writing experience. It began as a writing exercise. I was leading a creative arts program working with homeless youth and I had tossed out the line "princes and princesses of the streets." The idea rather stuck with me. I have always loved the Arthurian mythos. Maybe it's my British side popping through or being weaned on Monty Python and the Holy Grail as well as Excalibur (which I eventually watched another half dozen times while writing the books and called it research). Anyway, the idea became the basis of me attempting to do National Novel Writing Month and next thing I knew, I had the rough draft for *King Maker.*

Here's the other thing, I love crime fiction. George Pelecanos. Elmore Leonard. David Simon (who, technically, writes non-fiction). With the setting of my take on the Arthurian legends revolving around the lives of homeless teens and gang members in Indianapolis, the series has the pacing of a crime novel rather than a fantasy novel.

When all is said and done, acknowledging my love of horror, the scariest part of the series was the lives of the kids. In the series, magic becomes a metaphor for homelessness: it's all around us if we choose to see it.

Q: The mythic elements are metaphors then? The original Arthurian story seems a metaphor for statehood. Do you see it as a striving for order within your own novels?

Broaddus: Very much so. Two of the things King has to come to terms with is the fact that he's caught up in The Story and he's trying to bring reconciliation to his divided neighborhood. It's a burden he takes on himself because no one else seems to care enough to do anything about what' going on.

At the same time, the mythic/magic elements are treated as matter of fact. Of course, tainted drugs produce zombie drug users. Of course there's a dragon living in the basement of an apartment building. Of course there are troll hitmen or elf assassins running around. Basically, of course there is this magical underbelly to Indianapolis, its shadow self. All cities have one, but we'd rather pretend or be caught up in our constructed safe worlds rather than see it.

Q: Just curious: Have you read Sanders Anne Laubenthal's *Excalibur*? This is an Arthurian novel set in Mobile, Alabama. It was in the Ballantine Adult Fantasy Series. The editor Lin Carter said that when he got the proposal he didn't believe it could be done, but he allowed himself to be convinced. An Arthurian story set in Indianapolis also sounds pretty dubious. Did you have trouble convincing the editor?

Broaddus: I didn't and I read *so* much Arthurian material. *Le Morte d'"Arthur*, comic books (*Camelot 3000* and *Mage*), *The Once and Future King*, Peter David's *Knight Life*, research papers. The more I read, the more I became convinced that I could do anything I wanted with the story because the underlying mythos was so strong.

I had actually sent a different novel to Angry Robot. They rejected it (it was that second novel I had mentioned before), but they said that they liked my writing style. They asked if I had anything else. "Well, I have this novel I wrote for National Novel Writing Month which I just polished. It's *The Wire* meets *Excalibur.*" [i.e. the John Boorman film, not the Laubenthal novel—DS] They said "if you can make it work, we're buying this book." I sent them three chapters. They offered me a contract.

Q: Did you read any of the other medieval Arthurian material other than Malory?

Broaddus: Tons, including Welsh poems. It's one of the reason why there are so many characters in the series. I delve into a lot of the "side stories," for example, bringing in the Green Knight, the Red Knight, and the Black Knight, not to mention Tristan and Iseult.

Q: Is it the King Arthur mythos which is so universally applicable, or is this more a matter of Joseph Campbell's mono-myth about the Hidden Hero, which is found in cultures all over the world?

Broaddus: I think it's a bit of both. Campbell's mono-myth certainly plays a part in the cycle, but the mythos are so grand and expansive, filled with such drama and passion, that people simply relate to them. I had to be careful while writing the Tristan and Iseult storyline to make sure it didn't take over the entire book.

Q: I suppose if Tristan and Iseult threatened to take over the entire book, you could have let them have an entire volume to yourself. Surely the publisher would encourage this for a successful series.

Broaddus: From your lips…

Q: Have you felt any inclination to go the Charles Saunders route and address specifically African material?

Broaddus: Funny you should mention that. I've written several "sword and soul" stories, two of which feature a warrior named Dinga Cisse and the third featuring the heroine Lalyani. My fourth novel *Black Son Rising* felt like a love letter to Charles Saunders and will probably have a home before too long. The idea that has been noodling around in the back of my head has been to explore more specifically Jamaican material, which of course has its roots in West African traditions.

Q: What about the narrative voice? Do you have to wait until you can "hear" the story in your head, or can you just make that happen?

Broaddus: Now's normally the time when I would wax eloquent about "my muse" or the perils of writer's block, but my wife cured me of a lot of my writer's angst. It involved a "come to Jesus" type conversation where she reminded me that we can't afford writer's block because we have bills to pay so I better plant my butt in a chair, get over myself, and get to putting words on the page.

Once I have my notes, I can usually go. But a lot of those notes involve background on my characters, typically snippets of conversation, and description. So I know quite a bit about the POV character and how they sound before I put pen to paper. (Literally, pen to paper. I still write long hand.) Also, armed with my notes, it cuts down the odds of becoming stuck.

Q: I am reminded of L. Sprague de Camp saying that much of writing consists of "the application of the seat of the pants to the seat of the chair." In other words, self-discipline. Do you think you'd write any differently if you *didn't* have to make a living at it?

Broaddus: I'm not sure. There are some projects I might have passed on if the payday wasn't so good. Who am I kidding? I'd probably still have taken them. Taking on projects helps reinforce the discipline to be honest with you. With a lot of looming deadlines, I don' have the luxury to lie around or take extended breaks. Deadlines don't move all that much, so I have to stay on it. On the plus side, having multiple projects means that if I *do* get stuck on one, I can always switch to another.

I don't even get to enjoy what I call "the cigar moment": that moment when I type "The End" and have completed a project. I allow myself the evening for a glass of muse juice (Riesling), but the next day I know I have another project to get to.

Q: Let's talk about influences a little. Who are some of your favorite writers and how did they influence you? Was it a matter of your finding these writers at the right time?

Broaddus: Coming up, Stephen King influenced me on characterization. Neil Gaiman and Kelly Link on that sense of wonder and story. Octavia Butler on voice. Elmore Leonard on dialogue. George Pelecanos on plotting. Michael Chabon and Junot Diaz on style and prose. Amy Hempel…just because she's cool and I love her way with words.

All of them I found at the right time. I'm always looking for new books to read and writer's to learn from. There's this whole canon of words to choose from so we have this advantage of choosing from some truly great teachers. Then I kick myself for not discovering them sooner. Case in point, Walter Moseley's *Futureland.* That book rocked my world in terms of how to incorporate worldview into story.

Q: Tell me about projects you're working on now or plan for the future.

Broaddus: I have a massive "sekrit projekt" which I'm working on (Non-Disclosure Agreements and everything!). That should keep me tied up through the end of the year writing wise. Well, it should. I'm also doing the final prep on *Streets of Shadows* (Alliteration Ink), an urban fantasy meets crime anthology co-edited with Jerry Gordon and featuring such writers as Jonathan Maberry, Seanan McGuire, Kevin J. Anderson, Kathryn Rusch, and Tim Lebbon. I'm about to release a short story collection tentatively titled *Walkers with the Dawn* (Blackwyrm Books). I'd keep an eye on the Firefly RPG stuff from Margaret Weis Productions as well as the Storium storytelling game. Be looking for an announcement about my sword and soul novel, *Black Son Rising* (co-written with Steve Shrewsbury) soon.

Coming up early next year includes me wrapping up *Pimp My Airship: The Novel* (plus another short story collection of steampunk tales all in the same universe), a science fiction/crime novel tentatively titled *Serpent* (co-written with Jason Sizemore), plus a middle grade detective novel. There's about a half dozen short stories sprinkled among all of that I've already committed to also. That should be enough to kick off 2015.

Q: Thanks, Maurice.

JAMES P. BLAYLOCK

James P. Blaylock is certainly one of the pioneers of Steampunk. Whether he invented it or not is under discussion in this interview. He was in any case born in 1950 and is noted for decidedly strange, often humorous novels such as *The Elfin Ship, The Stone Giant, The Digging Leviathan, Lord Kelvin's Engine, Zeuglodon, The Last Coin, The Paper Grail, All the Bells on Earth, Knights of the Cornerstone*, etc. He won the World Fantasy Award for the story "Paper Dragons" in 1986 and "Thirteen Phantasms" in 1997.

←*·⚊··*→

Q: So, did you and Tim Powers invent Steampunk? Did you have any conscious awareness of doing so, or was it just something in the air?

Blaylock: This is a complicated question, as are all questions of origin, I suppose. Certainly K.W. Jeter has to be included with Tim Powers and I when it comes to inventing Steampunk. K.W. was a great instigator in those days, and it was K.W. who suggested to Powers and I that we read Henry Mayhew's brilliant London Labor and the London Poor, a book that functioned in its way as much of the inspiration for my novel *Homunculus*. That being said, many sf readers could point out that Michael Moorcock and Keith Roberts and possibly other writers had already written books that today would be regarded as Steampunk. When I wrote my first Steampunk stories I hadn't read those books and didn't know they existed. I had spent some time in front of the television watching *The Wild Wild West*, which I very much enjoyed, but I didn't at all associate it with what I was writing at the time. It was a western, after all, and not at all the world I wanted to inhabit as a writer, which was 19th Century Europe, primarily England. Not all influences are conscious, however, and certainly *The Wild Wild West* appealed to me for Steampunkish reasons that I didn't bother to define at the time, partly because Steampunk as such didn't exist. I'd been infected with a regard for 19th Century science, language, and trappings by reading Verne and Wells and Conan Doyle as a kid, and later on by dredging myself in Stevenson. I was bowled over when I was around 11 years old, give or take, and first saw *The Fabulous Baron Munchausen* and *The Fabulous World of Jules Verne*. Those films are quintessential Steampunk, and for me were monumental influences. When I wrote "The Ape-box Affair" (my first

Steampunk story, although K.W. wouldn't coin the term "Steampunk" for another 10 years), I was bingeing on both Stevenson and P.G. Wodehouse, and was caught up in the language and atmosphere of those bygone days— a literary bent I'd been on for the past several years at the university, where I'd read as much 18th and 19th Century literature as I could get my hands on, as did Tim. In short, I was primed to write Steampunk, and so were Tim and K.W., and we found ourselves hanging out together in Orange and Santa Ana in the 1970's, talking about our own writing, recommending books to each other, etc., and what came out of it was this early crop of stories and novels by the three of us, all with what came to be regarded as Steampunk sensibilities. Because of those publications, the three of us came to be regarded as the progenitors of Steampunk: we didn't regard ourselves as such until Steampunk had caught on, so to speak, and was developing the characteristics of the phenomenon that it became. I was amused when the term came into existence, but my understanding of it as a phenomenon (nice word) was clarified in the very early 90s, when I was invited to attend a Steampunk conference put on by the University of Bologna's Department of Utopian and Dystopian Studies, one day of which was dedicated to my work. Certainly they're a scholarly crowd, and certainly they considered the three of us to have invented the thing; I make it a point never to argue with scholars from high-toned universities. So...did we "invent" Steampunk? Something like that, although certainly we were standing on the shoulders of giants, whether we were aware of it or not.

Q: How did you feel when it came back in recent years, having transformed itself into a social phenomenon and generated a second wave of literature?

Blaylock: I was quite happy when it blew up, so to speak, in recent years. I had written my last Steampunk novel in the early 90s, and had no idea of writing anything more in that vein (nor any idea of not writing more). Some few years back I read a nifty collection of stories by James Norman Hall, titled *Doctor Dogbody's Leg*, which reminded me of how much fun I'd had writing Steampunk. I asked Bill Schafer at Subterranean Press whether he was interested in my writing a series of lengthy Steampunk novellas (or short novels) and he said that he was. I set out to write what became *The Ebb Tide*. The inspiration for the book had little or nothing to do with the growing phenomenon of contemporary Steampunk; it had everything to do with my reading *Doctor Dogbody's Leg*. So my second wave of Steampunk stories was coincidental with the cultural phenomenon, and I'll write the stuff when the craze has faded, given that I haven't lost my taste for it. Given that I first fell for the stuff as a ten-year-old when I checked *Twenty Thousand Leagues Under the Sea* out of the Stanton Free Library, the charm of the literature in one form or another has lasted me over fifty years. I doubt I'll abandon it any time soon. Even so, I'm happy to be suddenly living in a world in which editors actively want to buy Steampunk stories. I had more fun writing *The Aylesford Skull*, my most recent Steampunk novel, than I had writing anything else in recent memory, or so it seems to me now. I've got a new publisher for it—Titan Books—which is hearteningly enthusiastic about the novel and about Steampunk in general. So—speaking of the phenomenon that is Steampunk—it makes me quite happy. I love the whole idea of it. Despite the proliferation of Steampunk junk, the best of it is literally wonderful. If I stepped out of the house this morning and discovered that the general population was dressed in morning coats and beaver hats and crinoline, I'd have a wide smile on my face (although I'd still be wearing jeans and a flannel shirt; it was a gaudy era, and I'm not a gaudy kind of guy.)

Q: Hmm. I am reminded of something S.P. Somtow told me once about academic music conferences. If you, the creator, are faced with a panel of academic experts who regard you as the originator of what they study, then they will believe anything you tell them. Did you ever feel the temptation to, ah, elaborate a little bit in the presence of those high-toned scholars?

Blaylock: I might in fact have been guilty of that once or twice. One of the things that recommends literature as a university degree is that you can make crap up, and then find "textual evidence" to "prove" your assertions, thus assuring your A grade. If you're good with words, you can avoid real work (until you run into a professor who sees through it, which, luckily, happened to me). As for the conference in Italy, however, I couldn't afford to attend, despite my Italian publisher, Mondadori, offering to set up a soiree, signing, etc. We didn't have much money in those days, and there was no way I was going to Europe without Viki, my wife. The university offered something like 8 million, trillion lire as travel money, which turned out to be about sixty dollars and a few odd cents. I turned down invitations to conferences at the University of Volgograd and at Trinity College, Dublin, for the same reason. I was teaching at Chapman University at the time, but there was no travel/conference money for adjunct professors. Seems like a mistake to me now not to have gone, but at the time it was flat out impossible. Anyway, as regards the conference in Bologna, I was asked to talk about Steampunk as revisionist history, and I actually set out to write a paper. It seemed fun—potentially hilarious—that a guy who had grown up in Anaheim, California, and spent most of his time at the beach, whose idea of London was almost entirely cribbed from Dickens and Conan Doyle and was essentially twice-removed imagination, and whose idea of science was largely a product of Verne and Wells, had "revised" history in some regard. I wondered how a serious academic study of that strange business was in any regard sensible. Academic scholarship is often an inscrutable business.

Q: You might superficially conclude that Steampunk is the next Goth, only they dress better. But more seriously, what do you think is the appeal of fantasizing about the late 19th century and its technology? Why does this resonate so widely just now?

Blaylock: I suspect that the trappings of the 19th century resonate today because the world is literally being buried in throwaway products that are ugly and virtually useless to begin with and which are designed to fall apart and are outmoded before they go on the market. Because I'm attracted to conspiracy theories (the nuttier the better) I'm wary of buying into those theories, but it seems to me that there's a plot afoot. When my family was in Singapore a few years back, we all bought watches from a vendor on the street for three bucks apiece, which happened to be less than it cost for a Tiger beer in most bars. All four of the watches were stone dead within five days. Mine died on the flight home. Sherlock Holmes's pocket watch was made of sturdier stuff. A carpenter's square from the 19th century was built to last several lifetimes and was decorated with carvings of goblins and with polished brass inlay. (I'm imagining the goblins.) I'm a fan of the Arts and Crafts Movement influence on everyday things in those days, an influence that lingered well into the 20th century before dying out and leaving us with cheaply made plastic trash and high fructose corn syrup. Sorry to get carried away there. Personally, I'm attracted to the 19th century partly because science was still largely imaginary. Lost worlds, prehistoric monsters, Barsoomian-type rays, and a whole plethora of cool things were a dirigible ride away. (So were slavery and disease and abominable human cruelty, of course, but whereas the lost worlds have disappeared, slavery, disease, and cruelty have not.)

Q: Have you ever been to a Steampunk World's Fair or an event like that? What did you make of it?

Blaylock: I've attended several Steampunk conferences over the past few years, although never the Steampunk World's Fair. (Is there such a thing?) I found myself to be one of the very few people among the sometimes thousands of attendees who wasn't dressed up in Victorian fashion. I'm far too introverted to wear a costume of any sort. I was quite happy, however, that everyone around me was wearing fabulous clothing. I loved the whole business—robot dogs, automobiles that looked like immense snails, steam driven bicycles, clockwork gizmos. When I received the "It's All Your Fault" Airship Award at Steamcon in Seattle, I found it to be a strangely moving thing, even though it was 1/3 my fault at best, and, clearly, I owed that 1/3 to a host of books and people that influenced my writing, not the least of whom was my mother, who first hauled me down to the library when I was ten years old and steered me toward Jules Verne, and Viki, who during the early years of our marriage was off earning the weekly paycheck while I was hanging out in O'Hara's Pub in Orange with Tim and K.W. "working." I'm happy that something interesting came from all that beer and popcorn and wild talk.

Q: Well wasn't the 1950s just as much an era of ugly (often downright hideous) manufactured goods and planned obsolescence also? But there was no Steampunk then. It may be because they still believed (albeit nervously) in a bright future in those days. You know, a helicopter in every garage and vacations on the Moon. That vision is now just as much pure fantasy as Barsoom or *The Moon Pool*. I wonder, more seriously, if the popularity of Steampunk right now isn't a matter of a retreat from the future. We're no longer taking it seriously. We turn away to gaudy fantasies of what-wasn't rather than what-might-be. Your thoughts?

Blaylock: You're right, I think. I love the line in *Death of a Salesman*, when Willy Loman laments modern notions of whipped cheese. In many ways it was a Cheese Whiz world back then, and much more so today, even though we're all aware of the evils of processed food and planned obsolescence (which seems to me to be a plague). (Isn't Cheese Whiz similar to Peeps and Twinkies in that it never goes bad? Survivalists probably have crates of the stuff. A new cell phone is obsolete when you buy it, but Cheese Whiz is never obsolete in any regard. Makes you think... Maybe.) I remember being an enormous fan of the House of the Future when Disneyland opened in the 1950s (and equally a fan of Captain Nemo's submarine). I watched the Jetsons on tv. Orange County, California, in those days was still full of orange groves, and on a typical afternoon, when I got home from school, I'd grab a book, ride my bike to the end of the street (where I'd let it lie—no chain and lock necessary), walk a hundred yards into the orange grove, climb a tree, and read for a couple of hours in utter tranquility. That seems very much like a dream now. I had no idea that some of the best things in my world were rapidly passing away, and so it seemed quite possible that the future would be fairly cool. A few years later, of course, there were no orange groves left (although there's a "demonstration grove" near where I live now. It's near the freeway, so the trees are feeble and dying. They produce an occasional orange, though, which no one picks and eats.) Even then, however, I saw a vast gulf between that moving sidewalk, hover car future and the world that I lived in, which, orange groves aside, looked a lot more like *The Outsiders* than *The Jetsons*. There turns out to be plenty in the world to retreat from, I suppose. Raymond Chandler pointed out that everything we read, we read to escape. I was as likely to escape into *In Dubious Battle* as into *Mysterious Island*, but I did plenty of escaping into books and still do today. I'm a fan of what was as well as what wasn't.

Q: Aren't labels tricky things anyway? I've seen you *labeled* an "American magic realist." Does that actually mean anything other than you don't have a Spanish name?

Blaylock: I first saw that label attached to me a couple of years after my novel *The Digging Leviathan* came out, specifically in reference to the Roycroft Squires character coming past on a flying bicycle. Roycroft Squires was based on my pal Roy Squires, an L.A. rare book dealer. I changed his first name to Roycroft in the novel because of my interest in Elbert Hubbard and the Roycrofters, who wore enormous bowties. All of this seemed funny to me. That it seemed like magic realism to someone else seemed doubly funny. Bill Gibson told me that when he'd asked for the book at a Vancouver bookstore, the proprietor had given him a strange look and asked, "Do you know if it's supposed to be funny?" I found that funny, too. When it comes to academia and literary critics, I have the habit of agreeing with anything they say about a book or about me as a writer as long as it makes me sound erudite. "Magic realism" is an okay term in that regard, so I'll claim that it's true. Recently a reviewer referred to me as a post-modern writer—something having to do with Steampunk and dystopia, I think. That's another term that's okay in academic circles, and so I'll claim it, too. Perhaps I'll have hats embroidered. I've never cared for labels. Forgive me for dumping one more literary allusion into this, but it was Samuel Johnson who wrote, "… theory shall have little influence on practice." I seem to recall that he was writing about ghosts at the time, but I'll say that theory has never had the least influence on my writing. It's deadly, I think, for writers to take any label seriously.

Q: I've got a theory about literary theories, which is that when an actual practitioner of the art of fiction (not a critic or academic) comes up with a theory, it is self-descriptive and retrospective. Some writers, from Poe onward—everybody from Lovecraft to Hemingway—have written, sometimes at length, on the Theory of Fiction. But this tells us more about them than about fiction, actually. Lovecraft's description tells us a great deal about how he did it, but very little about how Hemingway did it, and vice versa. So do you think you could generalize a little about how you do it?

Blaylock: I'm happy to chat about it. Your last sentence reminds me a little of the Tom Waits song "Big in Japan," (which, of course, is meaningless unless you've heard the song.) I'll have to assume that I'm doing what I think I'm doing when I write, and I'll admit that I often get interesting effects when I'm not consciously trying to get those effects. I'll say for openers that I teach a grad class at the university titled "Techniques of Fiction," which is something like the "Theories of Fiction" class that I took as a student 40 years ago. I've always thought that there was a misleading element to any discussion of literary techniques, in that (as you pointed out) "techniques" are something we examine and categorize after the fact. No writer

I've ever talked to sits down at the desk thinking about techniques. It could be that Hemingway (since you've mentioned him) knew from the start that he wanted to write a story, say, in the objective point of view. When he wrote about the craft, he chatted about the usefulness of the objective point of view, about its…objectivity, and about how the objective narrator doesn't seem to manipulate characters. There's a more truthful outcome, or so he said. That's nonsense to my mind. Hemingway carefully chose every word that went into his stories and phrased his sentences in such a way as to manipulate the reader into believing in the objectivity of the narrative. Despite claims of objectivity, in fact everything in such a story is manipulation and contrivance, meant to give the appearance of objectivity: there's nothing at all objective about the result. So-called techniques are an attempt at the rationalization of things that are in fact closer to alchemy or magic. (Sorry for all that. I've been on sabbatical for 8 months, and I find myself lured more and more often into this sort of thinking. Feel free to edit any of this. I'm quite possibly in a verbose mood.)

So…to answer your question, I begin to think that I might have a story to tell when a character and setting (the one as important as the other) swim into view in my mind. If I also can hear the voice, literarily speaking, of the main character, then I'm moderately certain that I have a story to tell. I begin to imagine scenes that might occur given this character, with his particular way of seeing things, in this particular setting. These initial, imagined scenes suggest other scenes and other characters. When I can picture a dozen or fifteen scenes, then I can fairly effortlessly develop the rudiments of a plot, which I can use to sell the novel to a publisher, sketching the whole thing out by synopsizing the vital scenes. At that point I pitch the plot synopsis into the drawer and I don't look at it again.

The best stuff in a book or story, without exception, comes to me while I'm writing. I've found that I have to let the book develop organically (jargon alert) from that point on. These beginnings take several months, perhaps more if research is involved, and are characteristically a sort of schizophrenic conversation with my computer screen. I type in potentially useful ideas or questions, one thing leading to another. Fairly often I immediately accuse myself of stupidities, say abusive things to myself, etc. There comes a point in this dialogue when the shape and color and tone of the novel has become clear to me, when the characters seem to have become real in some sense, and I'm compelled to write the first scenes as such. I'll inevitably false start if it's too early. I revise as I write, editing yesterday's work first. By the time I'm finished with a novel I've quite likely revised or rewritten the first chapters 25 or 30 times, and I've discarded early suppositions because I've come up with better stuff. When I sent in the finished manuscript of *The Digging Leviathan*, which I sold as a hollow earth novel, I got a call from Susan Allison, my editor at Ace. She liked the book well enough, but she complained that I'd promised the hollow earth, and yet my characters had never gotten out of Glendale.

Q: Regarding Magic Realism, there is an indelicate quote which I will have to clean up a little before I can repeat it in the august pages of Orson Scott Card's magazine. I paraphrase Gardner Dozois. Suppose there is a voice in a part of the human anatomy whence voices do not customarily issue. If it is caused by aliens, that's science fiction. If it is caused by demonic possession, that is fantasy. If no one cares, that's magic realism. Gardner's version was funnier, but I think the distinction is valid. That is, if "magic realism" actually means anything, it represents the attitudes of non-scientific, non-skeptical cultures, in which what we would call "the supernatural" is taken for granted as part of daily life. It is the extreme polar opposite of the Lovecraft approach, in which hard-headed skeptics with a firm grounding in science go mad at some violation of natural law. Magic realism is basically saying there are no natural laws. Can this be a valid and deliberate approach to fantasy? Can it be something which somebody outside of the original South American context can deliberately assume for purposes of a story?

Blaylock: Gardner's definition seems to hit the nail on the head. (I have it on good authority that Gardner was once on a panel at a convention where he was asked a question regarding what constituted science fiction. I don't know whether the question came from the moderator or an audience member. Supposedly part of his answer suggested that one might write SF like Blaylock: "Is that a dinosaur in the bushes or a trick of shadow?" And leave it there, the reference to the dinosaur being enough to qualify the story as science fiction. Gardner is an insightful guy.) I have very little science in me. There was a time in my youth when I was a monumental tropical fish enthusiast, and could remember the genus and species of hundreds of freshwater aquarium fish, especially if they were bizarre. I'll never forget that the purple striped gudgeon is in fact mogurnda mogurnda mogurnda. That's as close to "science" as I've ever gotten. When I've had an opportunity, I've happily put a gudgeon or a leaf fish or a Surinam toad into a story, thereby infusing it with scientific… validity. When I was in physics class in high school, I confused mass with volume. My teacher explained to us that an astronaut hurtling through space would increase in mass as he approached the speed of light. I immediately pictured an enormously fat astronaut shoe-horned into his ship, bulging out through the portholes, a sort of giant balloon man, dangerously overinflating. I innocently mentioned this during the class discussion, thereby striking the teacher speechless and then moderately angry. It seemed apparent to him that I was making fun of him and of physics in general, something that I deny (unless I'm around scientific types, in which case I insist that I was only fooling). In fact I was entirely innocent, which made it clear that I had no chance of writing science fiction, and so I fell naturally into writing fantasy. *The Digging Leviathan* featured a mechanical mole built of a vacuum cleaner and parts purchased at a Sprouse Reitz dimestore. Ace Books put an SF logo on it, explaining to me that if a book had a machine in it, it was science fiction by default. Homunculus was science fiction because it involved vivisection and an animated skeleton (or so I suppose).

All that being said, I'm going to have to be careful with this question in order not to sound like a lunatic, although it occurs to me that it's too late for that. The truth is, I'm no rationalist or materialist or anything of that nature. I'm happy to believe in ghosts and in the paranormal, although in an eccentric and (in a literal sense) unpopular way. I wrote a story titled "The Other Side," about a character who is confounded by evidently paranormal experiences—small, inexplicable, irrational, useless things. That was the only story I've ever written that was virtually entirely autobiographical. There's a long record of very convincing plesiosaur sightings in the open ocean and in deepwater lakes, well up into the 20th century. Science has no truck with such nonsense, but I'm happy with it. Science had no regard for giant squids until a batch of them showed up one day, although mariners had for a thousand years reported seeing enormous sucker marks on whale carcasses. One day, maybe tomorrow, a plesiosaur will appear in Los Angeles Harbor, and science will take it on the chin once again. If Gardner's definition of magic realism is correct, then I'm one of those non-scientific, non-skeptical types that dwells on the fringe of the cultural norm. I'm not sure that one has to have come from South America or some other exotic place to qualify in that regard. In fact, I find southern California quite moderately exotic from time to time. (I've also read and reread Charles Fort.) The term "magical realism" has a highly intelligent ring to it, which makes it appeal to me. "That Blaylock is apparently crazy!" "Not at all, he's a Magical Realist."

Q: What are your writing methods like? Are you an outliner? Someone who starts from an image, or a word? You will recall how Tolkien one day jotted down "In a hole in the ground there lived a hobbit" with no idea what that meant, and all else followed. Are you like that, or are you one of these writers who wants to know where he is going first?

Blaylock: I'm an outliner, although not as ferociously as some writers I know. I'm generally prodded into thinking through a novel by a combination of setting and character, both being vitally interesting to me. I carry on a schizophrenic conversation with my computer for a period of several months, during which time the plot swims into focus and begins to reveal itself as a series of scenes. When I've got enough of them in my mind, I try to write an 8 or 10 page double-spaced outline, which I use to hustle the book to a publisher. Meanwhile I start in on the writing process, at which point I put the outline into the drawer. I rarely look at it again, because the nature of the beast is fixed in my mind. The best stuff, without fail, is suggested to me during the writing process itself, and very quickly the outline seems to be flat and uninteresting, hence my diminishing interest in it.

That's my method. One last thing: my first novel, *The Elfin Ship*, was pure shooting-from-the-hip. Lester del Rey agreed to buy it after telling me that it had a completely senseless, crappy, stupid plot, but that he'd send me a contract if I would throw away the second half of the novel and send him a plot synopsis that would work. There followed two or three pages of information informing me (not always kindly) about the nature of plots in general. My experience with Lester and Judy-Lynn del Rey was like one of those Scared Straight programs where enormous tattooed felons scream at fifteen year olds. Without them, however, I'd probably have become a beach bum.

Q: So, what are you working on these days?

Blaylock: At the moment I'm in between books—plotting out two new ones, actually. I've just finished thinking through a sequel to my recently published novel *Zeuglodon*, and I've got some notions for a new Steampunk novel swirling around in my mind. I'm waiting for it to stop swirling and stand still, so that I can see what it actually looks like. Two weeks ago I mailed in the manuscript of a short Steampunk novel to Subterranean Press—a novel titled *The Pagan Goddess*, which will be published as a companion volume to *The Ebb Tide* and *The Affair of the Chalk Cliffs* (ideally with J.K. Potter illustrations). Not long ago I got a new agent—John Berlyne of the Zeno Agency, London—who's a real taskmaster, and he's got the strange notion that I must write more. I plan to be cooperative in that regard.

Q: Thanks, Jim.

THEODORA GOSS

RECORDED AT THE WORLD FANTASY CONVENTION, SAN DIEGO, CA, OCT 30, 2011.

Theodora Goss is the author of *The Thorn and the Blossom*, which has just appeared from Quirk Books. Her first short story collection is *The Forest of Forgetting* (Prime, 2006). She has been nominated for the Nebula Award and the World Fantasy Award, and she has won the World Fantasy Award for "The Singing of Mount Abora" (best short story, 2008). She has also won the Rhysling Award for her poem "Octavia Lost in the Hall of Masks" in 2004. She lives in Boston.

◄─*─··─*─►

Q: Let's just start out with your background, who you are, and how you came to writing.

Goss: Do you want me to go through my life story a little bit? Okay.

Q: Well it is somewhat exotic. More than mine. I was born in New Jersey.

Goss: It is somewhat exotic. I was definitely not born in New Jersey. This does actually have quite a lot to do with my writing. I was born in Hungary, back in the Communist era. I left the country when I was, I think, about five years old. There was really no legal way to leave the country back then. So we officially escaped from a Communist country. That was one of the first things that happened in my life. So it's an exciting background to have. But I moved around a lot. We lived in Italy for a while after that and then we lived in Brussels, and then we came to the United States. Even when we were in the United States, we ended up moving a lot. I think because we were moving so much, because I always had to make new friends and get used to new places, one of the things I held onto during my childhood was books. I would read books and I would find a home in places like Narnia or Middle Earth, and they were always there for me in a way that geographical locations were not always there for me. I think that's why I started reading fantasy, or at least partly the reason that I started reading fantasy, that they gave me this sense of home, and they didn't seem strange to me. They didn't seem particularly unusual. I could understand that people were talking to dragons and things like that, because to me the real world seemed fantastical anyway, partly because I'd had such a sense of dislocation in childhood.

Q: Was English your first reading language?

Goss: No, actually my first reading language was French. So I started reading children's books in French, and it wasn't until I was about seven years old that I started learning English.

Q: So you must have grown up with French fairy tales. This might have been an improvement, because you didn't get the Disney versions.

Goss: I definitely didn't get the Disney versions. I grew up with not just French fairy tales; I grew up with a lot of fairy tales. What I got when I was a child were European books. We had European books in my house, books of European fairy tales, things that my mother had grown up on. We had an entire book of fairy tales from the Baltic area, I remember. We had them in English and in the original Hungarian. I guess they were originally in Hungarian. So we had these stories from Eastern Europe, and they are much, much darker than the versions of fairy tales that are told to American children. I hadn't really thought about this before, but that must have influenced me deeply, because when I tell fairy tales—and my fairy tales are for adults—they are much more dark. When you marry a bear, for example, that has consequences of various sorts. It's a strange, very real thing and not at all a kind of Disney thing.

Q: When I was growing up in the U.S., they very much had the attitude that fantasy of any sort is only for small children and it is something they are to be encouraged to outgrow, which would explain the trivialized versions. Isn't it true that in Europe they treat the fantastic with a little more respect?

Goss: I think that's true in a certain sense, though in an odd way, because my mother had grown up under the Communist system, the old folktales were given respect; but on the other hand there was this notion that literature for adults was supposed to be realistic. So I think that she always looked at my writing fantasy as a very odd thing. The kind of literature that she had grown up with was about workers and when you had American books that were coming to Hungary, they were John Steinbeck, about the plight of the American worker. There really was censorship of literature back in those days. There were books you could read and books you couldn't read, that were expurgated. But I think she had, without really thinking about it, grown up with the idea that literature was supposed to reflect real life. So she always looked at my writing fantasy and reading fantasy as a very *American* sort of thing. So it's interesting, the way that Communism had this impact on genre.

Q: Did they have any samizdat tradition? The Russians certainly did, which is where we get the word. I wonder if this didn't become a kind of forbidden fruit.

Goss: I think it did, actually. What you find in Eastern Europe now is that since the fall of the Berlin Wall there are a lot more people who are interested in fantasy and science fiction. I think that part of it is that it is associated with American culture for them, and it is associated with liberation, the permission to write what you want. They're very small movements, still, but it's interesting that most of the stories of mine that have been translated have been translated into Russian or Rumanian or Hungarian or Polish. They have been translated into Eastern European languages. Maybe it is because I have a connection with the area, but also there has been an upsurge of interest in science fiction and fantasy in those areas.

Q: Isn't it also interesting that most American fantasy is not about America? Some of it does, but most of it is not about Native Americans and magic buffaloes or whatever. It has castles and elves in it. It looks back to Europe.

Goss: I think that's partly because so many Americans came from Europe originally. Their ancestry comes from Europe. There is a way in which they brought their literature with them, brought their folktales with them, and their magical figures, and you haven't really had an incorporation of a Native American tradition into an American literary fantasy tradition. This is in some sense unfortunate, I guess. We had a panel on this at Wiscon. The more problematic aspect is that when you do have an incorporation of that tradition it is not necessarily by people who are brought up in that tradition. So they don't necessarily have the feel for it, and they can write it in ways that aren't very true to the original. At least these were some of the problems that we were discussing.

In some sense it is easier to write about Irish fairies, because they are more removed from us. But I think that we have a kind of immigrant fantasy tradition. We take liberally from the fantasy traditions of all different countries, and we mix stuff up. I heard complaints about how we mess up Irish fairies and do things to Irish fairies that people are looking at dubiously. But I think we have a very eclectic fantasy tradition.

Q: Maybe we even take fairies a little more seriously. I heard a great story from Michael Swanwick once. He and his wife were in Ireland, and they were looking at this stone circle that was in someone's back yard, and as they were doing so a ten-year-old boy came out and said, "What are you doing?" and he said, "We're looking at the fairy ring." With a look of absolute disgust the boy said, "Don't tell me you believe in *fairies!*" Is it possible that precisely because they don't have this sort of tradition in America, Americans look back to it more.

Goss: I think that's part of it. There is also a sense in which our lives are so urban now and so focused on the technological that we are nostalgic for a fantasy tradition that seems to link us to something authentic and something of the land. There are certain countries that stand in for that kind of authenticity, and Ireland is one of them. We have these beautiful images in our minds of Ireland as green and somehow enchanted and magical. It's a way for us to mentally connect back to something that feels real and natural in the middle of our lives, which are lived online and in urban centers for the most part.

Lupoff: There is an American tradition, but maybe for most writers it's as much of a stretch as writing about ancient Greece or something. In any case, it's only got a couple hundred years of depth. I am thinking of Stephen Vincent Benet or Manly Wade Wellman, or Orson Scott Card's Alvin Maker series. These are fantasies about white people in America. But you and I have never lived in a log cabin in the woods, now have we? So we are just as removed from that as we are from living in a castle.

Goss: What about Lovecraft? I mean, Lovecraft was not looking back to Europe in the same way that Poe was. Poe really was looking back to Europe for his fantasy tradition, but Lovecraft seems to have created something that was, for me, deeply influenced by what was going on in Europe intellectually in the last part of the 19th century, but on the other hand it seems very different from what anyone else has done.

Q: I think Lovecraft was looking back to his New England roots, back to the 17th or 18th century, often very overtly; but he was also looking forward and outward. He wasn't looking at the past at all. He was looking at the Einsteinian universe. Remember that he came at precisely the time when they discovered that those swirly things you see in telescopes are actually other galaxies. There was a time when astronomers thought that the universe was shaped like a mill-wheel, and those pinwheel things were just swirling clouds of gas, and not very far away. Suddenly, in Lovecraft's time, the universe got vastly bigger and much more chaotic. So the answer is that Lovecraft is looking *forward* through the perspective of the cutting-edge science of his day.

Goss: I think there is something very American about that. We're the ones who put men on the Moon, right? There's something that feels very American about the sense of uncertainty about the future, a kind of fear linked to the exploration of space. There is something to me that feels very much of this country. I say that because I grew up in Europe and there is a different feeling there. There is a different relationship to time, in a sense. You are so living in traces of the past. I remember going down in the metro in Budapest when I went to visit there, and parts of the metro are Roman ruins. There is such a tendency in Europe to look back at the past more than there is to look forward to the future. In a sense, the fact that we have such a short past as Europeans in this country—or as immigrants in this country, I should say, because obviously not all of us are European immigrants—we don't have that deep sense of the past; although Lovecraft also had a deep sense of a very weird past. I mean, he was looking back at an incredibly distant past which was a very non-human past.

Q: As someone put it, if the history of the Earth were written as a 150-volume encyclopedia, the history of mankind would fill the bottom half of the last page. Lovecraft had a keen sense of that kind of perspective. This also raises another point which may be relevant to the difference between European and American writing. I at least have the impression that there are no serious distances in England, and there is no empty land. But while flying to this convention, well, I seemed to pass over the dead sea bottoms of Barsoom, and I spent an hour and a half passing over the Grand Canyon. You can look to the horizon from that altitude and see no trace of human activity whatsoever. This isn't even just the case in the Southwest. There are placed in Pennsylvania where you can drive for hours and see nothing but forest. So I think this gives us a very different view of distance and land from the way Europeans see them.

Goss: I think that's absolutely right. I even feel it after returning from Europe, when I get back to the United States and I leave the airport. Everything's larger. Our roads are larger. Things are farther away from each other. We have a sense that there is simply more space for us to live in. Our houses are larger. You can drive five hours from Boston to New York and you are still speaking the same language, and the culture is really not very different. Whereas, if you take the town my father lives in Hungary, which is Debrecan, and you drive five hours south, you have crossed a number of different countries and you've spoken a number of different languages. So, things feel smaller there and it feels like there are boundaries around you in a way that it feels like there aren't in the United States. In some sense that can create a feeling of anxiety, to feel that sense of boundlessness, but it can also create a sense of possibility.

Q: So, what does this change in perception do to your fiction?

Goss: I think my fiction partakes of both. I think that there are parts of it that feel very European to people, and there are parts of it that are definitely American. I think I feel very free to cross boundaries of all sorts and to experiment. I think that's partly my rebellious Americanness. [Laughs.] I think there is something rebellious about us. And I also end up writing about the American South, which is where I actually grew up. I grew up in Virginia. I think that had an influence on me as well. There is something about the South and the fantastical, Gothic tradition of the South that I got growing up as a child. But there is something in the language I use. I have been told this, that I write in a way that is fairly precise, and I think it may be the way that you write when you learned a language as a second language rather than as a first language.

Q: So your first spoken language would have been Hungarian, then you learned to read French, and then you learned English.

Goss. Yeah, absolutely. I still have some of the children's books I had when I lived in Brussels. Yeah, I have crossed three linguistic boundaries. I still speak French, not very well anymore, because I have not practiced for a long time, but I still read French. I know a very little bit of Hungarian. Unfortunately not very much, about the amount you'd know if you were a five-year-old. But I think that having those languages has done something to my style. I am not entirely sure what, but it's changed it.

Q: Americans may be the world's worst linguists, but it was my experience anyway, that about the time you get to high school in this country, and you study a foreign language for the first time—and don't really learn it— you start thinking for the first time about how languages work, the syntax and grammar, such as the fact that in the Latin-based languages the modifiers follow the nouns, or that in German the verb at the end of the sentence comes. That sort of thing. Do you find yourself suddenly more conscious of language and how you use it because you know more than one?

Goss: I think that's true. I am not sure it's happened with me on a conscious level. Maybe on an unconscious level. I think I pay attention to the sound of language very carefully, and I am a writer who writes by ear. I think a lot about the way sentences sound. Another thing that has influenced my writing obviously is that I teach writing at the university level. I have been trained as a teacher of grammar and of style, so I am very conscious of the way I write, but I also write in a sense, by the sound. I think even of punctuation in terms of the way that it makes sentences sound. I don't know. Maybe even that comes a little bit from being a child and learning these different languages and being aware of the way they sound, because Hungarian, French, and English all sound very, very different.

Q: Speaking of other things you may get from childhood, what do you think you have brought from childhood into adulthood from fairy tales? Some people just read fairy tales as kids and then leave them. Obviously fantasy writers don't.

Goss: I think one is the displacement of the human. Human beings aren't necessarily the most important things in fairy tales. If you read a realistic novel, every single character is a human being. Human beings are very, very important. In fairy tales human beings are not necessarily the most important things. The wolf is very important, or the bull is really important, or the polar bear is really important. So one thing is the sense that human beings are not the only actors in the world. I think that as fantasy writers —Ursula Le Guin said something like this at one point—we have a sense that we as human beings are not living alone in the world. We can imagine ourselves into the consciousness of other beings, whether they are imaginary beings like dragons or animals of various sorts. We have a tendency to tell stories from the point of view of non-human characters, and I think that is very, very important. Especially nowadays, when we have so much power over the natural world, it is very important to be able to look at that world from a different perspective.

I think another thing I bring into adulthood from fairy tales is a belief in the possibility of all sorts of transformations. Fairy tales are about transformations and magical shape-shifting. Things change in fairy tales. I think that appears in my writing. I think fairy tales have given me an enormous freedom in writing. I can write anything that I can imagine happening. I can make women marry bears. I can have someone who is a reincarnation of someone who lived a long time ago. It's a sense that the boundaries of the real don't bind me.

Q: I also notice from your story collection, that in some of your stories the fantasy element is extremely understated, like in the "Letters from Budapest" story. I'm reading this and it's very authentic, but it reads like a realistic story about being an artist under Communism, and then there is this fantastic flourish at the end, which changes the meaning of everything, but sometimes it seems as if you've put in the fantasy element as a seasoning.

Goss: That's an interesting observation. I am not sure it is quite a seasoning. I think that what I see in the world around me is that there is a kind of fantastical element to life, and it underlies everything. Then all the realistic stuff happens on top of it. So I think I reflect that in my stories. There are stories of mine where somebody suddenly comes to the discovery that life is stranger than they think. I think that that's a discovery that we need to make, and that more of us could make. If we look at what science is discovering nowadays, bacteria living in conditions where we thought that no life was possible, for example. If we look at actual life, the actual real life around us, we will see that it is much, much stranger than we ever thought. We have this assumption that we understand life, and we don't. So I think that my stories, the stories that function like that, are stories that point out that you think you are living in one world, but it is not really the world you are living in, and there's often this moment of recognition that the characters go through, where they realize that the world is magical, and they didn't think it was.

Q: It's also a backward-looking moment, at least for the reader, because then the reader, because the reader understands that you're reading a slightly different story than you thought. All the events are still in the same order, but they have taken on a new meaning.

Goss: Yes, and that's fun to do. I think that one way that I think about stories is in terms of their shapes. The book that I just wrote, which is coming in January [of 2012] is a book that does that consciously in that it's a book that consists of two stories, so you can read each story individually, and each story should make sense individually, but when you read both of them, you get a larger story. So when you read the first story, you get one story, but when you read the second you end up re-evaluating the first story. I think that you almost have to read the first story again in order to look back and understand how the whole functions.

Q: What is the title of this book?

Goss: The title of this book is *The Thorn and the Blossom,* and it is coming out from Quirk Books. It's a project that one of the editors at Quirk asked me to do, and I was attracted to it because I thought of it as a sort of literary feat of engineering. I thought it would be fun to write two stories that interlock in that way. I told him I thought there were two sorts of stories that could do that. One is a mystery and one is a love story, and I chose to write the love story. So the love story is from the point of view of the two lovers, but they have different versions of events, and they tell you different things about the story. They give you different pieces information. So you can only tell the entire story once you have read both of them.

Q: Sort of like *Rashomon*, in which everybody tells the same story from a different point of view?

Goss: The editor actually told me right from the beginning, "Don't make it like *Rashomon.*" It shouldn't be the exact same story from two different points of view. There should be an element of mystery about it. There are parts of the story that are telling different events, so there are events you get in one story that are not in the other story. It's really about the lives of two people and how they live those lives, and how they interact with each other, and how each of them has their own life and their own story to tell. In a way, I thought of it as very much about how we do live our lives. Each one of us does have our own life and our own story to tell. They intersect in different ways, but you can never fully get another person's story. Each of us is living his or her own story.

[She shows an advance copy of the book.]

Q: This is a very strange looking book, physically. It opens up like an accordion. Would you explain the purpose of this?

Goss: This was his idea in the beginning, to create a book that opened like an accordion. It opens from one side, and that's one story, and once you get to the back you can flip it over and open it from the other side and it's another story.

Q: Like reading two sides of a scroll.

Goss: It is like reading two sides of a scroll. In fact someone has said to me that it looks like an ancient Japanese scroll, which is interesting, because what Quirk did was create a book which is in itself a work of art. And it's in a slipcase. There is going to be an e-book version, a Kindle version, but I am not sure it is going to be the same experience. This really is a book you want to hold in your hands.

Q: I imagine that at some point someone will want to do a mass-market paperback in a more conventional format, maybe back-to-back like an Ace Double. My first thought on seeing this is that if you put this in libraries, it's going to fall apart. It will tear down one of the folds, and then you will have two pieces. Would it work in a more conventional format?

Goss: I don't know. You'd have to talk to Quirk Books and ask what their plans are. I think that they are not necessarily thinking of doing that. But we will have to see how the book does and what happens to it.

Q: What else are you working on these days?

Goss: The next thing I am going to be working on is a novel. I wrote a short story a while back—You know another thing which has influenced my writing is my academic work. I just finished a Ph.D. in English Literature. The funny thing is that my academic work often leads to writing. So I was writing this doctoral dissertation, and one chapter of my doctoral dissertation is on *The Island of Dr. Moreau* and in *The Island of Dr. Moreau,* Dr. Moreau creates a woman out of a puma. This is the woman who ends up killing him. She is in turn shot by his assistant. Well, I decided to tell her story. So I wrote a story about the puma woman, who does not in fact get shot on Dr. Moreau's island; she makes her way to England, and becomes a sort of scientist herself. After that story I decided that she was such an interesting character, and I was studying mad scientists anyway, that I decided to write about all the daughters of the mad scientists. I wrote a story called "The Mad Scientists' Daughter." It includes, I think, six mad scientists' daughters, including Justine Frankenstein, which is the female monster that Frankenstein did not create in the novel but does create in my alternate universe. I have a sort of alternate literary universe. There was Mary Jekyll, for instance, and then Catherine Moreau, my puma woman, was in this story. It was published in *Strange Horizons*, and people responded to it very strongly. It was a finalist for a Locus Award. I decided that what I was going to do was write a novel with these characters in it. So this is a novel that is going to be about all the mad scientists' daughters, and what they do when they band together and form a club.

Q: Sort of the League of Extraordinary Gentlewomen.

Goss: Exactly. They're going to have adventures. I don't know how it's going to go yet. I have written the first few chapters and I have a lot of revisions to do; but the first thing that happens is that Mary Jekyll and consults Sherlock Holmes.

Q: When you write this sort of book, how do you get beyond the level of being too obviously made up? How do you get the reader involved emotionally, beyond the sheer novelty value as a neat cartoon? To my mind the graphic novel *The League of Extraordinary Gentlemen* never succeeded. It was just too obviously made up, a big in-joke. How do you get past that?

Goss: This is something I have been thinking about a lot as I have been writing it, because it would be very easy to write this as a neat cartoon, as a kind of adventure novel. I started out doing that and I realized that it was the wrong way to go. This is a book about a group of young women who know that they are monsters. Now, every teenaged girl in the world is convinced that she is a monster. I remember growing up as a teenaged girl and feeling out of place, feeling I didn't know what I was doing in the world, feeling a lack of self-confidence about all aspects of my life in the world. So I think the heart of this book is that it's about a group of young women who are, in fact, monsters, and yet they are also women like any other women out there, who are trying to find the same things. They are trying to figure out how they are going to live. They are trying to figure out how they are going to function in the world. Justine Frankenstein is seven feet tall. What are you going to do if you are a seven-foot-tall woman made of corpses in Victorian England? On the one hand, it can be very cartoony. On the other hand, you have to think about who this girl really is, on the inside, and you have to start getting into her head, and I think that's where the readers can start to connect with the characters. That is where I start to connect with the characters, when I start to think about who she really is and how she must feel being who she is.

Q: These are characters who are misfits rather than evil, aren't they?

Goss: They're not evil, but they are outcasts from society, and therefore they are people who don't necessarily accept all the social norms and codes around them, particularly in Victorian England. And they have different personalities. So, for example Diana Hyde is not exactly evil, but she is a chaotic force, whereas Mary Jekyll is much more law-abiding.

Q: This may be a bit pedantic, but what did you do about the chronology? *Frankenstein* is set about a hundred years before any of the others, so Justine Frankenstein should be quite elderly before she meets Ms. Hyde.

Goss: That's an excellent question, but what I decided in the end was that I didn't care. I was playing in an alternate universe, and in my alternate literary universe I was going to mix stuff up, because I wanted to create a different kind of story, one that didn't necessarily fit into the stories that had already been written, but one that played with them in kind of a postmodern way. In some sense, this is a Young Adult novel, although I am not consciously aiming in that direction, but it seems really odd to say that I am trying to write a popular novel which could potentially be a Young Adult novel in this post-modern vein, and yet that is exactly what I am doing. I am *playing* with this material. It took me a long time to get to that. I really worried about the chronology until I decided that, you know what, this is me playing with the material and that is what I am going to do.

Q: "Post-modern," such as this term means anything, seems to refer to writing which is consciously aware—and which reminds the reader—that it is writing, which gets back to the problem of how you avoid having it so obviously made-up that it doesn't seem like a story anymore.

Goss: I think that by writing characters that feel real to people, that is the way that you always get to a story that doesn't just feel like a bunch of writing. You create characters that feel real to your readers because they are psychologically real. So, in a sense, it is much less important to me to be technically correct on the chronology than to be right about what my characters are thinking and how they are feeling.

Q: This is what any fantasy does, isn't it? Any fantasy contains elements readers know are impossible. Middle Earth doesn't exist, so Tolkien had to bowl them over with his characters.

Goss: Yeah, although usually there is a kind of internal consistency. That's a good question—I guess there will be internal consistency in my novel if the chronology will work within the story itself. It's just the literary tradition that I am playing with. I think that is going to be a fun aspect of it. I have this elaborate training in Victorian literature, so I may as well use it for something, right? If I am going to be writing in that era, I don't want to write as an academic researcher. I don't want to have everything sound exactly right and get all the details right. That is not what I am going for. I am going for a fun, interesting story that readers can relate to.

Q: Thanks, Theodora.

BEN BOVA

Introduction: Ben Bova is best known as an author of numerous hard-science fiction novels, most recently the Grand Tour, in which he re-explores the Solar System planet-by-planet in the light of current scientific knowledge. The most recent of these is *Leviathans of Jupiter* (2011). He is also noted for the Sam Gunn series (collected as *The Sam Gunn Omnibus*, 2007), the Orion series, the Kinsman series, and for numerous stand-alone novels. He was a very successful editor of *Analog* between the years 1971 and 1978 (where he discovered, among other new writers, Orson Scott Card) and then fiction editor and later editorial director of *Omni* magazine (1978-82). He won the Hugo Award for Best Editor six times. He is President Emeritus of the National Space Society and served as president of the Science Fiction Writers of America.

←*·····*→

Q: Could you describe your beginnings? How did you discover science fiction? What made you want to write it?

Bova: I grew up in South Philadelphia during the Great Depression of the 1930s and, later, World War 2. I got turned on to astronomy when I was about 11: a class trip to Philadelphia's science museum, the Franklin Institute, included a visit to its planetarium. When they turned on the stars I became instantly hooked on astronomy. In those days (circa 1943) there were a few far-seeing people who dreamed of building rockets and flying to the Moon. I became fascinated with rocketry and astronautics. Then I found that there stories about doing such things. That's how I discovered science fiction. Mostly I read magazines such as *Astounding* (later renamed *Analog*). When I started writing, I wrote about what interested me: science fiction.

Q: Let's also talk about your science background. What did you do on the Vanguard project?

Bova: I'm not a professional scientist. My degrees are in journalism, communications, and education. I had the good fortune to become a protégé of the director of the planetarium, Dr. I.M. Levitt, who led me to read widely in the sciences. I became a newspaper reporter, but when I learned that the U.S. would attempt to launch an artificial satellite during the International Geophysical Year (1957-58) I talked myself into a job as a technical editor for the Glenn L. Martin Co. (now Lockheed Martin Corp.), on the basis that Vanguard would be very much in the public eye, and the project would need someone who could understand the engineers and translate what they were doing into prose that the general public could understand. I stayed with the project through the furor of Sputnik, Vanguard's dismal failure on its first attempt to launch a satellite, and finally through three successful satellite launches. I also met Arthur C. Clarke when he came to the Martin plant to gather material for a nonfiction book he was doing about "the first man-made satellite of Earth." Arthur and I remained good friends until his death.

Q: Were real rocket engineers and such people interested in science fiction in those days?

Bova: Yes, some of them were. Many of them went into technical careers because they read science fiction in their youths.

Q: So how did you discover the science fiction community?

Bova: I'd been reading science fiction, and trying to write it, for years and years before I found out that fandom existed. I was working as a technical editor on the Vanguard project, at the Martin Co. just outside Baltimore, when David Kyle phoned me. He had heard about me through a mutual friend; I had no idea who David was. He told me that he was helping to make arrangements for the World Science Fiction Convention that year (1956, if memory serves) in New York City. I had no idea that there were science fiction conventions. David asked if I could bring a couple of engineers from Vanguard to speak at the convention. I recruited the two top engineers on the project, and that Labor Day weekend we drove up to New York and the Biltmore Hotel.

We rode an elevator to the floor where the convention activities were taking place. The elevator doors opened, and there were fans of all sorts and descriptions, many of them in costumes of one sort or another. And smack in the middle of all this bustle was a seven-foot tall poster of some sci-fi monster, with Forrest J. Ackerman standing beside it, happily reading a copy of his own magazine, *Famous Monsters of Filmland*.

My engineers were gray-flannel-suit types, narrow ties and button-down collars. They did a one-eighty and ducked back into the elevator. I had to tug them out, literally by their coattails. They were *very* apprehensive. But once I got them to the auditorium where they were to make their presentation, they were introduced to Arthur C. Clarke, Willy Ley, and others whom they knew by reputation as authorities in the field of rocketry. They settled down and gave their presentation. I must say that it was so dry that a lot of the audience got up and left. But they had a good time afterward with Arthur, Willy, et al.

Q: How long were you writing before you got anybody interested in anything you wrote? Did you get some of those legendary, long letters of rejection from John Campbell?

Bova: The first letter I ever got from Campbell was a reaction to a letter of criticism I had sent about the scientific accuracy of a story he'd published. His letter began, "Okay, wise guy." It went on for several pages, and gradually I realized that John was challenging me to write a better story. Eventually I did.

The first short story I ever sent to a publisher was bought for a magnificent $5.00. This was a local magazine in Philadelphia, my home town. I cashed their check and rode the trolley car to see these magnificent people. Alas, their offices were padlocked! The magazine had gone broke. I wondered if my $5.00 had busted them. But it taught me an important lesson: Cash all checks immediately. Don't wait for the company to fold.

I wrote my first novel in 1949. It was never published; probably a good thing. I struggled for ten years, learning my craft the hard way. My first published novel was *The Star Conquerors*, which came out in 1959.

Q: What was your relationship with Campbell like? Were you one of those writers whom he took to lunch and then pitched ideas to?

Bova: John Campbell was very kind to new writers, very solicitous. And he was a fountain of ideas. He spent the better part of his life striving to get writers to produce the kinds of stories that he wanted for *Astounding/Analog*. He discovered new talent and worked ceaselessly to develop it. He took me to lunch whenever I visited New York. He liked to challenge writers with intellectual puzzles, and many's the time a group of us sat around the lunch table trying to figure out the answer to his latest conundrum. John Campbell was one of a kind. What we call science fiction today is, in large part, what John decided the field should be.

Q: Did you ever have any difficulties with John Campbell's reported dogmatisms? There was a time when he was insisting that psionics was the essential "science" every SF writer should know. Your writings do not suggest you ever shared this view. How did you cope with the fact that this brilliant, mentoring figure could fall for things like the Dean Drive and the Hieronymus Machine?

Bova: I think the talk about John's "dogmatisms" has been overblown. He never insisted that I write about certain subjects or include one of his pet hobbyhorses in any story I sent him. When John was first hired to edit *Astounding Stories*, he asked his boss, "What happens if I don't get enough good stories to fill the magazine?" The boss fixed him with a stern gaze and replied, "A good editor does." I firmly believe that from moment on, John spent his energies on encouraging, cajoling, badgering writers into producing good stories for *Astounding/Analog*. His famous crotchets, such as the Dean Drive, et al., were a technique he used to get his writers to think outside the box, to try to go a step or two beyond themselves and produce new concepts. He never rejected a story of mine (or anyone else's, I daresay) because it didn't include whatever hobbyhorse he was riding at the time.

Q: How did it feel to fill his shoes? How did you become his successor?

Bova: Fred Pohl once remarked, after hearing someone introduce me as the man who filled John Campbell's shoes, that I also filled his chair. I think was referring to the size of my butt. Be that as it may, it was exciting to be the editor of *Analog*. The management of The Condé Nast Publications, Inc., certainly provided me with all the encouragement they could, and Katherine Tarrant stayed on to help me find my way. Kay had been John's assistant since he'd started on the magazine in 1937.

How did I get the job? When John died so suddenly, the management asked Kay Tarrant to draw up a list of contributors to the magazine who had written both science fiction and science fact. Kay, in turn, asked half a dozen of the magazine's major contributors to draw up such lists. Apparently my name was on each one of them. A year after I started at *Analog* I asked the man who had hired me—who was now the president of Condé Nast—why he had picked me. After all, there were much more distinguished people available for the job. He told me that none of the "suits" in the company's management knew anything about *Analog*—except that it made a modest profit every month. They had been content to let Campbell run the show, and continue to bring in a profit. When he got the various lists of potential successors, he told me, he made it his business to read some of the fiction and some of the non-fiction that each person had written for the magazine. "Ben," he exclaimed, "you were the only guy I could understand!" Score one for an apprenticeship on newspapers, where clarity is vital.

Q: When you became editor of *Analog*, did you deliberately setout to do things differently? I can tell that as a reader at the time, the change seemed pretty dramatic to me. It had always seemed strange that *Analog* had not featured Larry Niven regularly, and as soon as you took over, it did.

Bova: Actually, I tried to hew pretty close to Campbell's system. It was very successful, after all. Like John, I personally read all of the incoming manuscripts. I was fortunate enough to discover writers such as Orson Scott Card, Spider Robinson, Vonda McIntyre, and others. I helped to boost Joe Haldeman's fledgling career by publishing segments of what turned out to be his novel *The Forever War*. (I was able to help Joe Haldeman get his first novel, a YA titled *War Year*, published.)

But John and I were not the same person. I naturally had slightly different tastes, and I felt that *Analog*'s readers would be open to a slightly wider variety of stories. And so they were, although a few of the old-timers complained about hints of sex in Haldeman and Fred Pohl's *The Gold at the Starbow's End*. It struck me, though, that *Analog*'s readers had nowhere else to go! Even if the magazine changed a bit, they would stick with *Analog* because that was the only place they could find the kinds of stories they enjoyed reading. I learned that I could get out in front of the readership by a few paces, and they would follow me. On the other hand, there were marvelous stories that I had to reject—some of them by close friends of mine—because they were too far from the *Analog* type. I published some of those stories when I went to *Omni*. Even over a span of several years, the writers had been unable to find a publisher for them.

Q: Did you also try to feed ideas to writers the way Campbell did? I gather that part of his technique was to start a friendly Socratic argument, perhaps taking an outrageous position to stimulate thinking.

Bova: I did that on a few occasions, although I found that the stories pouring into *Analog* had enough new ideas in them so that I didn't have to do much prodding. That wasn't my style, anyway. I remember once asking a few writers what the world would be like if Germany and Japan had decided to go for world domination commercially, instead of militarily. Gene Wolfe responded with, "How I Lost the Second War…" A neat story in which Volkswagens and transistors conquer the world. I bounced another idea off several writers, who gave me nothing but blank stares. So I wrote the story myself; it was the first of the Sam Gunn stories.

Q: Now I know it was always the rule that the editor of *Analog* could not write for *Analog*, but were you able to go on writing fiction while editing the magazine?

Bova: Since I'm mainly a novelist, I continued writing novels, although the workload at *Analog* cut into my writing time considerably. My one regret about taking the *Analog* job was that I was unable to serialize my novel *Millennium* in the magazine. John and I had talked about it, and he liked what he saw of the novel. Incidentally, I had to write an editorial every month. That was demanding, too: being brilliant every thirty days.

Q: So, tell me a little about being fiction editor for *Omni*. How did that happen?

Bova: After seven years of editing *Analog* I retired from editing. My income from writing supported me nicely, and I had always wanted to be a full-time writer. So I left *Analog*. In the meantime, Bob Guccione and Kathy Keeton (the woman Bob eventually married) showed me their plans for a magazine they called *Nova* and asked me to edit it for them. I declined, telling them I would love to write for their magazine, but I was retiring from editing. Then they asked me to recommend a fiction editor for *Nova*. I recommended Diana King, who had earlier been my assistant at *Analog*. They hired Diana, who ran off to get married just as the first issue of *Omni* (nee *Nova*) was going to press. I got a call from Guccione, who told me that he didn't have a fiction editor and it was my fault. I agreed to sit in at the fiction desk until Bob and Kathy could find another editor. I enjoyed the job immensely. Among other delights, I was able to buy stories that I had rejected at *Analog* because they didn't fit the hard-core science fiction criteria. Within a year I was editorial director of *Omni* and having the time of my life. I had deliberately kept my salary low, so that I could walk away without any financial problems. But the perks were fantastic! My wife, Barbara, and I traveled the world first class. Finally, after four years, I tendered my resignation and—at last—turned to writing full-time. *Omni* was selling more than a quarter-million copies per month at that point, with an estimated readership of five million.

Q: Did you have any sense, as editor either of *Analog* or *Omni*, that you could lead the field and reshape it in some desired direction? In both cases you would have had some leverage, since you were editing the highest-paying market in the field. We all know how John Campbell recreated science fiction in the first ten years or so of his editorship. So did you have any sense of doing something similar?

Bova: No. By the time I became editor of *Analog*, the field had matured—largely thanks to Campbell's unceasing efforts. My aim at *Analog* was to continue what Campbell had started, widening the choice of stories a bit because I felt that a new generation of readers was ready to accept stories that were more mature in dealing with sexual relationships. At *Omni* I could publish stories that were outside the "hard sf" type, because *Omni*'s readers were much more varied than *Analog*'s.

Q: Let's talk about your writing a little, and related matters. Most of your SF has been very much of the hard-science type. I take it you must find the frontiers of science stimulating for story creation rather than inhibiting, as some writers do. Is there any secret for turning a scientific notion into a story.

Bova: I write "hard" science fiction because I've been interested in scientific research since I was a pre-teen. I started by being turned on to astronomy. This led me to rocketry and astronautics—and to reading science fiction. I have worked with engineers and scientists most of my adult life. So when I started writing seriously, naturally I wrote about what—and who—I knew best. I find that the nexus where scientific research and politics interact is not only interesting story material, but vitally important to the success of our society and the well-being of everyone in it. If there's a secret to turning a scientific notion into a story, it is to understand the science, and understand who it will help, and hurt.

Q: Do you feel that science fiction has any didactic or educational purpose? I know you have been a long-time advocate of space exploration, and of course much of your fiction—notably the recent series in which you have visited the planets of the solar system one by one—certainly seems to be tailored to encourage further interest in this area. Is it possible that what some fans have called "the Gernsback Delusion" (the idea that science fiction exists to teach and stimulate interest in science) is not a delusion after all?

Bova: I think that stimulating interest in science is a byproduct of science fiction, not its primary purpose. The primary purpose of science fiction, like any type of fiction, is to show ourselves to ourselves. In science fiction we can use exotic backgrounds and unique moral dilemmas to reveal the workings of the human soul. However, I don't think it's a coincidence that many youngsters have been turned on to science by reading science fiction. Some of those kids grew up to walk on the Moon. One of the things that science fiction stories accomplish is to show readers the wonders of the universe, and the thrill of discovery. Science classes in school can be dull, because science courses of necessity have to begin with the basics. Science fiction stories can skip over the basics and show how exciting the quest for knowledge can be.

Q: So do you have any sense that some current science fiction has lost its nerve and is turning away from the future? What's to be done about it? Or are we doomed to be overwhelmed by urban fantasies, alternate history, and Harry Potter knockoffs?

Bova: I think you're seeing the glass half-empty. Science fiction ideas and ideals permeate the entertainment industry nowadays. True, the "hard core" stuff is only a small percentage of what the SF field is publishing at present. But to me, that's the heart of the field. As the audience for SF has expanded, naturally the field has widened. Which is cause, which is effect? I think there is still some good "hard" science fiction being written, and read.

Q: What are you working on now?

Bova: It's another novel in the Grand Tour series, titled *Farside*. It's about building an astronomical facility on the side of the Moon that never faces Earth, and will be a bridge that moves the series beyond the solar system.

Q: Thanks, Ben.

RICHARD A. LUPOFF

Richard Lupoff has had a distinguished and varied career since the early 1960s, when he and his wife Pat co-edited the Hugo-winning fanzine *Xero* and he was an editor for Canaveral Press, overseeing the republication of much of the work of Edgar Rice Burroughs. His first book was a non-fiction study, *Edgar Rice Burroughs, Master of Adventure* (1965; revised 1975). His first fiction was the 1967 novel *One Million Centuries* (revised, 1981), after which he ranged from the satirical *The Sacred Locomotive Flies* (1971) to the experimental *Space War Blues* (1978) to a fantasy based on Japanese mythology, *Sword of the Demon* (1977). Other SF, fantasy, or related novels by Lupoff include *The Triune Man, The Crack in the Sky, Circumpolar!* and *Countersolar!* (both of which anticipate Steampunk by decades, *Sun's End, Galaxy's End, Into the Aether, Lovecraft's Book* (un-abridged reissue as *Marblehead*), *The Forever City,* and *The Comic Book Killer.* He has also had a distinguished career in mystery fiction.

Q: To The best of my knowledge, for all you've had a long and illustrious career in science fiction, you haven't gotten rich at it any more than I have. That must mean that either we are paragons of selfless virtue, or that ultimately, the SF writer has to be in it for something other than the money. Would you agree? Do you find that the same enthusiasm you must have felt as a young fan can still sustain you after all this time?

Lupoff: I'm not sure that we ever fully understand our own motives for life choices. My enthusiasm for science fiction has deep roots in my childhood. We'd experienced a number of family tragedies and my brother and I found ourselves shipped off to a truly dreadful military/boarding school. If you've ever seen one of those horror movies about this environment, let me tell you that they're essentially truthful depictions, except that conditions are far worse than you can imagine.

Talk about tyranny and oppression! This was during World War II and the early years of the Cold War, we were supposedly fighting for freedom and democracy and here was an environment that was based on the very opposite of those principles. Any parents out there contemplating educational "opportunities" for your offspring—listen to me: do not—*do not!*—do this to your children!

I'd always enjoyed fantastic fiction in all media—children's books, comics, motion pictures, radio. Television wasn't a factor in those days. Trapped in those nasty surroundings, I found in the alternate realities of the far future, of distant planets, of alternate time lines important solace. This was escape reading of the highest order.

My heroes were the authors and editors who filled the pages of *Galaxy, F&SF, Thrilling Wonder Stories,* and the early inexpensive anthologies like Judith Merrill's *Shot in the Dark,* Groff Conklin's *The Science Fiction Galaxy* and the anonymously edited *Avon Ghost Reader.* It seemed the most natural course to want to emulate my idols, and I was submitting short stories to our school paper and to my favorite professional magazines by the time I was in my teens. The paper accepted my offerings, as I was the editor. The prozines turned me down, but I received wonderful, encouraging personal letters from Anthony Boucher and Mick McComas. God bless their beautiful souls!

Well, sixty years later I can't honestly say that I have the same degree of enthusiasm that I had back when Harry Truman was President, but something of it survives, and I hope always will. Every time I open a jiffy bag and get my first look at a book of my own, or at a magazine or anthology in which I have a story, I do turn into a teenaged fan again, at least for a little while.

Q: Would you describe the beginnings of your career, how you made the transition from fan to pro?

Lupoff: Those early unsuccessful attempts to sell short stories were pretty discouraging, but I never gave up the dream. I even started a novel while I was in high school, but only got a couple of pages written before I realized that I was in over my head.

Every few years after that I'd take another shot at selling, always with the same results.

But in the early 1960s I was lucky enough to land a job as an editor at the fondly remembered Canaveral Press. With that job as my credential, I found myself hobnobbing with other editors and writers—lunching with Larry Shaw of Lancer Books one day, with Don Wollheim and Terry Carr of Ace Books another. Talking about problem authors and artists like the great Roy Krenkel. Roy was a delightful person as well as a brilliant artist, but he refused to install a telephone in his home and he lived out in the suburbs. There was no email in those days, of course, so if you wanted to talk with Roy, procedure was to send him a dime via snail mail. Then if the weather was nice he would walk to a phone booth and call you up!

Around this time I remember James Blish sitting in my living room one afternoon, listening to me bitch about not being able to sell a short story. "You should write a novel, then," he told me. "Novels are easier than short stories."

I found that hard to believe, but I decided to give it a try—writing a novel, that is—and turned out three chapters and an outline of a book called *One Million Centuries*—and it sold! Thank you, Mr. Blish!

Q: It *was* a very different time, wasn't it? It was a time when any science fiction paperback sold a safe amount of copies, almost regardless of what was in it. There was a stable short-story market. Wasn't it an easier time to get started and get noticed in science fiction than today?

Lupoff: Oh, yes, it was a very different time in the publishing world. Anthony Boucher had written an essay about publishing science fiction, in which he compared this to publishing mystery fiction. At that time—early 1950s—science fiction was still predominantly a magazine field, while mystery fiction had switched over in large part to books several decades earlier.

Boucher said that any genre book, clearly labeled with the right icons—smoking gat, tough guy in fedora, sexy babe in slit skirt for mysteries; spaceship, tentacled alien for science fiction—if attractively packaged and distributed, was virtually guaranteed a successful sale. But there was also a ceiling above which it would not go.

Omit the icons, Boucher said, publish the book as just "a novel," and you forfeit the guaranteed loyal reader base—the fans. But you also remove the ceiling and the sky's the limit. You could blow to the top of the best-seller list, or you could flop disastrously.

Time has proved Boucher 100% right.

Incidentally, just a few years after Boucher wrote his essay, Don Wollheim told me that every Ace Book sold 25,000 copies. Didn't matter who the author was. Some might sell faster and others slower, but Ace printed 25,000 copies of every title and every title sold out. Isn't that amazing!

I don't know whether it was actually an easier time to get started, though. Of course there were many more science fiction magazines, something like thirty of them at the peak of the early '50s boom, so there was a huge market for science fiction, especially for short stories and novelettes. The market for novels was much smaller, although the leading magazines often ran short novels "complete in one issue" or longer ones as two, three, or four-part serials.

There aren't many science fiction magazines left today, but there are plenty of science fiction book publishers. In fact, more than ever if you include the low-end independents that rely on computerized, print-on-demand production. They don't pay very well but they make it easier than ever, I think, to get your foot in the door.

Q: So, did you get noticed?

Lupoff: I guess I did. The fan-turned-pro phenomenon was quite prevalent in those days. The whole science fiction community was pretty small, and when a fan's byline started appearing on magazine contents pages or on the spines of books, there was often a "welcome to the club" type of response. Marion Zimmer Bradley told me that when she sold her first novel a lot of her fellow aficionados took the attitude that she was "just a fan who got lucky," while the established professionals accepted her without reservation.

As for my personal experience, I think it was fairly atypical. As a fan I'd been in a very active circle of New Yorkers who included a thoroughly mixed group of fans, pros, and fans-turned-pros. Larry Shaw, Don Wollhein, Terry Carr, Ted White, Dave van Arnam, James Blish, Algis Budrys, Lee Hoffman, Lin Carter—the wall of separation between fan and pro was very thin and permeable. I had one foot in each camp for several years before I felt the need to choose, and I chose to be a professional.

Q: Where does Edgar Rice Burroughs figure into all this? You were working for Canaveral Press, a publisher of both reprints and previously unpublished ERB material. You wrote a book about him, *Edgar Rice Burroughs: Master of Adventure*. May we safely assume that ERB was a major enthusiasm and influence for you at this time?

Lupoff: As I was growing up I associated Burroughs with low-budget Tarzan movies featuring an overweight, over-the-hill Johnny Weissmuller, and crudely drawn comic books. When I started reading science fiction pulps I kept coming across letters from fans mourning the lack of new Burroughs stories. That was my first inkling that he'd even written science fiction. But Burroughs had died in 1950, so that question was moot. Or so it seemed to be.

Then when I became a new husband in 1958 my bride happened to read *Tarzan of the Apes* and told me that there was more to Burroughs than I'd realized. I started reading his books and realized that she was right. This led to the whole Canaveral Press experience, which I dearly loved. It was the best job I've had in my life. And I even got to read—and publish!—some previously unpublished Burroughs manuscripts.

My first novel, *One Million Centuries,* was a sort of Tarzan story turned inside out. Instead of a white man plunged into a world of blacks, my hero was a black man who had grown up in a white-dominated world, plunged into—a world of blacks. As an author I realized that I was much more interested in the psychology and the sociology of my characters and their relationships, than I was in describing physical adventures.

Without being over-analytical, I think that's been true of my work throughout my career. I'm not an ideologue; I'm a story-teller. But I think my stories are driven by characters and relationships far more often than by events. I've worked in many fields: science fiction, fantasy, horror, mystery, and mainstream fiction. I've even written a couple of westerns. But as

Ed Gorman said in a recent essay, whatever genre I'm working in, what I really write are "Lupoffs." Other commentators have said very much the same thing, and I find it a highly flattering evaluation.

On the other hand, my onetime agent resigned—maybe I should say, "fired me," but I won't—over this issue. He insisted that I did action scenes well and wanted me to play to that strength. He wanted me to write what I call "helicopters strafing the White House" books. Stories packed with action, set on a large stage and for heavy stakes. I wanted to write smaller, more intimate stories. Stories about ordinary people living more-or-less ordinary lives. Yes, even if they led those lives on other planets or in the year 600,000 CE. The kind of thing that Philip K. Dick used to do so well.

As you can see, there wasn't much future in that relationship, although my "ex" and I are still good friends and even get together on a project now and then.

Q: Might it be that the problem with SF publishing today is that we've lost the protection of genre? You and I can remember when such things as R. A. Lafferty novels or collections of Avram Davidson stories, or a book as odd as David Bunch's *Moderan* could be routinely published in mass-market paperback—a fantastic notion today. It must have been that any science fiction book sold an adequate number of copies then, regardless of content. This no longer seems to be true, and all too much as is a result no longer publishable, except in very small presses. Have you any idea why this is so?

Lupoff: I think we can look at that problem in both a "narrow-band" and a "broad-band" view. In the former case, I refer you back to Anthony Boucher. When science fiction was a cottage industry with its own limited but fanatically loyal following, virtually any science fiction book had both a floor beneath it and a ceiling above it. With any kind of decent packaging and distribution, it was almost impossible for a genre book to fail, but its success was also limited.

Editors could publish quirky books—you mention Lafferty and David-son, two wonderfully talented, very distinctive writers—and get away with it. Both Don Bensen and David Hartwell told me at different times that they published populist adventure novels—they specifically mentioned the works of Lin Carter—in order to subsidize a book like *A Double Shadow*. That was several decades ago, the author was Fred Turner.

It was a very odd novel. I believe it was the author's only published science fiction. The idea was that a terraformed Mars a thousand years or so in the future would support a culture in which a science fiction writer would produce a novel set in that future's future. You see how daring this was. I thought the book was a brilliant success, its publication was one of the few times that the term *tour de force* is really justified, but it made hardly a ripple at the time.

Do you think it could be published today? I doubt it—unless one of those miniature publishers you refer to took it on as a labor of love.

The shelves at Dark Carnival, the science fiction bookstore near my home, are covered with images of future wars and space operas and other strictly low-end or entry-level science fiction. Most of it is inspired by TV shows or big screen productions. What we like to think of as mature science fiction is strictly alien to readers who think *Han Solo Meets Lieutenant Uhura* is great literature.

Seeing things more broadly, the whole publishing industry—in fact, the whole media world—is in the midst of a revolution. You can sit on a commuter train and watch a movie on your smartphone, you can download music or videos on your desktop or laptop or your Dick Tracy Wrist Radio. An author can turn a raw manuscript into a professional-looking pdf and email it to a POD publisher and have finished copies of his book in a few days.

Electronic readers have been kicking around for at least twenty years but after a long struggle to establish a place for themselves, they have finally caught on. Instead of loading your suitcase with a dozen fat volumes before you head to the airport you can load 'em onto your Kindle or iPad or some other reader and you're ready for that big business meeting in Chicago or the beach chair under the palm tree in St. Thomas.

What's next? Where will all this lead?

It's easier than ever to get published, thanks to POD. And harder than ever to make a living at it!

Q: I wonder what you make of the entry about you in *The Encyclopedia of Science Fiction* (Clute and Nichols) which seems to suggest you've done all these pastiches and never found your true voice. Do you feel any sense of frustrated ambition? Or is it that when you borrow tropes from Edgar Rice Burroughs or whomever this is more in the form of a metafictional commentary? We have, after all, Ed Gorman's testimony that you write unique "Lupoffs" in whatever genre you venture into.

Lupoff: Ed Gorman said that in his introduction to my collection of mystery stories, *Killer's Dozen*. I was very pleased with Gorman's insight, and in fact a number of readers and critics have been making the same point lately. About time, sez me!

It's true that I've written a certain amount of parody and pastiche, much of it collected in *The Compleat Ova Hamlet*. This is done usually as homage to writers whom I admire and whose works I enjoy—Fritz Leiber, J.G. Ballard, Arthur Conan Doyle, H.P. Lovecraft, Rex Stout, Jules Verne. There's even a website that insists that "Jack Kerouac" is a pseudonym of mine, or maybe that Richard Lupoff is a pseudonym of Kerouac's. Some fun!

But in fact this amounts to just a small fraction of my total writing. With all due respect to Messrs. Clute and Nichols, I know damned well that I've found my voice. Somehow they haven't heard it, which I regret, but that's not my problem, it's theirs.

Anyone who thinks I'm an elusive writer who hides behind masks of others can find the real me easily enough. Read *Marblehead,* a massive mainstream novel that I wrote in 1976. It got entangled in a snarl of publishers, editors, and agents, disappeared for thirty years, then resurfaced in 2006. One of those new POD-oriented micropublishers, Ramble House, finally brought it out and it got rave reviews everywhere from *Locus* to *Ellery Queen Mystery Magazine* even thought it isn't science fiction at all and isn't really a detective novel.

If you want to read a "real" Lupoff science fiction novel, pick up a copy of *Sacred Locomotive Flies* or *Sun's End* or *Galaxy's End.* Those latter two were intended as the opening and middle volumes of a science fiction trilogy. The first of them was a big success—multiple mass paperback printings, great reviews—but the second was packaged so horrendously that when I saw an advance proof of the cover I pleaded with my editor to have the book redesigned. I warned her that, as planned, it was going to die the death.

She refused, and the book flopped, and my punishment for being right was the cancellation of my contract for the third volume!

One more suggestion: read my mystery novels about Hobart Lindsey and Marvia Plum—*The Comic Book Killer* or *The Emerald Cat Killer* or any of the six novels that came between those.

If you can't figure out who I am by the time you've read those books you'd better demand a refund from the Famous Detectives School.

Q: I am sure that the Frederick Turner book would *not* be possible from a major publisher today, and was only possible then because a dedicated and idealistic editor pushed for it, and very possibly pulled the wool over his boss's eyes a little bit. These things do happen. I was astonished to see Greer Ilene Gilman's *Moonwise* published by a major publisher, for example. It happens because somebody believes that the book is more important than just the next sales report. Possibly nowadays, with sales tracked by computers and the buyers for the big bookstore chains being all-powerful, this sort of thing is going to happen less and less often. What can this result in but the impoverishment of the field, and of the culture generally?

Lupoff: You raise a pretty dismal prospect, and I'm afraid you're right. But I wouldn't give in to total despair. There are still dedicated editors in the business and one would hope that the next time a *Double Shadow* or a *Moonwise* comes along one of those editors will decide to take a chance on it, and will not only publish the book but will get behind it and—pardon my crass terminology—support the product. Alternately, an editor might use some commercially-oriented space operas or future war novels or teenage vampire or zombie stories to subsidize a piece of real literature.

Incidentally, to the best of my knowledge *A Double Shadow* did die the death, alas, and I've never heard peep from its author since that splendid book was published. But *Moonwise* won all sorts of prizes and I hope this means we'll see more books from Ms. Gilman.

Q: Or, to really rub it in, consider the following eccentric (but masterful) writers: Avram Davidson, R.A. Lafferty, David Lindsay, Clark Ashton Smith, Austin Tappan Wright, and David R. Bunch. If these writers were new, starting out now, do you think any of them would be able to have careers?

Lupoff: That depends on how you define the word "career." I'm sure they could all get published today. Well, maybe not Wright, simply because *Islandia* is such a huge book. They might have to go to small presses but they could certainly get published. But could they make a living?

Darrell, remember that there was a time when I was a starry-eyed fan whose fondest ambition was to become a professional science fiction writer. The same is probably true of you. Let's pause to tug thoughtfully at our long white beards and wipe away a nostalgic tear.

Okay, back to the issue at hand.

Time was, seriously, when the idea of anyone's being a real, full-time, professional science fiction writer was quite beyond the pale. You can pick up old copies of *Imagination* or *Thrilling Wonder Stories* and read author biographies in them, and they all contain sentences like, "When not writing science fiction, Herman MacGruder earns his living as a sanitation engineer for the City of Detroit."

I invented ol' Herman there, but consider: H. Beam Piper was a track walker for the Pennsylvania Railroad. Hal Clement was a high school science teacher. Isaac Asimov was a college chemistry professor. Clifford Simak was a newspaper editor. Rog Phillips was a night watchman. Bertram Chandler was a steamboat captain. James Blish was a public relations flack. Fletcher Pratt was a respected military historian. Eric Vinicoff was (presumably, still is) a federal bureaucrat. Elizabeth A. Lynn is both a tax preparer and a martial arts instructor. With a little research we could extend that list indefinitely.

Somewhere along the way—I think it would be in the late 1960s or '70s—science fiction started to hit the big time. I suspect that it was the film *2001: A Space Odyssey* that was largely responsible for this. Prices started rising and almost overnight it became possible to earn a living writing science fiction. But that seems to have been a bubble, and like the housing boom of the 1980s, it has burst and left a lot of people sitting in the wreckage of their careers, wondering what went wrong. It's tragic, but you pick up the pieces and move on, there's nothing else you can do.

And of course there are a few of us who are still making a living from science fiction. Maybe they're really that much better than everyone else, or maybe they're just lucky, or—well, it's not for me to say. But for the overwhelming majority of science fiction writers, it's back to the future all over again. You either have a day job doing—well, just about anything!—or spread your writing across multiple genres—science fiction, fantasy, horror, mysteries, thrillers, you name it.

Q: You're involved with editing a small press yourself. Could you say something about that? You mention that small, POD presses make it possible to get anything into print rather easily. Yes, but has anyone solved the promotion problem? If there is no promotion, and no one knows to seek out these books, how are they to reach more than a few dozen readers?

Lupoff: A few years ago I came across an odd little book by Harry Stephen Keeler published by a little press called Ramble House. I was so taken with the book that I sent a note to the publisher, a man named Fender Tucker. One thing led to another and Ramble House wound up publishing my novel *Marblehead,* which became a bestseller by the very modest standards of the small press world.

Eventually I did a little volunteer editing for Ramble House, and Fender was so pleased with my work that he asked me to take on an imprint of my own. That was an offer I couldn't refuse. I asked Pat to partner with me on it, and after a search for a name for the imprint we settled on Surinam Turtle Press—in honor of a creature whose ugliness is rivaled only by its laziness.

Unfortunately we don't have any budget with which to buy properties, so we've had to rely on a good many excellent but forgotten works by authors like Gelett Burgess. When Burgess is remembered at all it's for his light poetry and children's books—he created the famous limerick about the purple cow—but in fact he was a first-rate novelist and his books hold up remarkably well after a century. We've done seven or eight of his books, and every one has real merit.

I've also been able to issue or reissue a number of books, either through Surinam Turtle Press or its parent company, Ramble House, that might otherwise languish. For instance, Jim Harmon was a rising young science fiction writer of the 1960s who contributed short stories to many of the magazines of the era. He was also one of my mentors, a brilliant teacher of fiction technique.

But early on he switched gears and became a distinguished cultural historian. But he'd left behind an unpublished science fiction novel, *The Contested Earth.* I was delighted to publish that book. There was Fox B.

Holden, a '40s and '50s pulp writer whose one novel, *The Time Armada,* was serialized in *Imagination* but never had a book edition. I was able to secure rights from surviving members of the Holden family and we published the book through Surinam Turtle Press.

There was Mack Reynolds' very first novel, *The Case of the Little Green Men.* This book is a wonderful romp through the fan community circa 1950, leading up to a murder at a science fiction convention. Thanks to Mack's old friend Earl Kemp and Mack's son, I was able to get rights to issue this book, which had been out of print for almost sixty years. And there was *Sideslip,* a fine little science fiction—hardboiled hybrid by Ted White and Dave Van Arnam. I got rights to this book from Ted and from Dave's widow, and we reissued it.

Then there's Jon L. Breen, regular book reviewer for *Ellery Queen Mystery Magazine.* No way I could persuade Jon to write a book for me, for no advance. But he was willing to compile a volume of his past essays and reviews that we published as *A Shot Rang Out.* It's a marvelous book.

I do wish I had the budget and the staff and the know-how that it would take to get these books onto the shelves of a thousand bookstores and into the hands of a million readers. We're making some progress in that direction, getting into some retail stores, distributing through on-line book dealers and getting listed on sites like Amazon.com and B&N.com, but we've barely scratched the surface and it is a very tough job.

Q: So, what are *you* writing these days? Are you still able to get anything out from the major publishers?

Lupoff: My most recent books have all been collections and they've all been from small companies: *Visions* (from Mythos Books), *Quintet: The Cases of Chase and Delacroix* (from Crippen & Landru), and *Killer's Dozen* (from Wildside Press).

My next book—it may be on sale by the time this interview sees pixels, it's already listed for sale on several websites—will be back to the big publishers. It's a mystery novel, *The Emerald Cat Killer,* from St. Martin's Press.

Beyond that I've got enough projects lined up to keep me busy for many months, if not years. *Rookie Blues*—a cop novel that's about 80% complete, that I put aside a long time ago and want seriously to get back to... *Villaggio Sogno,* a fantasy novel based on a short story that I wrote for a Mike Ashley anthology... *Beneath the Karst,* an adventure novel with vaguely Lovecraftian overtones... *Transtemporal!,* the long-delayed wrap-up of a trilogy including *Circumpolar!* and *Countersolar!*... and *Dreams,* the concluding volume of my three-decker including *Terrors* and *Visions.*

I've also accumulated a lot of shorter nonfiction pieces that ran in magazines ranging from the old *Ramparts* to *F&SF* to *Locus* to Andy Porter's

Algol/Starship, and more recently in online periodicals like Arnie Katz's *VFW* and Earl Kemp's *eI*. A couple of publishers have approached me about putting these together as a sort of critical compendium crossed with an episodic autobiography. It's a monstrous chore, but I would like to do it if I can.

A lot of these projects are by way of tying up loose ends that have been dangling for years or even decades, but somehow when I shave in the morning that fellow who peers back at me from the mirror isn't the energetic twenty-something who started all these enterprises. I may not get them all finished in my lifetime, but I want to complete as many as possible.

Q: Thanks, Dick.

JAY LAKE

RECORDED AT THE WORLD FANTASY CONVENTION, AUSTIN, TEXAS, NOVEMBER 4, 2006.

Q: So, who *is* this mysterious and multiply-talented Jay Lake, who seems to have come out of nowhere, publishing thousands of stories all over the place in the past few years? Where did you come from?

Lake: I sprang full-blown from the head of Zeus, back around 2000. He emerged from the Aegean waves.

Q: I suspected as much.

Lake: Are you looking for a serious answer?

Q: If you would. I imagine there is more to it than just that. Did Zeus have a headache afterwards?

Lake: The very long answer, which I can give you very shortly, is that I was born and raised outside of the United States, in the Third World. So I grew up without television, which is very unusual for a person my age. This was before satellite TV and VCRs. It was all books, all the time, from as soon as I could read, which was about the age of four.

So I have always been very book- and writing-oriented. I wrote fairly consistently right on through the '90s, in my twenties, without ever publishing anything. I went silent in 1998 when my then-wife and I adopted our daughter, and didn't write anything for about three years. At that point I had not sold anything, but I probably had written a couple hundred stories over the course of some years and submitted a number of them. I had a nice collection of rejections. And at the very end of 2000, when I came back to writing—my daughter was a little older, so I had time again; I had emotional energy again—I had somehow gotten better. In April of 2001 I sold my first short story, which came out just about this time [early November — DS] in 2001, so we are just past the fifth anniversary of my first appearance.

At that same time, in 2001, I had made a decision for no other reason other than sheer foolishness, I suspect, that I wanted to write a story a week until I got better. I wrote a lot of bad stories, but I also got a lot of practice, and I got better.

Q: This is the Ray Bradbury method. He wrote a story a week. He has said that what you do then is burn the first million words.

Lake: I actually figured out once that the first story I sold began at about word 850,000, and the stories I started selling consistently were somewhere around word million. Atb this point I am closing on two million words. I am probably writing three or four hundred thousand words a year right now. So, I've maybe passed two million words by now.

Q: Are you selling three hundred thousand words a year?

Lake: Now that I am selling novels, yes. I've actually managed to sell three novels this year, only one of which was written when I sold it.

Q: In what categories?

Lake: Right now I seem to be selling primarily in fantasy. I've got a two-book deal with Tor for a high-concept fantasy about a clockwork Earth orbiting the Sun on a brass track. It's kind of distinctive. It isn't like anything else. The only way I can describe it is *Ringword* for fantasy geeks. The other series I've got going is with Nightshade Books, with a book called *Trial of Flowers.* That is a New Weird China Mieville kind of book. That one just came out about a week ago. It's for sale here at the con. The Tor book will be out next June. Since they are both two-book deals, each will have a book following a year later.

Q: Do you think the phrase and category "New Weird" actually mean anything?

Lake: Not in the slightest. It's a lot like "Slipstream." We're monkeys. We like to label things. There's red fruit and yellow fruit and green fruit, and you don't eat the green fruit, right? So we have to call it something. So, I don't think New Weird is a movement. It is at best something of a common style. Again, like "Slipstream," the term is used more by people who aren't doing it than who are doing it. I threw it out as a label so that you or someone reading this interview could say, "Oh, that's the kind of book it is." We need to know that. Otherwise bookstores would have just one giant shelf, alphabetically, and that would be kind of annoying.

Q: That's the way it used to be and some people insist it was the good old days, before everything split up into genres and categories.

Lake: Well, sure, if you're willing to go through all that. But I work in marketing in my day job, and marketing is all about categories and segmentation. People don't want to take the time to sort through everything that is out there. They want to understand what they are looking at.

Q: I make the argument that today there is no mainstream in American publishing. There are only categories. The literary novel contains several genres.

Lake: Sure. It's naturalistic fiction, John Updike or something. But I agree with you that it is still a genre in its own right.

Q: If, for marketing purposes, a fantasy novel is what is published as a fantasy novel, and a horror novel is what is published as a horror novel, my guess is that if this were fifteen years ago, when the horror category was much stronger, you'd be trying to publish as a horror novelist.

Lake: Yeah, given the kind of stuff I write. There is a lot of psychosexual tension in my work, for example. But, you know, genre classification is like the Potter-Stuart method of detecting pornography. I know it when I see it. This thing is fantasy because I point to it and say it is fantasy.

Let me give you a simple example. I had a story that ran *Interzone* last summer called "The American Dead." It's a post-apocalyptic story about an American kid who lives inside a mausoleum in a cemetery, and he sells scraps out of old porn magazines for money to survive. It's like *On the Beach* for poor people. I have had interest in reprinting it from science fiction, fantasy, and horror markets. I find it kind of odd that the same story can be seen across all three ways, but that's exactly what you just said. It's what the market thinks today. What it thinks five years ago or five years from now will be different.

Q: What Third World countries did you grow up in?

Lake: Taiwan, Dahomey, and Bulgaria, which is actually a Second World country.

Q: Other than the fact that you didn't have television, how did this influence the sensibility of what you write?

Lake: Landscape. Two things: landscape and culture. I think the vast majority of Americans, people who grew up in one place or a small number of places, especially if they only stayed in one region of the United States have a tendency to assume as all people do that their experience is the default experience of being a human being. So they don't see what the world's like if you life in a place that is largely not white or largely not wealthy, or doesn't, say, have electricity or schools. So that sense of the acculturation of the other is something that a lot of Americans miss out on.

The other thing is landscape, the idea that the world looks and feels different. The physical alienation is, I guess, like cultural alienation. Once you travel a lot of places you realize that the localized physical geography actually varies quite widely.

I've been on safari in Kenya and looked at Mt. Kilamanjaro. I've been in the old Dutch forts in Tainan. I have stood at the ruins of Karakorum in Outer Mongolia. Every place I've gone I've seen something completely different. That gives me a sense of the fantastic, of alien, in writing. It helps me in both science fiction and fantasy because it gives me a descriptive vocabulary that I wouldn't have otherwise had.

Q: You can also get some of that in the United States. Here we are in Texas, which looks a whole lot different from Pennsylvania. You go farther out, into Arizona perhaps, and it's a genuinely alien landscape. Tint it red, add a few cratrs, and it could pass for Mars.

Lake: Absolutely. You can do that all over the United States. Last weekend before this one, I went to North Dakota, because I had never been to North Dakota and it was the only state I had never visited. To say I've been to North Dakota doesn't mean I've been to all of North Dakota. I only drove around the eastern end of the state. I have a sense of a widely varying geography. But, quite frankly, most people never even get that far. Someone who was born and raised, let's say, in Pennsylvania, may never even get to Arizona. So they haven't had that experience.

Q: Are you able to pick up and use local lore, say, a scary Bulgarian legend that no other American writer knows about?

Lake: [Laughs.] Like the Witch of Melnik, for example? Yeah, yeah, sometimes. I had a lot of experience with Chinese myths and legends when I was a gradeschool kid in China. I went to an American school, but we had a big Chinese culture element, because that's where we were living. Honestly, for me sometimes it is the physical details.

For example, in Bulgaria there is a city called Velicoturnovo, which means Old Turnivo. "Velico" means old in Bulgarian. It looks like something out of a fantasy illustration. It's in a canyon, built on top of what we would call mesas in the United States. The Bulgarians don't call them that. Each little piece of the city is walled, so it's literally castles on top of tall pillars of rock. And inside the walls, there is sort of Bulgarian-Revival, quasi-Turkish, quasi-French architecture. It's like a mutated verion of late 19th century Paris surrounded by a medieval wall. When you go up there and visit it, the people will tell you that when the Turks ran the place, when somebody got out of line, they didn't bother with prison. They just threw them off the wall, 120 feet down to the stones at the bottom of the canyon. You walk through these places and you hear these stories, and you take that back home and you internalize it. But I internalize wherever I go. I live in the Northwest now. I've internalized Mt. Hood, for example.

Q: Would you say that what a fantasy or horror writer does is fantasize experience?

Lake: I don't even think that's true. I think most of the experience in fantasy and horror is real experience. It's just told through a lens of distortion.

Q: I don't mean in the sense of imagine experience, but making real experience strange, in the sense that Mervyn Peake was raised in China, and Gormenghast has a good deal to do with China, particularly the Forbidden City, but it is *not* China.

Lake: Yes, exactly. What I personally think is that the world is plenty strange on its own, and one of the things we do as writers is bring that strangeness out. Most people won't see the strangeness. Most people don't see things, except what they expect to see. Part of being a fantasy or horror writer is violating people's expectations about what is going to be in front of them.

Q: Horror writers often say they're doing this to disturb people. Are you do this to disturb people or to enlighten them?

Lake: I'm actually doing it to entertain them. I don't *mind* disturbing people. That's a form of entertainment. But I don't think I've ever set out just to set someone's hair on fire.

Q: There are certainly horror writers who would be proud of doing exactly that.

Lake: And there are readers that want that. There are whole sub-genres of horror that exist pretty much for that purpose. That would be slasher horror, I guess. That's not my particular cup of tea. On the other hand there is some pretty bizarre and perverse stuff in my new book that will disturb some people. But that's not why it's there.

Q: What did you grow up reading that influenced you and made you turn out to be the writer you are?

Lake: [Laughs.] Gosh, everything. The King James Bible. Mack Bolan's Executioner series, *Dune,* the Andre Norton Forerunner juveniles and all the classic Heinlein juveniles, which my library had. When I was in the fifth grade I took it upon myself to read the entire works of William Shakespeare, most of which I did not understand in the 5th grade; but it was interesting.

Probably two of the most important things I read as a kid, in terms of setting me on my course, were, in 6th grade I decided it would be agood idea to read *Dhalgren*—I am still not sure why—and it was also the year my mother gave me a copy of *The Lord of the Rings.* It was the first of God knows how many times I've read that book.

This was much later on, but the particular moment I realized I was going to become a writer of fantastic fiction—although it took me the better part of twenty years to follow through—was when I read Gene Wolfe's *The Book of the New Sun* when I was in college. I felt, Oh my gosh, you can do that with the language!

Q: That's a very high bar to set for yourself. I think a lot of us only aim to be half as good as Gene Wolfe.

Lake: I'll be amazed if I ever get to be half as good as Gene Wolfe, but I am not going to get there if I don't keep throwing myself against this wall until I find a way over it.

Q: Certainly it is true for any writer that you'll never achieve what you are aiming for, but if you don't aim high, you will end up very low indeed.

Lake: This business is founded on idiot-persistence. Nobody does it because it's easy or possible to make a lot of money.

Q: By way of idiot persistence… what are your writing methods like?

Lake. [Laughs.] I spend a lot of time thinking about writing when I am not writing, but when I am writing, it is purely bend my head down and type. So I will prethink a story. Novels I will outline. Short stories I will not, because outlining a short story just turns into writing it, so I will just go ahead and write it.

Typical of what will happen to me is I will have an idea, and the idea can be extremely trivial in terms of what it takes to get this started. Let's say that there's a secret code in which information about the true origins of the human race is embedded in the bumps on people's ears. That's all. I was actually talking about that yesterday. So I have this highly metaphorical thing in my head in what I call the Cloakroom of Ideas. It's like a meat locker. I hang the idea there and then it comes back to me a day a week or a month or a year later—and some of them don't—and then I write the story.

If it's a novel, instead of the cloakroom, I also write an outline, probably to sell it, but also to organize my thoughts, because I need to get a lot more detail. But when I am actually ready to write, and I sit down at the keyboard, I just start writing and I type until I am done. I am a very fast writer. I draft 2000-2500 words an hour, so I can write a short story in a sitting, unless it is a novella. Even a novel takes me one to two months to pump out a first draft. I don't edit at all when I am writing, other than grotesque typos that I might stop and fix. Even if I know it's wrong, I just go, because that way I keep the flow of the story, the flow of my voice. And then, after I am done the amount of editing it requires depends on what's going on in the story, how many mistakes I've made or not made. But I get my best voice and my best-regarded stories out of writing quickly out of my gut, rather than thinking about it.

Q: Ray Bradbury supposedly has sign over his desk that says DON'T THINK.

Lake: That's exactly right. I can tell you about the number of writers I've gone on a retreat or a workshop with, and they start to write with pen and pad or a laptop, and they start to write…tap,tap,tap… "Oh God, that's shit!" and then they back up, and they write or they scribble, and two thousand words later they have a page and a half.

What a freakin' waste. But that's some people's process. If that's your process, I'm never going to tell you you're wrong, but I think that one of the things that *sells* fiction, both short fiction and at the novel level, is strong voice, at least in our field. There are fields where voice may need to be transparent, but typically not in spec-fic, not in fantasy and horror, and really not even that much in science fiction. And strong voice comes best when you write fast and you don't think. That's when whatever makes *you* distinct as a writer comes out, and the chattering monkey editor in your head is duct-taped in the closet with the door locked.

Q: Doesn't this also give you a propensity for writing in the first person? After all, the whole point of first-person is to capture the voice of the narrator. Once you have that, point of view and much of the structure fall into place. Does it work this way for you?

Lake: It used to a lot more than it does. I think I have just gotten to a point in my evolution as a writer where I actually mostly prefer tight third to first. I don't think I would even want to write a novel in first-person. Never say never, but I wouldn't touch it right now. I don't think my agent would touch it either.

In short stories I still do it some, but sometimes I think that what I am after in voice is not so much the voice of the character as the voice of the story itself. Every story has an implied narrator which is external to the explicit structural narrator that's built into the person of the story. That implied narrator has a voice. So the story can have something in the kind of word-choices that happen and the kind of grammatical structure that the story engages in that is independent of what is going on with the narrator.

Then problem with first person—you're right—it's very defining, but it is also very limiting. If you have a first-person story about a character who is for some reason very limited—they have a head injury, they're mentally challenged, they're an alien and they don't understand the environment or the language—of necessity you're going to be limited to their capacity in telling the story. I like to go to third because I have a lot more choices about what I do.

Q: Even there you are limited by the conceptual world of the story. I would say, at least, if the story is set in ancient Greece, you do not say "they came charging in like an express train."

Lake: Oh, absolutely, but that is language sensitivity. I had a guy in a workshop one time. I was critiquing a story, and he had a phrase—this is a very simple example of that—he said something about "the German shepard lay down to stand guard." I had trouble getting him to see what was wrong with thst sentence, because he was reading "stand guard" in its metaphorical sense, as in to watch over something, and I said, "You cannot lay down to stand. You just can't the language doesn't work." That would be like having the phrase "charging like an express train" in a story about ancient Greece. That's context, but every story has context. For me, one of the great sins is the way people use the word "okay" in fiction. "Okay" has a very specific cultural context.

Q: I suppose that since this interview is for a magazine devoted to horror, I should bring this up: if you actually did want to scare the crap out of people in a story, how would you do it?

Lake: I think that the thing that scares people the most is the familiar.

I think that sex is one of the scariest things, if you distort it in certain ways that make people uncomfortable. I think that religion is a very scary thing. I don't need zombies crawling from the sea bottom. I don't need things from outer space. What I need are people you think you can trust who, it turns out, you can't. I don't think there is anything more frightening than having a family member turn on you, or having a process of your own body and mind turn on you.

I have written a few of what I hope are bone-scary stories. My story "The Goat Cutter" was reprinted in *The Mammoth Book of Best New Horror* over the the UK and has been reprinted a couple other places. It's very much about religion and sexuality. The things that we think are part of ourselves, when we turn them around, are far more frightening than those externalities.

Not that I'm above writing a good zombie story. I love 'em.

Q: You could always do humorous zombie stories.

Lake: Yeah, yeah. Zombies are so pathetic. They need so so much help.

Q: Just like mummies.

Lake: Exactly. I want to write a story about a dyslexic zombie that goes hunting for guys named Brian. [In spooky voice] Brians, brians, brians!

Q: Would you agree that, all considerations of publishing aside, the scary story is always going to be with us, that it is eternal?

Lake: I think it's the first story. If you go back to a bunch of Neanderthals or Cro-Magnons sitting around a fire at the mouth of the cave, what are they talking about? They're talking about what made the stick crack out in the shadows. The two earliest stories that you get are why lightning strikes and that thing that is going to eat you, because at that level scary stories are teaching stories. Beware of the darkness. Beware of the thing in the shadows. Beware of the tooth that glimmers. I think that fantasy arises naturally from scary stories, all forms of fantasy, and I think that religion arises naturally from scary stories. What do you have if you go back in literature? You have *Gilgamesh,* the *Bible,* the *Odyssey.* Fantasy and religion.

Q: I think there's an important distinction. There's a question of whether the audience is aware that this is made up. You can argue that Homer is not fantasy because it was intended to be believed. Thee were Homeric fundamentalists in Antiquity who said, "If Homer says the Indian Ocean is landlocked, it is." People would point to their ancestors in the *Iliad.*

Lake: I am aware of the concept of magical thinking. I can read about the Cyclops and say that this is obviously fantasy. There are perfectly good physiological reasons why there are not twelve-foot-tall men with eyes in their foreheads. But I realize that that is not patently obvious to a classical Greek reader.

Q: My feeling is that there's an element of both. Homer is telling his good yarns on the way, but ultimately the story turns on the religious and moral ideas.

Lake: Every storyteller embellishes. Anybody who has ever told a bar story punches up the details. Why in the world would Homer have done less? Even if he told what he believed to be true about the Trojan War and about Odysseus, why wouldn't he have punched it up to make it interesting? That's an oral tradition. Again, it's a campfire story, even at that level.

Q: Have you ever wanted to do an oral story, for performance?

Lake: I think that would be great. I am one of those people who, late at night at the party, is telling weird stories anyway. I've had many stupid, strange things happen in my life and some of them are funny.

I had a story in that was in *Realms of Fantasy* two years ago, called "The Angel's Daughter," that got me a letter from an oral storyteller in Florida, someone who went on the festival circuit, asking me for permission to use it as part of her repetoire, as a spoken-word story. Now, would I want to write a spoken-word story, or take up the delivery of spoken-word? It would be cool, but it would be a sideshow. I am about the written word.

Q: Can you give an example of a strange thing that happened in your life that you turned into a story?

Lake: [Laughs.] Wow...the mind boggles. I use so many pieces. Gosh.... Well, I had a neighbor who died in a pornography fire once.

Q: His collection caught on fire?

Lake: Yeah, and he asphyixated from the burning ink. It's funny, because I rarely write directly about the things that happen to me. I write indirectly about them, at great length. "The Goat Cutter" is partly about my experiences on my mother's goat farm, dealing with her goats. Goats are nasty SOBs. I don't know if you've ever dealt with goats up close in person. They're *way* too smart. So I wrote a story that partly about sacrificing goats, because I had a goat that I took after with a book once. She butted me in the nuts and apparently wanted to mate with me and kept chasing me around. That's not all that strange a story, but it all feeds itself.

Q: Then again, you could have written a story about what would have happened if she succeeded.

Lake: Yeah. Then I would be the father of a very nice little satyr.

Q: Then, what motivates the goat to want to do this?

Lake: That was the part that I never understood. But, I don't hate livestock. I actually think goats are kind of cool. I just don't want to be standing next to them. I don't know what motivates a goat. I don't know what motivates a cat. I don't know what motivates most people. Sometimes when I am writing it is just to find that out.

Q: I wonder if the purpose of writing sometimes is to make up an explanation for such things.

Lake: You know the game. You're sitting in a restaurant and a group of people comes in. It's not obvious what they are. It's not Mom and Dad and four kids. What do you do? You figure it out. You parse the family. You may be wrong, but you never know. Those people must be siblings. That guy's never looking at that woman….

Q: And that one has been dead for weeks but he's still moving, and these two reproduced by fission and have hidden tentacles.

Lake: Exactly. Did you see how his eyes glowed?

Q: I have relatives like that.

Lake: [Laughs.] We won't talk about my cousins.

Q: Are you related to the degenerate Whateleys? Speaking of which, have you read much Lovecraft?

Lake: Not in years. I had a Lovecraft phase when I was a kid. It's kind of when I went through a Poe phase. Then I went from there to reading E.R. Eddison and William Morris, and somewhere along the way I got stuck on the second half of the 20th Century and have not gone back.

Q: It sounds as if you were a child of the Ballantine Adult Fantasy Series, like everyone else.

Lake: Yes. Well, there you are. That's all I had. Books were everything to me. I moved every year or two. I never knew who my friends were or who my friends were going to be, so books were everything.

Q: I could ask you the meaning of life.

Lake: Forty-two.

Q: That's the answer, but what is the question?

Lake. Oh, damn. Actually I have a semi-serious comment on that. I have spent most of my life working in high-tech and marketing. I have a child. One of the reasons I'm a writer s that when I croak, they're not going to chisel on my tombstone, "He wrote good press releases." If they do, that's going to be a sad thing to say. But if I can write something that reaches out to people the way some of those other writers reached out to me back in the day, then I have fulfilled the meaning of my life.

Q: It's not vanity. It's a sense of mission.

Lake: Exactly. It's a purpose. My highest purpose in life is raising my daughter to be a successful adult, but that's a transient purpose too, because eventually she will leave me. Everything I write leaves me, but then I write something else. That is a process that never ends unless I choose to end it.

Q: Thanks, Jay.

WILLIAM TENN (PHILIP KLASS)

Note: This interview was recorded at Paracon, a convention held in State College PA, in, I think, 1978. It has remained unpublished until now because, while Phil Klass graciously granted me his time and gave this interview, he insisted that before it could be published, he would go over the transcript. A reasonable enough request, in fact standard practice in the interviewing trade, but, alas, for all I sent him the transcript right away, he promised to get right back to me on it, he never did. Even twenty years later, he remembered who I was and promised to get right back to me on the interview. But he never did. He seems to have been really, really bad at getting specific things done. So, while this interview was intended for the Ted White *Amazing,* it only appeared in *The New York Review of Science Fiction* in 2010. As far as I can tell, there is nothing here that Phil Klass would have disapproved of, except perhaps a turn of phrase here and there. He comes off very well in it, as a writer of intelligence, integrity, and passion.—DS

Q: You stated in a speech today [at the convention] that with the exception of a very few stories, you don't like what you have written. Why is that?

Tenn: Why were there exceptions? You mean why shouldn't I object to more? Or how come I don't like most of what I have written?

Q: Yes. Mostly this last.

Tenn: I think that any writer who says he likes most of what he has written is either a liar or a fool. To begin with, your standards have to be much higher than anything you could possibly achieve if you want to achieve anything. I hate to mumble things about the reach having to exceed the grasp, but that's crucial. So this is true in general, I think, of most people, of most writers. I've known a few who go to great length about great things they have written, and who are their own critics, and examine their work in terms of comparison and contrast, and all that. But the writers who I have always respected look back on the things they've done and feel that most of its failure. I can't imagine Shakespeare, for example, in the full flood tide of *King Lear* or *Hamlet* feeling that he had done remarkably good work, say, in *King John,* or in any of the earlier plays. It just seems to me that you grow, you improve, but most of all you develop as a person, and it's the development as a person which counts more than anything else.

When I was a child, I thought as a child, and when I was a child I wrote as a child. When I began writing I had a totally different view of myself, of what writing meant, and I was a substantially different person. These things have changed. Therefore I don't like many of the stories that I wrote during that period. This is a general statement. I'm coming to the more particular now.

Q: Well, what were you doing at the outset that has changed?

Tenn: I wrote for a long time to sell, and I tried to do the best work I could, but I was trying to sell and I was trying to please editors, to please others, and I came to the conclusion that it's the worst thing a writer can do. I've always believed, and I teach my writing classes, that there is such an equation to writing as I-Thou, which I stole from Martin Buber, of course. He uses it in a different context. But you're not going to get either end of the writing equation, the necessities of the creator and the necessities of the audience—both must be kept in mind. I think that I was perhaps a little too aware for too long, because science fiction was a pulp medium, because in most of what I was doing in that form, I was a little too aware of the audience. When I began writing things that I wanted to write, a lot of editors didn't like it. In fact the things that I like best were not well received at the time when they were done. "Null-P," for example, was not highly thought of until years had passed. Kingsley Amis mentioned the story in *New Maps of Hell*, and then people began writing about it and anthologizing it. That was one of the stories that I like, and I want to do many more like it. And nobody appreciated it at the time. So I found myself typed because I was supporting myself writing, though I had held other jobs, but also because I felt that the audience was so very important. I was doing things I thought the audience liked. They wanted me to be funny, so I was funny. They wanted me to be a farceur, so I was a farceur. Basically I've always been interested in satire rather than farce, rather than sheer burlesque. I gave people what they wanted and I wasn't even aware that I was compromising. I think that when you become aware that you are, you make a fundamental decision. You become aware that you're giving people what they want instead of what you want to do. You announce to yourself once and for all what kind of person you are. When I made the announcement to myself I decided I didn't want to give people what they wanted and what I *didn't* want, fundamentally, and I turned away from the writing I had done. I found it very difficult to continue working.

Q: Isn't it possible to reach a happy combination where instead of slanting your material to your audience, you find an audience that wants to read what you want to write?

Tenn: Sure. This is basically what I have always tried to do, almost from the very earliest days. But first, this is a theoretical construct. You search for the audience that wants what you want to do, but you don't communicate directly with the audience. First of all, this is rarely discussed, this problem here that I mention. It is rarely discussed when writing is ever discussed. You're dealing most of the time not with an audience, but with a representative of the audience, to wit, an editor, and the editor may be completely wrong about what the audience wants or he may be wrong about what the audience wants from you particularly. It'll take years for that to be discovered. The editor is essentially projecting his own personality to the audience. So that's one problem. You try to do this, but there's another thing, I think the crucial problem a writer faces. It's not a writing problem. No problems are writing problems or artistic problems in the end. They're personal problems, and until you find out for certain who you are and what you can do, you might very well be finding audiences that are not valid for you. The same problem applies to finding someone to love, in relating to people. Most of the time you're operating with some kind of a personal fantasy about who you are and what kind of a person you should live with. Most people don't marry mates; they marry private fantasies. The man marries a woman he always dreamed of as someone he wanted to have in his house, or he marries the woman he always dreamed of in terms of how other men might envy him, or he marries the woman who would make him a great writer or a great person. They don't marry individuals because most people are living in fantasies of one sort or another about themselves. It takes an awfully long time to find the barest fingernail's worth of truth about yourself. I don't know the truth about myself, but I know something that I didn't know before, and as a result I know audiences I can no longer write for. I wouldn't *dream* of writing for certain audiences in science fiction. I wouldn't dream of trying to write certain things and attempting to embed in alien work things that were crucial to me.

Q: What audiences wouldn't you write for anymore?

Tenn: To begin with audiences that exist at the moment, I would never try to write for the sword and sorcery audience, or for any audience that is in any way related to the sword and sorcery audience, any audience that's interested in a replay of Robert E. Howard, or, a writer I admire much more, the early Fritz Leiber. I can't do that sort of thing. It's not important to me, and yet there was a time when I wanted to write in every area and I tried to write that sort of thing. And I would no longer dream of trying to write for the space opera audience, for any kind of essentially action-oriented audience, because the statements I have to make don't have much to do with action. They have to do with rather crucial things about the world. I doubt very much I would try to write for any audience now where there is an editor who sits astride communications between me and the audience, that is, an editor with a very strong personality who will represent the audience to me. Then so far as I'm concerned, I'm enhancing the editor's image, will, desires, creation, and not my own. These are just the beginning things I would mention. I would not now write for any audience for which I don't feel an initial tenderness and understanding.

Q: What if those audiences desire your work? Would you leave them high and dry?

Tenn: Yes. That's no problem. I mean, it's horribly flattering to be wanted, but when what someone wants of you is not real or important to you, which you can't honestly give without disaster to yourself, you're being asked, really, to damage yourself. I have a comic side to me. I've always loved the comic, but I'm not *only* a clown or comedian, and when I'm constantly being asked to come on funny, as I have been, two things happen. Either I get very tired of the creative act in the first place and something inside of me stops doing it, or I keep doing it with the feeling of more and more strain, and I've learned to stop that. I can't do what I can't do, in other words. I can't be what they think I am; I have to be what I know I am. Here I may be making a terrifying mistake. It's all too easy. There's always the clown who wants to play Hamlet, and there's the tragedian who wants to be the clown. It's all too possible that the individual may make a mistake about what he does best, but all I can say is that if the individual makes the mistake, at least he's betting himself. He's betting his whole life, his whole spirit, and I haven't found I've done wrong that way. I've found as a matter of fact that *every damn time* I've written what was not wanted and was not liked by a given editor, and sometimes by the audience, *I've* been right and they've been wrong, in the long run.

Q: At what point did you come to realize that you were writing for the wrong audience, or that something was seriously wrong?

Tenn: Well, may I say that I've realized that at every point in my career, at every point in my life? I realized after I sold my first story to John Campbell, which was a bad story, by the way, and it was an attempt to write the kind of story that John Campbell would like. I hadn't met him yet, but I had read the magazine. Well, there were elements in it that I still like—that was a story called "Alexander the Bait." Then John Campbell invited me to have lunch with him, and I was terribly excited because after all this was my intellectual father, and over lunch I found out three things. One, he was as brilliant as I thought he was from the material I'd read by him in the magazine. Two, I discovered that he was genuinely my intellectual father, and that he had created a large part of my mental life. And, three, I discovered that I wanted to leave home if he was my father. I found that I couldn't live intellectually in the same room with Campbell. That was my first discovery, and that story wasn't even printed yet, but my God, he was the editor of the best science fiction magazine there was. I swallowed all that knowledge and I tried to write for him. I discovered it about Gold at *Galaxy,* an editor with whom I felt very close and who flattered me and pleased me and pulled some of my more interesting work out of me, but who didn't want what I did best. There was one man who wanted what I did best, and Heaven help me, I gave him very little. I gave him least of all the editors I knew, and that was Tony Boucher. Tony wanted what I wanted, and he wanted that constantly, but at the time I had an agent who didn't think *Fantasy and Science Fiction* was a good market. At this time this was the poorest paying of the markets in the field, and so I didn't do very much for Tony, and I'm desperately ashamed of it today. Everything I did for him I'm very proud of.

Q: What did you hope to accomplish in your writing, as opposed to what you actually did accomplish? Did you have conscious standards then, of which you fell short?

Tenn: Yes and no. It's very difficult to say. Only once or twice in my life did I write something which I didn't consider good while I was writing it, that is, things I wrote only for the market, and when I did I paid for it very heavily by not being able to write for a long time afterwards. Most of the time I didn't write things that I thought were not worthy. I thought I was doing the best I could. I felt that if I were writing space opera, for example, that I was properly experimenting with space opera as a form, with what could be done with it. And when I wrote something like "Down Among the Dead Men," which Horace Gold called a tour-de-force because he'd asked me for a space opera and I'd written a space opera in which almost all the space opera action took place off stage, I was very proud to achieve that, a sort of E.E. Smith great space war story in which nothing really happened. I wrote another space opera for Fred Pohl. He hadn't really asked for it, but again I was curious about the problem, something called "The Deserter." It's not nearly as good as "Down Among the Dead Men," but again all the action takes place off stage, and the story focuses on one aspect in one case of a deserter from the army. But I didn't consciously write this way. It was just that I allowed myself to respond to flattery, to respond to money, to make up all kinds of things which to myself and for myself enabled me to write things that I didn't want to do.

Q: What did you want to write?

Tenn: Fairly early on, I had written one story, "Brooklyn Project," which was not written for Campbell, by the way. It finally appeared in *Planet Stories* and broke their rule that no story in the magazine could take place on Earth. It was a satire. It was a satire against what was later called McCarthyism, and that was written for a magazine that Ted Sturgeon and Groff Conklin were supposed to get going but never did. Once I wrote that story I knew what I wanted to do in science fiction. What I wanted to do was write satire. I wanted to use science fiction as a vehicle for satire, and nothing else, not really, because it's a *magnificent* vehicle for satire. That's not all it can be or all it is, but it's what it means to me, and I kept on sneaking satire into my work and having editors tell me—Howard Browne at *Amazing* said this to me, Horace Gold said this to me, John Campbell said this to me once—that the pulp magazine equivalent of satire is what closes on Saturday night, and they didn't want it. I was aware of this, and even though I knew that's what I would like to write, I felt that I was indulging myself by writing satire. It was too much fun.

Q: Didn't you ever worry that after the object of a satirical story, such as Joseph McCarthy, has vanished, then the story will lose its value?

Tenn: Well this has happened to several satires I've written, among them "Brooklyn Project." That's one, and that was written about pre-McCarthyite, a pre-McCarthy McCarthyite, that kind of investigation. There's a story, "Null-P," which was written about the early Eisenhower years and the Truman years, and Kingsley Amis commented in his book *New Maps of Hell* that it didn't seem to be based on anything that was really happening in American life, and of course he was dreadfully wrong. It also happened to a story of mine called "The Liberation of Earth," which was about the Korean War. First, it's good satire, and I think this is important for most good satires, "Brooklyn Project" has almost never been out of print. It keeps being reprinted. "Null-P," even though everyone has forgotten or else didn't know that it was written about the Truman years, has stayed in print. Many people have anthologized it and it's a well-liked story. Finally, "The Liberation of Earth," which was a satire on the Korean War and which in those days could only be published after everyone else in science fiction had rejected it. It was purchased by Bob Lowndes who paid me a half a cent a word on publication, and he told me he was only buying it as a favor, simply for my reputation because he wanted a story by me in the magazine, and nobody liked it for years. "The Liberation of Earth" come into its own about five yeas ago. It was constantly being anthologized as a Vietnam War story. And so, what difference did it make? The statement in there is still valid, and my feeling is that most of us don't know what Swift was satirizing with the big ends and the little ends in *Gulliver*, and yet the book is a very strong piece of work because the satiric intention comes through and has survived. Somehow it remains a wonderful commentary on man. If I can achieve that ever, I'd be pleased even if the object of the satire no longer existed. No, that never bothers me in the slightest.

Q: Do you see any difference between what for lack of better terms are commonly called satirical values and story values?

Tenn: The essential story value is drama. I think that a really strong satire must be a really strong story. I'll say this. The reason why satire frequently closes on Saturday night, especially bad satire, is because it's too overt. The writer is trying too hard to attack and not enough to dramatize, to make clear as you must make clear in any piece of writing, fiction, non-fiction, science fiction, straight fiction, the essential dramatic story elements. So that is perhaps the chief reason why there seems to be a conflict, but there is none. Satiric story value is basic story value. There is another reason, perhaps, why satires frequently fail as stories, and that is that the writer misses what someone described of Jane Austen, who wrote satires on the society of her period, that no matter how harsh her caricatures, underneath it all lay the thought, "Well aren't they dears?" A good satirist never gets away from this, and I don't know if I have ever achieved good satire. I've tried, but you have to love people in order to make fun of them, and all too frequently people who write satires are releasing hatreds rather than love. That's what satire is. You write satires because you love so much that it hurts, and you don't want to see what's being done to what you love. If you write satire only out of hatred, you're writing polemics. You're writing political tracts, and those things will never live.

Q: When you found that you weren't writing what you wanted, you stopped writing, in science fiction at least. Did you go anywhere else?

Tenn: I tried to write in other media. First of all I've always written in other areas, and I've not always published in other areas, but I began writing a series of memoirs, some of which were published in men's magazines, for example *Rogue, Dude, Gent,* some of which were very cheap. I was experimenting with the form. I now find that a lot of what I want to do is in memoir form. I began writing memoirs. I began writing a lot of non-fiction. One of my articles, "Mr. Eavesdropper," has been anthologized and republished as much as any one of my stories. In fact I've written two articles. "Mr. Eavesdropper" appeared in *True* in the summer of 1967, and is now in *Best Magazine Articles 1968* edited by Gerald Walker, who is an editor on the *New York Times Magazine.* It's a damn good piece of work if I say so myself. I like it as much or better than any of my stories. It's a fine portrait of a specific man, and a very fine picture of a certain area of our world, and it enabled me to deal satirically with certain elements. Now I've done a bunch of other articles, but that's been the best. Most people in science fiction don't know about it. I wrote an article which is not nearly as good as "Mr. Eavesdropper" for an electronics magazine, but which has been translated perhaps twenty times. It's constantly being republished. I've written a number of stories which are non-science fiction, and only one of them was really any good, but I've been doing these things. And very recently I've been writing scholarly articles on science fiction. I did stop writing science fiction almost completely in the period of 1963-1964 up to very recently, largely because at that time SFWA was formed and I wasn't a member of it, and I felt it was being used by certain individuals to develop their careers, and I didn't like what was coming into science fiction, which was a little-magazine quality. Just when the little-magazine quality was dying in the world of general fiction, science fiction discovered it and picked it up. I didn't like that. I didn't like the people who had begun to dominate the field, and I didn't like the emphases they made, so I withdrew for a period of time. But I believe in science fiction as a form very much. I believe in its social necessity. It is a form most peculiar to the present. I believe it is the form of modern man and it is the form which modern man will write. I'm not sure I'm a modern man so I'm not quite sure I should write it.

Q: It seems to me that during the period in question the field broadened considerably. Might there not be a larger audience for what you want to write merely because there is more diversity?

Tenn: I do not think there's a much larger audience. I think that a lot of the people writing are doing much more interesting things that we used to be able to do years ago. I'm very pleased to see that. I also like a lot of the younger writers on the scene. They're less self-conscious about writing science fiction. They're not apologetic and they don't give a damn what they're doing. They feel that if they do their best and they have any talent it's got to be literature, whereas the older writers are still apologetic. I like a lot of what's happened, and I feel the audience has expanded somewhat. I don't know if it's been good for science fiction. I tend to think that the expansion has been away from the things that make science fiction an exciting form, that made it an intellectually exciting form. I think it's been the sort of thing that has to some extent taken away from science fiction. It has tended to emphasize certain kinds of stories which have really very little to do with the fundamental qualities of science fiction.

Q: What kind of story would this be?

Tenn: They type of story which essentially harks back to a magic past, either in terms of developing that magic past, or trying to extrapolate that magic past into the future, a past of nobility, a past of magicians, a past of strange things that are unexplainable and wonderful and yet happen, a past where the quest story still occurs and Grendel emerges as an unexplainable monster, not from within the marsh but on some planet or other, a past of exotica and incantations, and a past where the social forms that occur are ancient social forms and not novel ones that relate to man's future, a past in which technology in all its aspects—not just chemistry and physics and engineering, and not just biology either, but the social sciences and aesthetics—are not developed the way they should be in terms of where man might be going. Where the future is not considered with excitement.

Q: It seems to me that you're not talking about science fiction here, but pseudo-medieval fantasy.

Tenn: I've seen a tremendous amount of pseudo-medieval fantasy masquerading as science fiction. Let me give you an example of what I mean. I'll speak here about a major piece of work, a very substantial piece of work from the past—Asimov's *Foundation Trilogy*. Asimov's *Foundation* is something which belongs to a much earlier period of science fiction and it's a very substantial achievement. Even though the first volume is superb, the second part deteriorates quite a bit, and the third one is very poor. But the flaw in *Foundation,* the absolutely unnecessary flaw in it even at its best, is the concept of an emperor. There is no genuine need to make it an emperor, to make a proper galactic empire. There are various other forms which would have centered on rule by one man, an oligarchy, which could perhaps have come to an end. But Asimov did there was go too directly to the past. Now this, however, is not to criticize that first volume of *The Foundation Trilogy.* It is a superb thing, but the exciting part of the trilogy is history as a genuine science, history that can be used as a resource, and almost as a technology. That's the exciting part of the story. The repetitive part of the story, the most unimportant part of it, is the material that deals with the emperor and a court constantly lurking in the background of the story. Now that's minor. In *The Foundation Trilogy* you don't notice it, especially in the first volume, because it's brilliantly done and you're caught up in the scope of the thing. But *that sort of thing* has been used and expanded constantly. There is very little awareness that changes do occur. As for example, we have a government today which is not that much very different from governments that men have had in the past, but the government by committee that we have, by legislative committee, the government by executive departments we have, is substantially different in many respects. It has a momentum of its own, and this deserves to be examined in terms of the future. The relationship between this government that we have and the government by the Communist Party of the Soviet Union with its various bureaus, with its presidium, for example, over all, its various local manifestations—these are the things that are worth looking at in terms of where they might go some time in the future, and many science fiction stories I've read in recent years just don't seem to be aware of this kind of change and of these developments.

Q: Isn't it also true that the change likely to occur in the next, say, four hundred years will be so great that no one can imagine it, and thus writers have to fall back on existing models?

Tenn: First of all it is the business of science fiction to imagine and make the effort, even if failure occurs. Second, and more important, history has to be the guide. It is not accurate. It is not sound and it doesn't suffice, but it's the only guide we have. Of course we use history, but it's a question of which models you select. Which models *do you notice?* This is the important question for a science fiction to ask when he's dealing with government. Which models seem to pertain to expanding, developing societies? Which models? How many societies in our history have been intellectually expansive and have existed under very narrow despotisms? I'd say few. At least there are forms of democracy. It may be democracy for the minority, as in Greece, as in Venice, but the city states, for example, that grow throughout history, and tended to develop peculiar commercial and scientific empires, by and large were places where one operated by a committee, rather than under the rule of one absolute monarch. These things, I believe, have to be noticed, and they're not, all too frequently, by writers who are dealing with the future. And I'm not only talking of government—and this is very important. I wanted to get to this. I am talking of stories which do not anticipate the future with excitement. I am talking of stories which by and large are locked in the past or examine developments in the present, developments which will expand man's freedom and man's abilities—which look on these developments with hopelessness and horror. I'm speaking of stories which worry about what I call aristocratic things as opposed to popular things. What are popular things? Those which will feed more people and give more people a comfortable life. Now I may not like those things but I have to recognize that those are the things which deal with the popular—in the sense of pop*ulous*—whereas the aristocratic things are those which a coterie of people who want to preserve their way of life, who want to revere the past, the traditionalists, are jealous of. And by and large throughout the western world, I strongly feel, we are developing more and more what I tend to call a mandarin society. Writers more and more are members of the mandarin society. They're mandarins. They look to the past and they look to the values which existed in their early lives, or which they believe existed once upon a time, which they admire. This is not true of the bulk of man and women on our planet. Science fiction was tremendously successful and tremendously exciting because the writers were not traditionalists. They did not belong with the aristocrats of literature. They were not mandarins. Now I think they have become that.

Q: You mean they've developed their own tradition and become stuck in it?

Tenn: I think to some extent that's true, but more that they have left their tradition and coalesced with the tradition in western fiction, particularly American fiction, which is a dying tradition. Nobody reads fiction in this country very much. Science fiction was read because it was an exciting form. It's not nearly as exciting as it used to be, largely because the writers have made a rendezvous with literature and become accepted by the establishment. Heaven help me, that's what I wanted more than anything else, but now I think it's a bad thing, a damaging thing anyway.

Q: What can be done about it? If the establishment respects SF, it doesn't seem likely that the field can ever become disreputable and healthy again.

Tenn: I'm not interested in cures. I am setting an example of historical necessity—to that extent I'm still a Marxist—and if you happen to be writing in a form which takes a certain turn because of the historical pressure, there's nothing the form can do. There is perhaps something the individual can do in his work. He may have to write in a somewhat different form, which is one of the things I believe I have to do. The things I wanted to do in science fiction I now can express in somewhat different forms. I believe I can criticize this society more successfully in other forms. Among other things, by the way, I was a radical and I tried to express what were known as radical thoughts in science fiction for a long time. Today these thoughts are being expressed by everyone. They're attacking the political if not the literary establishment easily, casually, all the time. I want to attack another establishment which nobody else is attacking, the establishment of the communications industry, the establishment of the mandarins who think they're radicals, and I can't do that too easily in science fiction anymore, I don't believe. So I want to do it outside the field and I attempt to do it in other forms.

Q: Does this mean that science fiction will decay the way the American mainstream has, because it will become conventional?

Tenn: I think it will. Yes, I do. The American magazine science fiction will wither, but I think science fiction develop elsewhere. I think that just as American science fiction picked up a form which had been developed in England and France and possibly even in the Soviet Union and Czechoslovakia, as our science fiction dies, as it becomes respectable and accepted and aristocratic, so another nation which is exciting and excited, which is hungry and which is pushing, and where there is some measure of popular will expressed or at least felt, will pick up our science fiction and develop it, will take it over, and it'll be a vulgar and exciting form, but I think it'll be real. Yes, I *do* think that it must die here as things stand at the moment. But there can be changes, God help us. I can see all kinds of possibilities that might create new directions for science fiction in America, but currently I see little. It's too respectable. For example, the kind of excitement that I knew back in the science fiction magazines of the '40s and '50s I saw expressed in the pornographic underground comic of about eight or ten years ago. People like Crumb are doing things which had been done in science fiction and they had the kind of community, an excited community, and were building on each other's work in the way I described in my article, "Jazz Then, Musicology Now" because they were jazzy. They were not writing for the ages. Unfortunately the movement did not last for long. They've been co-opted by Madison Avenue, almost all of them very fast, and some by the establishment. But *that* was a movement which was very similar in terms of its liveliness, its excitement, *and* its non-acceptance by the establishment. Another such movement which has also been co-opted and has since died was the underground press, so-called, all over America, where interesting and unusual writing was done. That's left its mark upon the world. The so-called New Journalism is at least partially a product of that, and again this is a kind of disreputable movement where the people who wrote didn't expect to be reprinted, much as the people who wrote science fiction when I was writing it—My God, we knew we were writing for pulp magazines and we knew it would never last—never expected their work to find its way into various books. This lack of permanence, this desire to read other people's work to build on, was what made it so, not so thrilling but so constantly inventive, and so lacking in self-consciousness. Self-consciousness is the death of real art. Now science fiction has become like the rest of American literature, terribly self-conscious, posing like mad, standing against the backdrop of literary history and saying, "Consider my relationship to this form and that. Consider where I am in the development of literature." This is self-consciousness, which is death. There were brief forms which don't have this, and science fiction may develop a freedom from it again, but it doesn't have it now. All of which is not to say that I'm not happy about it, because after all I'm interested in the scholarship of science fiction. I'm interested in its being accepted. I'm interested in taking it seriously, but I still recognize that as a creative writer I have almost no place to go.

Q: Aren't you then destroying your own outlet for creativity?

Tenn: No, I'm responding to my interests in the pressure of history. But the kind of science fiction I want to write about is the least respectable. I'm not destroying my own outlet.

Q: But your own outlet has disappeared anyhow.

Tenn: No, my own outlet hasn't disappeared. It is dwindling, you might say, but my feeling is that whether I'm writing criticism, when I talk about science fiction as I am to you, when I talk about it to scholarly audiences, I am emphasizing the kind of science fiction that I feel is most viable and genuinely healthy. In a very real sense I am doing what I can to point to the qualities in science fiction, the qualities, for example, that I've described as consciously living in history, in a history of man, past, present, and future, which is the essential quality of science fiction, and it's that kind of science fiction that I write about and talk about, and in a sense am trying to keep alive.

Q: Will you ever write science fiction again yourself?

Tenn: I have a couple of unpublished stories which I have not sent out. One I sent out only once, to *Playboy,* and I didn't like their reaction to it so I retired it, and also I got kind of unhappy about science fiction. Also, more of my time has been involved in organizing a writing program at Penn State, so I have done less writing, but I have been working. I just haven't found any place where I'm happy to be published. That's one of the problems. I don't like the science fiction magazines as they are right now, and I'm sorry about that, but I wouldn't be happy to be published in them. The only place in science fiction that I might be pleased about being published are the anthologies of new material published by people like Silverberg, Carr, and Knight. The trouble with these is that publication in them takes a couple of years. I think it is dreadfully important to a writer to be published as close as possible to the date of his completion of a story. I think as he grows as a writer, his work changes as it appears. He notices it in print and it affects him. When he has material which is not going to appear for two years, he feels frequently that he's writing in a vacuum and its not a good thing to have happen. It was bad enough in the earlier days of *Astounding* when Campbell sometimes took seven months to publish a story. But he also took as little as four months or three months, and it was one of the things that was very important and very exciting. Somebody was reading your work and commenting on it and you were reading it, and noticing how it looked in print. If you're waiting two or three years for something to appear, it's almost as if you're writing for the desk drawer. It's as if you're writing for a censor who won't allow your work to appear. Of course writing for the desk drawer is a good thing to do in a censor-ridden society, but it doesn't enable a writer to grow as he should. So even the good anthologies are not a satisfactory place to be published in.

Q: Well, we still have two monthly magazines left, *F&SF* and *Analog,* both of which can get a story into print pretty quickly.

Tenn: Yeah, and I don't find them as exciting these days. Science fiction has moved from the magazine phase and the short story phase, which is a great shame because I think it is its most successful in the short story form. It's moved from that into the book phase, and most of the work that's being done in science fiction is being done in book form. I don't read the magazines. If I read anything, I read books, and I occasionally read stories in Silverberg and Knight anthologies. I think that many of the young writers in them are doing interesting things. I think that although I may not agree with their emphases, Delany and Zelazny, and certainly Haldeman are doing good things. But the writer I find most fascinating now is Ursula K. Le Guin, and the piece that she had in Terry Carr's *Best SF #4* really sent me.

Q: "The Ones Who Walk Away from Omelas"?

Tenn: "The Journal of Therolinguistics." Something about an ant poet. I don't remember what the full title was, but it was a very, very strong piece of work and it was genuinely science fiction. [Klass is referring to "The Author of the Acacia Seeds and Other Extracts from the Journal of the Association of Therolinguistics," which originally appeared in Carr's *A Fellowship of Stars,* Simon & Schuster, 1974.—D.S.] That other one you mentioned—what was the name of it?

Q: "The Ones Who Walk Away from Omelas."

Tenn: That's right. That's an example of the kind of story I don't recognize as science fiction. It is pure parable, and it really is a backward-looking story even if it's beautifully done. I salute it as a piece of writing but as far as I am concerned it's part of the entire structure of science fiction that's leaning away from whatever made it. And the only place science fiction can turn, and I want to use this as another kind of summation, when it turns away from anticipation of the future, when it turns away from a sense of living in history, the only place it can turn is a nostalgia for the dead past, and that's what that story was.

Q: Thank you, Mr. Klass.

KIM STANLEY ROBINSON

Kim Stanley Robinson is probably best known for his Three Californias series (*The Wild Shore, The Gold Coast,* and *Pacific Edge*) and his Mars trilogy (*Red Mars, Blue Mars, Green Mars*). Other novels include *Icehenge, The Years of Rice and Salt, Antarctica, Forty Signs of Rain, Galileo's Dream, 2312, Shaman, Aurora,* etc. He has won three Nebula Awards, two Hugo awards, one World Fantasy Award, six Locus Awards, a British Science Fiction Award, and a John Campbell Memorial Award. His doctoral thesis was on the novels of Philip K. Dick.

＋＊┄＊＋

Q: Could you give us some sense of your background, who you are, where you were educated, and (that life changing moment on the way to Damascus), what made you realize you wanted to be and could be a science fiction writer?

KSR: I was born in Waukegan Illinois, same town as Ray Bradbury, in 1952, but my parents moved us to southern California when I was three. We lived about ten miles from Newport Beach, and I spent a lot of my childhood and youth at the beach. I also loved sports, music, and reading. I had an English teacher in high school, Catherine Lee, who encouraged my interest in Shakespeare and poetry, and this caused me to pay more attention to the idea of studying literature. I went to the University of California at San Diego, and began as a history major but quickly changed to literature, figuring I would be a teacher, which is what I eventually became: I taught freshman composition for eleven years, both in grad school and then for a few years after I got my PhD.

My life-changing moment in terms of science fiction happened early in college, when I finally realized that science fiction was a full-blown genre; in my high school years, the town libraries had sf in its own section, and I never noticed it, and thought Jules Verne (who was in the regular fiction section) was just like anyone else, although very interesting. I also want to mention that I adored Madeleine L'Engle's *A Wrinkle in Time,* which I read when it came out, but I had no idea it was part of a genre. But in 1969 I checked out a Clifford Simak paperback, *The Goblin Reservation,* and enjoyed it and went looking for more. I started reading sf alphabetically, as I read everything in those days, so I quickly discovered Asimov. Pretty soon I was off to the races, and sf became the genre for me, and at that time (around 1970) the New Wave was going full steam, and I fell in love with New Wave science fiction. The older stuff wasn't as appealing to me. I shifted from writing poetry to writing poetry and science fiction stories, and after a few false starts I got a story that seemed okay to me ("In Pierson's Orchestra," later the first chapter of *The Memory of Whiteness*).

Around that time I expressed my interest to one of my professors, Fredric Jameson, who it turned out was a science fiction fan also, though he only told this to people who shared the interest, as far as I could tell. He was the first to show me a *Locus*, to which he subscribed; and he suggested I visit Willis McNelly, a professor at Cal State Fullerton, which also housed the Philip K. Dick archive. McNelly was friendly in the classic sf way, and recommended that I come back and see a Harlan Ellison lecture, and ask Ellison for the address of the Clarion workshop, which I might want to go to. When I did that and asked Ellison for Clarion's address, in front of hundreds of people, Ellison grilled me at length, and only later gave me the address when I came up afterward. I thought the whole evening was great, and drove back to San Diego determined to apply to Clarion. I applied and went in 1975, after a year at Boston University, and Damon Knight bought some of my stories, and I was on my way.

Q: I heard a rumor about you at the time, to the effect that after your early successes in Damon Knight's *Orbit* you had to "retrain" yourself before you could sell anywhere else. Is this true?

KSR: No, not at all. Damon was a very ecumenical editor and I wasn't thinking about what he wanted, only what I could do. He didn't buy all my stories, only a few, and if I wrote one and he didn't buy it (I was very slow while going to grad school, and didn't produce very many) I couldn't sell them elsewhere. Finally that broke when Ed Ferman and Terry Carr bought stories from me, admittedly after Damon had stopped buying for *Orbit*—possibly Damon would have bought those too, I don't know—but in any case *Orbit* was done, and I began to sell elsewhere, but without changing anything in terms of my stories. I was still just trying to do what I could.

Maybe this rumor started because I mentioned once or twice that it took me a few years to untangle everything that had been said at my Clarion. Six teachers in six weeks, 24 fellow students; it was a lot to take in, and after a while, I realized I didn't even want to. I wanted what I wanted, which came from reading literature for my BA and PhD, and in sf, loving most the New Wave. Much of what was said at Clarion was not right for me. After I sorted that out, and started writing entirely new stories, those stories seemed better. But it was probably all just part of the process: Clarion, Damon, my reading and writing, the work on PKD for my dissertation for Jameson (I had returned to UCSD at that point), and my love of the New Wave writers.

For sure Damon was nothing but a positive force in my life. He was a great teacher as well as a great editor, and he believed in me. I think now that he gave me my twenties—I mean he gave me the feel of my twenties, the sense that I could be a professional writer—he gave me that when I was 22 years old, and I never looked back. Everything I did after that was constructed around that idea. So I owe him a lot, far more than I can give back or even express.

Q: Your stories tend to have a classical feel to them, even the ones in *Orbit*. A pretty far cry from much of what was in *New Worlds*. So how do you think the New Wave actually did influence you?

KSR: I see what you mean by this, and it's true; my stories aren't much like the ones from *New Worlds* in the the Moorcock years. I think it can be explained in a number of ways. 1) I could only write what I could write. No matter what I liked as a reader, when I wrote I was constrained by my own abilities and interests and tastes. Then 2) I read Proust's great novel *Remembrance of Things Past* in the late 1970s, and that taught me that high modernism was not just stream of consciousness conveyed by fractured syntax and therefore difficult language. Proust's sentences were long but crystal clear, very much in the French Enlightenment tradition of rationality and forensic analysis of emotions, etc. It was a different version of high modernism, somewhat the opposite of Joyce. I was understanding my model, New Wave sf, as the introduction of high modernist techniques into the old sf ideas, with the addition of some new social material as well, and what I saw in Proust was a new way to do it, by focusing on clarity above all. This fit with my own natural sensibilities, and gave me ideas about my own way to do "post New Wave" stuff. Also, 3) I began to realize that I was using the term "New Wave" to refer to a period rather than a style; what I meant by the term was really everything in the years 1965-1975, which I regard as a high point, maybe the highest point, in SF literary history. So I'm not thinking of Moorcock's *New Worlds* when I say New Wave, but rather that whole period, including all the usual suspects, then also Le Guin and Russ, Wolfe and the Strugatskis and Lem and Disch, but also Vance and Niven and Anderson, etc.; the whole gang across the whole spectrum of styles and approaches. Tremendous work was being done in those years, and I thought of it all as New Wave. And for sure, that period of sf influenced what I wanted to do myself.

Q: I can of course easily look up your age, and I see you are about 6 months older than me, so I'd guess you were exposed to some of the same things at the beginning. I remember *The Goblin Reservation* too, but I read it as a serial in *Galaxy*. Were you reading the magazines? We both can remember *Orbit* but do you also remember John W. Campbell as a contemporary figure, albeit at the tail-end of his career? Did you read *Analog*?

KSR: No, I didn't read *Analog*. I thought of John W. Campbell as a figure from the 1940s, and didn't read any magazines at all, and didn't know that fandom existed. Everything I knew about sf I learned from the paperbacks, usually used paperbacks. But that, from 1970 on, was enough. The paperbacks gave me the whole history of the field, repackaged in many cases, but pretty comprehensive too. What I missed and didn't know existed was not the literature, but the community and the culture. When I came to Clarion in 1975, my classmates were amazed at my ignorance. They would do the "this parrot is not dead it's only sleeping" routine and I'd be on the floor laughing and saying "You guys are so funny, I can't believe you can make that stuff up!" and they'd say, "It's called Monty Python, Stan," and I'd say "What's Monty Python?" and then they would be the ones laughing. But of course in those six weeks they brought me up to speed.

However, after Clarion I returned to San Diego and went back to grad school, and stayed focused on academia and the beach. I didn't get *Locus* or go to conventions until about 1982, when my sales to *F&SF* and *Asimov's* made me more aware of the magazines, the community, SFWA, and the conventions. I started to meet the writers of my cohort and go to conventions, but then my wife and I moved to Switzerland, so we disappeared from the American scene for a while, but got to meet the British sf community, also the French and Italian sf communities, all of of which were great fun. When we moved back to Washington DC in 1988, I became a more typical member of the SF community.

So for the first ten to fifteen years of my career, I was somewhat of an outsider to the field, but not too much, because I went to Clarion, and in truth the paperbacks had the whole genre in them.

Q: I tend to think of the New Wave as a period, too. How does awareness of the history of the field affect you as you write? When I was at Clarion, there were people who seemed to think it was really a bad idea to clutter your mind up with all that stuff. There was even resentment when I told somebody who was writing short-shorts that he should study the work of Fredric Brown. They seemed to think that ignorance was an actual virtue and would lead to originality. I still think it is more likely to lead to the re-invention of the wheel. So do you feel that you are part of the main edifice of science fictional tradition, and is this a burden or an asset?

KSR: I definitely feel like part of the science fiction tradition, and I'm happy about that. Ever since World War Two sf has been the best realism of our time, especially in the USA, and then, more and more, everywhere. So it's a great tradition and continues so.

I also think it's very helpful to know the tradition, and not just the canon that everyone has read, but also one's own personal favorites, the books that you keep no matter what. All that reading does help to avoid re-inventing the wheel. For me it's just another aspect of being an English major, which I've stayed my whole life, in effect: I like literary history and criticism, and getting a feel for the changes through the decades of fiction, and getting to know the work of the great writers. It's one of my chief pleasures. So it isn't just the science fiction tradition but the larger literary tradition that I enjoy and think is important to know.

And knowing the sf tradition gives me ideas. I'd like to write a novel in each of the sub-genres that interest me. By now I've tried many of them, and I don't want to ever repeat myself, so I'm running out of sub-genres, maybe, but that's okay. The thing to emphasize here is that reading the sf tradition has given me lots of ideas, and more importantly, a way to structure my ideas in a structure larger than my own thinking. Genre is an enabling structure, but how can you use it if you don't know it?

One thing to add here, is that sometimes a writer can come in from the outside and with little or no knowledge of the science fiction that has been written before, add something to sf that has precisely the values of originality and strangeness, of newness. One example is Cecelia Holland's *Floating Worlds*, which brings to the planetary romance the greatness of Holland's historical novels, and resembles her *Great Maria* more than it does generically aware science fiction. But for every positive example like that one, there must be ten examples of people who come in and do something quite bad that is partly the result of their ignorance of what's been done before. The thing to do here as a reader is to stay open to the good outsider attempts, and don't worry about the bad ones. Those might even make quite a splash in the larger world, but you can in a chapter or two get a sense of whether they are any good or not.

Q: At the same time, your work seems to be more engaged with the real world than a lot of science fiction we see (and have always seen). It's the difference between, I suppose, early Heinlein and Captain Future. Your work is often distinctly political. How do you balance any didacticism with art?

KSR: I like writing fiction that is in the sf tradition, but can work for any reader who happens to pick it up. That's a matter of subject and style, a kind of openness to outside readers, I guess you might call it, but I'm not sure how that is created, as it is a fuzzy business, and really you never know much about who is reading your work or why. I see an extremely wide set of reactions to my books.

One working principle for me is to think that the more "realistic" a fiction seems, the more it will engage the reader. So I often try for a "reality effect," but mostly this is an effect. No fiction is particularly realistic, so it is not the main virtue to try for. But it can enhance other things you want to do.

I come out of the American leftist tradition and regard all art as political, so I am happy to be called a political novelist, though it is a redundancy. An apolitical novelist would be a weak thing, being in fact a status quo political novelist, possibly unaware of the political level of their work. I always assume the more you are conscious of in your project, the more your unconscious impulses can flourish. So I do my best to keep various kinds of balance, and I often comfort myself with the example of Proust, the thought that his novel is very political, in its support of Dreyfus and its attack on class snobbism, etc. So even the most artful novel ever written is very political.

This balance of didacticism and art is hard, I think, and what I want more than anything is to write good novels, and I am not a consistent or coherent political thinker anyway. So I try to give my various characters different political views, and let them defend those views well, and keep my hand on the scale as invisibly as I can. In my Mars novels, it helped that I myself was undecided on the Red-Green question. And I believe there are many different possible political routes to a good human result, so I've tried to express that too. In my climate trilogy (now re-released in a single-volume compressed version as *Green Earth*) I took it as a given that climate change is coming; I don't regard that as a political opinion, however. That wasn't being so much didactic as realistic, paying attention to science.

So, I hope to make art that is not too didactic and yet includes politics. It is for sure a balancing act, and it's possible to lose that balance, but I try.

Q: You've also got to balance it with science. Your Mars books of various colors are surely the most detailed and scientific novels ever written about the colonization of that planet. You must also be excited about the expanding frontiers of human knowledge, not just a novel as politics. Or is all knowledge likewise political?

KSR: No, I am interested in science as science, something distinct from politics, which I take it is about arranging relations between humans. That's always there in everything we do, but there's also this matter of science exploring the universe that is not us, and inventing different ways of looking at us and our interactions with each other, the planet, and the cosmos.

Then also, science as practiced in this civilization (STEM, science technology engineering and mathematics), has a kind of utopian political project to it that I find very interesting, because I like utopian efforts. Science tries to understand the world better in hopes of making us more comfortable in it, as for instance in medicine, a very important science. All the sciences seem to me a kind of empirical or pragmatic utopian politics, attempting to finesse the power struggles and go right for what helps us. But that can never quite work, so it gets bogged into the rest of all our efforts, tangled with them and mangled by them.

Over and above that political element of science is what you call the expanding frontiers of human knowledge, and yes, I find that exciting. It's an expansion that creates many new stories, and telling those stories is the work of science fiction, maybe even one definition of science fiction. I think it's Asimov's: the human impacts of technological change, isn't that how he defined science fiction? It's a good definition. New stories are not hugely easy to generate if you don't pay attention to the sciences, so again, science fiction is the right place to be in our era; it's the realism of our time, and the most exciting literature, the place where you get what Damon called "the sense of wonder." All fiction has always wanted to create that sense, so focusing on science fiction today makes sense in many ways.

Q: I note with some dismay that a lot of science fiction seems to have given up on the future. You obviously have not, but some has. Why do you think this is? After all, we are living in a moment in which the universe has suddenly been shown (as opposed to hypothesized) to contain thousands (and by implications billions) of planets. It's the biggest expansion since the discovery that those points of light in the sky are other suns. Surely this should awaken anybody's sense of wonder and possibility.

KSR: Well, I'm thinking the space program as practiced so far has shown that although there are many planets in this galaxy, they are all out of our reach. Then, if you focus on our current moment on Earth, you see climate change and the massive injustice and inequality of global capitalism, which wants to be the law of the planet forever, and is trying to do that with mortgages and debts of all kinds, in effect buying the future. So the real situation is enough to generate a huge amount of fear in the young. Their prospects look bad. And let's say that science fiction is always really great at capturing the mood of young people when they contemplate their own futures. Recall Jack Williamson, isolated on a ranch in frontier New Mexico but thinking, "We're going to the stars!" and having that optimism and excitement. Today a young person could be thinking, "The planet is wrecked and I'm competing for jobs with people who get paid a dollar a day." Not so encouraging! And so we get the YA dystopias. They're popular because they express people's fears so well. The global political situation causes these stories to manifest as expressions of our fears.

Then we still also want to express our hopes, which are always there, stubborn and persistent, even if subtle and small. So we need utopian fiction too. And there is some of it. It's what I've often tried to do, basically to portray positive futures, so we have something to orient our efforts in the present, and can express our hopes as well as our fears.

Q: If we can go a little further into the politics, do you think the world could, within a lifetime or so, evolve something better than capitalism?

Utopianism is one thing, but can we actually get from here to there, particularly when so many powerful people are making a short-term profit off the present system? Will it take a crash to change things?

KSR: Good questions. We need some kind of post-capitalism so badly, that I hope it can be invented and implemented—or simply implemented in hodgepodge style by successive tweaks without an overarching theory, as often happens. Laws change and history does happen, so the process is real, and the need is there. Capitalism as currently practiced exteriorizes the costs of the damage to the biosphere's natural resources and support systems, and this isn't realistic, in terms of long-term sustainability; and it also unequally distributes surplus values, so you get immiseration, the precariat, and the infamous one percent, the oligarchy that hopes to buy governments and forestall significant change. They have a lot of money, so it will indeed be a wicked political battle.

Raymond Williams discussed the idea of the residual and the emergent, so that capitalism is a mix of feudalism and whatever comes after it; and whatever comes after it will therefore include some aspects of capitalism as its residual. I've been thinking that if the necessities of life were all public utlities, and the work of civilization some kind of landscape restoration and biosphere balance, and adequacy for all, then the residual could be a market in toys and games and diversions. Capitalism on the margin, so to speak. People who want that risk, pressure, and urge to innovate, all the things capitalism exemplifies, could focus it there where the stakes are not life and death, with death for the losers (meaning the 99 percent and the planet).

Getting from here to there: crucial, and hard. Mainly, politics. But it's worth looking at the book *Why Civil Resistance Works* to contemplate politics as mass actions too, I mean more than voting and talking. Economic non-compliance, mass action, and so on.

This brings me to your question, will it take a crash to precipitate real change; it may be true, but I hope not. And we have the 2008 crash as a model. We didn't take advantage of that one, but we did nationalize GM, one of the biggest companies in the country. And we almost nationalized the banks. That would be the good move, next time. If finance itself were a public utility, it could get very interesting; that's a post-capitalist thought. So I think we need to be ready to do that, by discussing it. I'm going to write sf about it, which is my way of joining the conversation.

Q: Ultimately, though, isn't a story more about the experience than the idea? That is, not so much about the idea of a terraformed Mars, but what it's like for individual characters to live there, and the emotions of this being shared vicariously with the reader.

KSR: Very true. Novels are about characters and experiences. The social sciences call this "thick texture" which is not a bad term for it. But in the context of our genre, I would describe it by saying novels are forms of time travel and telepathy. The reader gets to be transported into other times and places, and crucially, into other people's minds. This is the magic of fiction. If that mental traveling doesn't happen for the reader, then all the ideas in the book are reduced to just that, mere ideas. Thin texture, maybe. We're always immersed in ideas, and political opinions are flying about like flies, but the experience of time travel and telepathy is rare enough to be valuable in a different way. So, I try to focus on novels.

Q: By way of a collapse I was thinking of something more like the French Revolution, which, of course, did not turn out very well. I don't think the original revolutionaries foresaw Napoleon as emperor. Likewise, Mao may have succeeded in getting rid of the remains of the feudal order in China, but I don't think he foresaw that in a generation the Party itself would chuck this Communism stuff and go whole-hog capitalist. Surely revolutions have a way of surprising us. And surely the science fiction writer's job is to imagine how social change might bring about results that no one otherwise thought of, right?

KSR: I've been thinking about more recent revolutions as being more likely to model the ones to come. For sure revolutions are wild and can eventually result in terrible regimes. They're dangerous, but we are in a situation where we kind of need one (or more). So I've been looking at books like *Why Civil Resistance Works* [by Erica Chenoweth and Maria J. Stephan —DS] and thinking about the crash of 2008, and how when the next bubble bursts and we are on the edge of financial collapse, we might seize that moment and turn it into a kind of virtual, democratic, legal or semi-legal revolution. But your final point is undeniable: such a social change would very likely bring results no one has thought of. That's history for you.

Q: You focus on novels so the characters have room to come to life? Why can't you do that in shorter works? In your early career you certainly did, in the pages of *Orbit*.

KSR: I guess it can be done in shorter works, although the word count makes it hard. But for me the problem with short stories comes not from trying to portray characters, but simply in coming up with short story ideas. They're not the same as novel ideas, and it seems like all my ideas these days are for novels. I'd like to do more short fiction, but a particular kind of idea has to come to me, or I can't do it. So, I keep looking. Recently I wrote one, for the first time in several years, but it's only two thousand words and is not exactly a character study.

Q: So, seriously, if you want to put on your prophet's hat for the moment, what do you think the world will be like in 2050?

KSR: That's 35 years from now, so it will still be a mixed picture, meaning human civilization won't be clearly disastrous or obviously and definitely on its way to balance and sustainability. The two possibilities are both so stranded together and full of momentum in their different trajectories that I think 2050 will look and feel kind of schizophrenic. So in human culture, the environment, and people's minds, there will be enormous stresses, a feeling that a race is on between utopia and catastrophe, a sense of wildness and revolution, stupidity and greed, but also huge potential. Anger and hope. So: like now, but more so. An exacerbated now. This of course is a kind of easy vague call, almost your classic straight-line extrapolation, which is usually wrong. Especially since, at our current pace, we will by then have burned the 500 gigatons more carbon we can before we raise the temperature globally by 2 degrees C., and therefore will likely be cooking our home by the year 2050. So, even granting we cut back on burning carbon, which hopefully we will, the situation in 2050 may feel like a permanent emergency—life with the hotel fire alarm ringing your ears, all the time.

Q: Let's talk about writing methods. Are you an outliner or someone who just jumps in with an evocative scene or even a phrase? Did you know that your MARS series was going to be that extensive when you started it?

KSR: I did know the Mars series was going to be a trilogy, or at least a single long novel. I thought it was a single novel, and yet had not yet gotten to Mars and had written 200 pages (early draft work), and my new agent Ralph Vicinanza said to me, "Stan, we call that a trilogy." That was fine; I wanted a broad canvas.

I don't outline, but I do usually have scenes in mind that are scattered through the story, like islands in an archipelago. I know I want to visit all of them, so I have to design a plot that will get me to them in a plausible way. Most of the work of figuring out the story happens along the way while I figure all that out. It's a process of exploration, and works for me; there's a certain amount of tension as I write my novels, but in a productive way. Could call it excitement rather than tension, in any case it definitely engages my full attention. Even after all these years I have no sense that I know what I'm doing, although I do now have confidence that if I persist, something will result. Mostly it still feels like exploring. I like the work.

Q: The thing I've most obviously neglected to ask you concerns your thesis on Philip K. Dick. Given that you wrote such a thesis, you must have thoroughly mastered his work, so was his work a major influence on yours? Did you ever meet or correspond with him?

KSR: I read all of PKD's published novels, and while I was doing my dissertation on him, visited Cal State Fullerton, where his papers were kept in 24 boxes, basically unsorted. This was around 1980, and he had sold his papers to Cal State Fullerton in a deal brokered by Willis McNelly. McNelly got Cal State Fullerton to give PKD $500 for his papers, which allowed PKD to afford to move from northern California to Orange County, leaving a very chaotic part of his life behind and transitioning to its relatively calmer end phase. In the 24 boxes were about 10 mainstream novels, all since published, and some significant fiction fragments, letters, etc. It was quite a trove, and I struggled to sort it out and read some of the mainstream novels, to get a sense of them for my dissertation. I did not do a completist job; there wasn't time.

I really like PKD's fiction, and reckon that about a dozen of his novels are truly brilliant, also often hilarious, and there are flashes of wit and insight among many of the other 35 or 40. I used to say there were 37 published novels, but that was in 1981 and I've lost count of how many more have been published since then. A lot, for sure. To me, what mattered in his work was the structural matter of his third person limited point of view, roving from character to character, and also the jamming together of lots of different sf elements into one story. So, mainly matters of form, with the first more important to me than the second. Then in terms of content, I like his anti-capitalism, and his focus on ordinary people. Also the portrait of California that emerges from all his books taken together. These were the aspects of his work that spoke to me. I don't think of him as a major influence, but definitely a benign minor influence. His classic move, the "reality breakdown" as I called it, is not something I'm much interested in. Although in his work it can be spectacular.

I never corresponded with him. I intended to send him my dissertation, with the hope he would like being written about in that way, even if he didn't like what I actually said. A few years earlier he had gotten mad at Fredric Jameson and Peter Fitting for describing him in the context of Stanislaw Lem, and writing about him from a Marxist perspective (I think that was his beef, anyway) so I was not confident he would like my dissertation, but I was going to send it anyway. But he died two months before I finished it, which was a horrible surprise for everyone, or at least to those not aware of his health problems.

I did meet him once. This too happened on the night of the Harlan Ellison appearance at Cal State Fullerton. PKD and Avram Davidson were in the audience, sitting together just a few seats from me, part of a full hall of about 500 people. After Harlan read the first half of his Kitty Genovese story, and gave a hilarious monologue, there was the question-and-answer session during which I asked my fateful question about Clarion. Later PKD stood up and told Harlan how much he appreciated Harlan's raising of the level of respect for science fiction among the general public. It was a statement rather than a question. Harlan was obviously moved. Afterward I ran into PKD in the hall outside the auditorium, and I said, "Mr. Dick, I really liked your novel *Galactic Pot-Healer*." He looked at me like I was insane, nodded and passed on without a word. But I was glad I had spoken to him.

Q: What are you working on now? You mentioned a short story, but what's the next big project?

KSR: I'm writing another novel. This one is about major sea level rise as a consequence of climate change, and takes place in lower Manhattan. I'm having fun with it.

Q: Thanks, Stan.

STANLEY SCHMIDT

Dr. Stanley Schmidt has been a professor of physics at Heidelberg College in Tiffin, Ohio. He began to publish science fiction, in *Analog,* in 1968. His first novel, *The Sins of the Fathers,* was serialized there November 1973-January 1974. His other novels include *Newton and the Quasi-Apple, Lifeboat Earth, Tweedlioop,* and *Argonaut.* He has been editor of *Analog* since 1978 and been nominated for the Hugo Award every year since. He has also edited numerous anthologies, most of them derived from *Analog.* He has recently announced his retirement from *Analog* and his intention to get back to more writing.

⟵⊶⋯⊷⟶

Q: Describe something of your background. Introduce yourself to the readers.

Schmidt: These days probably most people think of me as "the editor of *Analog*," but while I'm uncommonly pleased to be that, I still think of myself as a writer who currently edits, and take any chance to remind people that I'm a writer too, even though they don't see me in that role as often. According to readers' polls (and then-editor Ben Bova), I was one of *Analog*'s most popular contributors during the 1970s, having begun selling stories here while I was in graduate school (and not sure whether I was allowed to be doing it). Since becoming editor, I've still published occasional stories (sometimes here, more often elsewhere), and several books, including five novels, some nonfiction, and a bunch of anthologies. Editing the magazine takes a lot of time and the same kind of energy that I need for fiction writing, so I haven't been very prolific in that department lately. But eventually I hope to get back to doing more of my own writing, conspicuously including fiction. In the meantime, I can't resist mentioning that most of my earlier books are still available, either from the original publishers or as print-on-demand or e-books through FoxAcre Press.

Q: How did you get interested in science fiction, and at what point did you realize this was going to be a major part of your life's work?

Schmidt: When I was about nine years old, my father (a third-generation reader of *Astounding*) commented that while I was reading a wide variety of nonfiction from the bookmobile that came to my rural school once a month, he thought it would be good to have some fiction in the mix, too. "I've tried," I told him. "It's boring."

"Maybe you should try some good *science* fiction," he said.

"You mean the crazy stuff with the rockets and robots?" I said (having been somewhat brainwashed by the prevalent attitudes of the early fifties, even though he'd taken me to see *Destination Moon* and I was fascinated by his comment that this was stuff that could really happen).

"It's not all crazy," he said. He handed me three volumes of early *Astoundings* that his uncle had bound and said, "Read what's at the bookmarks." I did, and two Weinbaums and a Padgett later I was hooked for life.

I didn't try writing SF until the seventh grade, when I had a friend with similar interests and aptitudes and we egged each other on. But I had started writing fiction much earlier, when a wise second-grade teacher encouraged me to write stories instead of wasting time rehashing material I already knew. Those were mostly about things like big-game hunting in Africa (adventure in exotic environments, even if not SF!), and she sometimes sent me to the principal's office to let him read them.

By the ninth grade I had become sufficiently emboldened, and learned enough about the procedures, to start submitting stories, which, not surprisingly, got only printed rejection slips. I kept doing so off and on in the next few years, with the idea that someday I might learn enough and/or get lucky enough to sell one. I knew enough about the realities of trying to make a living as a writer that I never expected to do so, but I did see it as an enjoyable sideline for the indefinite future, and if it happened to generate some income too, that would be a bonus. From junior high on, my career plan was to be a physics professor, teaching and researching for a living, while freelancing as a writer and musician but not trying to rely on either as a primary income source.

And, though I never dreamed that I would actually get the chance to do it, the thought did cross my mind that John W. Campbell's job must be a lot of fun.

Q: Let's talk a little about what you did before becoming editor of *Analog.* Schmidt: I grew up in southwestern Ohio, with periods in urban, rural, and suburban surroundings, and up to a point pretty much followed the plan I've already sketched. I majored in physics at the University of Cincinnati, got a Ph.D. from Case Western Reserve, and got a job (which I liked much better than I expected to) as an assistant professor of physics at Heidelberg College (now Heidelberg University) in Tiffin, Ohio—while continuing, as planned, to freelance as a writer and musician. I started Heidelberg's first courses in astronomy and science fiction, teaching the latter with methods shamelessly stolen from John Campbell and his successor Ben Bova. That had the side effect that in the process of helping my students learn about SF, I was also teaching myself to be a Campbell-style editor. I enticed Ben out as a guest speaker and to visit my class, and he says that's what made him want me to replace him when he left as editor.

Ben was an important influence in other ways, too. He encouraged me to write my first novel, *The Sins of the Fathers*, and I had what may have been the first-ever sabbatical for the purpose of writing an SF novel: *Lifeboat Earth*, a sequel to *Sins*, much of which appeared as a series of novellas in *Analog* before it all came out as a book.

One of the requirements for being granted a sabbatical was an agreement to stay with the college for at least three years afterward. Ben left *Analog* just one year later, so while I really wanted his job, I feared I would have trouble getting out of my faculty contract at Heidelberg. It was a gratifying and humbling surprise to have fans who happened to be lawyers coming up to me at a convention that summer and offering their services gratis if I needed help. As it turned out, I didn't: fortunately (for me, if not for anyone else) the college (like many) was having financial problems then, and I think they were glad to get rid of anybody they could without a lawsuit.

Q: How much do you think you were influenced, as a writer, by John Campbell before you came to have his job?

Schmidt: Immensely. I had always enjoyed reading stories from many sources, but *Astounding/Analog* was the one for which I felt a special affinity. In reading its stories (and John's editorials) I was constantly trying to understand how the pieces I especially liked achieved what they did, with an eye toward learning to do something comparable of my own. When I finally caught John's eye enough that he started giving me personal feedback, I learned more about storytelling from his first half dozen rejection letters and a few long conversations than from all the classes and books I'd seen before. And not just writing: the way he worked with me as a writer was the main model for the way I now work with other writers (though there are some significant differences between his style and mine).

Q: Well, technically what you got was Ben Bova's job, but you must have felt the ghost of John Campbell at your shoulder when you became editor. Was it like that? Were readers expecting you to be John Campbell? I know Ben has told some funny stories about how some of them refused to believe Campbell was dead, and *Analog* would get letters along the lines of, "Hey John, this Bova character seems to be intercepting your mail."

Schmidt: There were times when I would have liked nothing better than to have John's ghost at my shoulder; I would have liked to ask his advice. But I'm reasonably sure it would have been, "You're on your own, kid."

Lloyd Biggle once told me somebody asked him, "But can Schmidt fill Campbell's shoes?" I liked Lloyd's answer: "He doesn't need to. He has his own shoes."

But of course there were some funny incidents involving readers not understanding or accepting a changing of the guard. I got occasional letters addressed to John for at least the first ten years. And I *immediately* started getting letters lambasting me for ruining the magazine, even though for the first few issues I was running almost entirely on inventory I inherited from Ben. It was at least five months before readers saw an issue that was actually "all mine."

Q: Since *Analog*, more than any other extant science fiction magazine, has an enormous weight of tradition behind it, how did you balance that tradition with a need to keep up with the SF field and the times? The wrong editor could either change the magazine so much he alienated the core readership, or allow it to turn into a fossil. Obviously you have done neither.

Schmidt: I've never felt particularly respectful of, or bound by, either tradition or a need to "keep up with the times" (in this or any other field). But I do view the magazine as having a core personality that maintains a certain continuity even as it evolves with passing time—just as any human being does. The reason it works, I think, is that

I'm as close as you can find to a "typical *Analog* reader" (not that there really is any such thing). My basic philosophy has been to try to make the magazine the one that I would like to read if I had to buy my own subscriptions and could only afford one. I would not stay long with a magazine that either kept doing the same thing over and over, or kept haring off in all directions just for the sake of novelty or because somebody else was doing it.

Q: How did you also manage to keep up the *Analog* tradition of unorthodox science without slipping down the slippery slope that leads to Dianetics, the Dean Drive, and the Hieronymus Machine?

Schmidt: I share John's interest in giving exposure to unpopular or "non-establishment" ideas that look as if they might have some merit, but I'm less inclined to getting all enthusiastic about things that haven't really made a very strong case for themselves—perhaps at least partly because I spent more time than he did actually working as a physicist. I recognize that scientists can get so locked into a generally accepted way of thinking that they need to be shaken up by being exposed to something else from time to time.

Of course, there simply isn't time to pay much attention to *every* offbeat idea that comes along, and most of them really aren't worth it. So you have to be a bit selective about both the ones you pay attention to and the ones you choose not to. In doing that, if you only pick things that eventually turn out to be winners, you're probably being too conservative. If you pick only things that are soon forgotten, you're probably too gullible—or too much of a contrarian for contrarianism's sake.

I've given some space to "cold fusion," mainly by way of commenting on the clumsy way the initial announcement was handled and the stubbornly defensive response of many establishment scientists, who systematically refused to even look at anything that might be evidence. I'd say the jury's still out on that one; it looks as if there may be something there, but nobody is quite sure what.

On the other hand, we also did some of the first (and, according to K. Eric Drexler, some of the best) popular coverage of nanotechnology, which has already established itself as one of the most important and promising fields of scientific and technological

research. We haven't yet seen the most spectacular forms suggested by early speculations about it, but it's still young and my personal hunch is that it will eventually do things that are hard for even the leading current researchers to envision. After all, how credible would Charles Babbage have found the computer on which I'm writing this, or the internet through which I'm sending it to you?

Q: Nevertheless, even the most open-minded scientist or editor needs a working crap detector. The history of our field is littered with real embarrassments, like the Shaver Mystery. (A series of stories published by Ray Palmer's *Amazing Stories* in the '40s, which purported to be "true," all about sinister underground beings called "deros" which manipulate our minds, etc.) But I note that John Campbell, credulous though he seemed at times, never fell for flying saucers, for instance. So are there some things which are just too obviously silly to pursue? I don't see articles in *Analog* about the Bermuda Triangle or Ancient Astronauts, and I am glad for it.

Schmidt: You don't see those articles because nobody has ever offered me one containing evidence or arguments strong enough to take seriously. And while I've published one or two fact articles about how what we think of as the universe *could* be an artifact within a larger one, I've never felt the slightest temptation to treat "creation science" (or its dressier version, "intelligent design") as if it were actually science. It just isn't, and the arguments people have occasionally used to try to convince me otherwise were so slipshod you couldn't even refute them logically—there was no logic in them to latch onto.

Q: What do you think about the "educational" aspect of science fiction? Can it really popularize new ideas and influence the world around us in a positive way, or is this merely the "Gernsback Delusion"? At the last Nebula Weekend I heard astronaut Mike Fincke say, "We went into space because science fiction writers told us to." So, do you as a science fiction editor (and writer) have any sense of didactic mission?

Schmidt: I don't think of it as a "didactic mission," but I certainly do think that science fiction can and does inspire readers, especially young ones, to "make it so." I know it can happen because it happened to me: I became a physicist largely as a result of reading science fiction, especially in *Astounding/Analog*. It also happened to many other scientists and engineers I've known. Many of them have gotten so involved in their own research careers that they no longer have much time to read SF, but the interest is still there. A few years ago I was invited to give a colloquium on "Science and Science Fiction" in the physics department of a major university, and the professor who organized it told me later it drew the largest audience of any colloquium that year.

I am a little concerned that we may not be doing that job as effectively as we used to, because it's most likely to have long-range effects on young readers. We're not getting as many of those as we used to, or as many as we'd like, in part because their attentions are being siphoned off in so many glitzier directions. And it's harder to evoke a sense of wonder in generations who have become jaded, almost overnight, about realities that were pure SF when we were growing up.

Q: Related to that, I've noted a very disturbing trend, which maybe I exaggerate, though some (Gregory Benford for instance) would probably say I do not. The whole culture, even science fiction writers, seems to be turning away from the future. There is less interest in space travel. I hear agents tell me they can't sell science fiction anymore, except military SF series. (Shawna McCarthy said so in one of these interviews a couple issues back.) We see steampunk and alternate history, all about alternate pasts and things that *didn't* and *couldn't* happen. Do you have any sense that the speculative impulse itself is flagging? Has Vernor Vinge's Singularity scared everybody off? If so, what is to be done about it?

Schmidt: I think this is a very real concern, and one of the reasons SF writers and publishers need to find new ways to stimulate positive thought about the future. The Singularity may or may not be a major factor in the widespread attitude shift. A bigger one may simply be that everyone is constantly barraged with propaganda about how terrible the problems we now face are, and too many have knuckled under and pretty much given up on trying to build a great future and resigned themselves to just playing with all the neat toys we have now while they can. Some science fiction, I'm sorry to say, contributes to this defeatist attitude by vividly portraying ugly, depressing futures without offering constructive ways we might prevent or fix them. That's the easy way out, and something we don't do much of in *Analog*. It's painfully easy to imagine ugly, depressing futures; it's harder, but much more rewarding, to imagine plausible alternatives and ways to get to them. That's what we try to do, and I hope it will inspire at least a few young readers to make them happen.

Q: Is it possible that science fiction is a victim of its own success?

People take the idea of, say, other planets so much for granted now that the discovery of hundreds of real exoplanets doesn't seem to be generating much excitement. Folks have been seeing that on *Star Trek* for decades.

Schmidt: Certainly it's harder to evoke a sense of wonder than it used to be, given that so much of our everyday world is full of things that we now take for granted but would have been strictly the stuff of science fiction—or, in some cases, not even imagined by science fiction—just a few years ago.

The problem really has at least two aspects. First, to a casual observer, the difference in content between SF and reality just doesn't look as big as it used to. Second, and to me more disturbing, is that so many people aren't grasping the distinction between having read or heard about something in speculative fiction and seeing it in the *news*. They should be getting excited about exoplanets because they're now, for the first time ever, known to be *real*, whereas *Star Trek* was just entertainment. I don't understand how so many people can fail to grasp the enormity of that distinction, but somehow they manage.

Q: Or is the problem perhaps the reverse? People realize the exoplanets may be there, but we aren't going to be visiting them any time soon. So they give up.

Schmidt: There may well be some of that, too—but then, how many people ever really cared about visiting them? The SF community—by which I mean people interested in seriously speculative, science-based fiction and in making its promises real—has always been a small part of the general population. That's still true, even though we see SF bestselling books and "SF" movies that make a lot of money oftener than we used to.

Or, to look at it another way, maybe the problem began with the end of the Apollo program. Back then, a lot of the general public was interested in space, but I think only a few of them were interested in it for the right reasons. Most weren't looking toward a major outward expansion, but only toward the much more trivial goal of winning a race with the Soviets. Once that had been done, they saw it as an end rather than the beginning it should have been, and started looking for other fads to follow.

Q: I don't imagine you, as editor of *Analog*, just passively sit back and wait for the field to develop. John Campbell certainly did not. But give that nobody will ever be in the kind of monopoly position he was in back in the mid-'40s, when he edited what was *the* adult science fiction magazine, which had no serious competition. So how does an editor lead these days? Do you have editorial lunches with writers and pitch ideas to them?

Schmidt: I certainly do, though the meaning of "editorial lunch" has shifted over the years. Writers no longer live in New York, or even visit it, as often as they used to, so I don't have as many working lunches there. But

I still have lots of productive lunches and dinners at conventions, and much of the same kind of dialog conducted in black-and-white at high speed despite great distances by e-mail. Like Campbell, I sometimes throw out ideas that I think a particular writer would enjoy exploring and do a good job. And sometimes I get a story that I think has a lot of potential but also has problems, so I tell the author what bothers me about it and challenge him or her to come up with a way to fix it that we both like better. Discovering and developing new writers is the single most rewarding part of this job, and I've developed a knack for recognizing potential even before I've seen a story. Occasionally I've sprung for an editorial lunch with somebody who hadn't yet sold me a single word, because I knew they would, and this was a way to accelerate the process. And no two writers are alike. That's one reason I like to meet them face-to-face as soon as possible, because the better I know their strengths, weaknesses, and quirks, the better I know what kinds of things they'll be interested in and do well.

Q: What do you think are some of the most fruitful areas for speculation just now, i.e. cutting edge science that can be turned into good stories?

Schmidt: A lot of the best possibilities are in the related areas of biotechnology, nanotechnology, and cognitive science. I've heard some people say that nanotechnology has been played out and it's time to move on to other things, but this seems to me like telling a hypothetical SF writer in 1900 that electricity has been played out and it's time to move on to other things. All the signs are that this is going to be a big part of our future, and if you choose to assume it isn't, you'll need to justify that. Cognitive science is an area where we've barely scratched the surface. One of the biggest benefits I got from writing my nonfiction book *The Coming Convergence* (shameless plug!) was a greatly increased awareness of just how differently nervous systems work from most of the things we call computers. And, as the title of that book suggests, many of the most fruitful possibilities for SF writers to explore come not from simple extrapolation of any one science, but from the convergence and interaction of two or more—like the three I've already mentioned.

And let's not forget that one of the oldest fields is just full of new possibilities just waiting to be explored. All those recently discovered extrasolar planets, for instance: every one of them is a whole new world, as big and complicated and diverse as the one we live on. From this distance we know just enough about them to know that many of them are quite different from any we've read about before. I'd love to see writers take us in for close-up looks at some of them, so we can see what they might really be like, and what might happen to people trying to explore or develop them.

Q: So, now that you are leaving *Analog* after 34 years, what do you feel you have accomplished?

Schmidt: The thing about which I'm happiest is that I've managed—with a lot of help from some very talented staff, the publishers who've provided a home for it, and above all the writers, artists and readers—to keep the magazine alive, growing, and still the kind of magazine I think it should be. I've often said that my overriding editorial philosophy was

to try to make *Analog* the magazine I would subscribe to if I had to buy my own subscriptions and could only afford one. I think I've done that.

Q: And, presumably this will give you more time for writing. Do you have any particular projects planned?

Schmidt: Quite a few, actually, beginning with a novel that I've been trying to

finish for a couple of years but haven't had time to build and sustain the momentum it needs. Now, I hope, I can. And I'd like to do more short fiction, without waiting for an editor to call me up and invite me to do something for a themed anthology. In particular, in the ten years before I became editor, I was one of *Analog*'s more frequent contributors, and the readers often seemed to like what I was doing. I'd like to try to do that again—if I can get past this new editor!

Q: Thank you, Stanley Schmidt.

LARRY NIVEN

Recorded at Eeriecon, April 30, 2011.

Q: What do you think is the most fruitful area for science fiction speculation right now?

Niven: I'd have to say exoplanets. Mind you, I don't dig very deep into medical speculation, or other areas of science. I prefer astrophysics. Exoplanets keep turning up and they're wonderful.

Q: I think there are now over a thousand of them known. What I wonder is why more science fiction writers don't seem to be excited about them. You'd think we'd be seeing an explosion of outward-looking, space-oriented SF, and we're not. Any ideas?

Niven: I've done a little of it. There was speculation in one of the magazines about other earths. It seems that Earth is at the lower end of the range of possible masses. Earthlike environments will be on planets two or three or four times the size of Earth. Some of them will have formed out where water is frozen, and they will have water shells tens of miles thick with exotic forms of ice at the bottom.

Q: Not very useful for human colonization.

Niven: No. It doesn't sound like they'd have land masses. But that's easy enough. I'd give them a life form that forms floating coral islands.

Q: Are you writing anything like this?

Niven: I did that in a short story, but I could do more of it. There's lots of room.

Q: There seems to be a malaise over science fiction today. A lot of SF writers seem to be losing interest in other planets and outer space at precisely the moment when these are the most exciting. I am wondering what is going on.

Niven: I wonder what is going on too, but the truth is I can't read everything, so I have no reason to think that what I am reading is representative. I read collections of the best short stories of the year and keep up that way. There are some good writers out there. There is some speculation on planets, although the really ambitious writers seem to go right to the end of the universe.

Q: I wonder if the public might not be just taking space travel for granted. How old do you have to be now to remember when there were no spaceships?

Niven: I think you've almost put your finger on the solution, that space travel is being taken for granted. It is the immense expense that is being taken for granted, the loss of the ability to visit other planets as human beings. Writers have to go through too much planning and thinking and research to come up with something that would even make the trip. There's less story left in the end.

Q: Isn't that essentially the writer's job? Where is the new Hal Clement, who would be doing all this at vast length?

Niven: A writer's job is whatever he will accept as his job. The writers of today are choosing from wherever the inspiration comes from. They don't plan out where they are going, most of them.

Q: In a conversation with a magazine editor who will remain nameless, I remarked that he needed more explicitly science-fictional imagery on his covers. How about a spaceship? He replied that he didn't want people to think the magazine was devoted to nostalgia, as if the future is behind us now. So, is the culture itself losing its interest in the future?

Niven: The culture itself is facing the fact that spacecraft cost tax money. Too many boondoggles already. We have lost faith that we can search the universe easily. That is some of us have. The rest, they go as far as we went, and then keep on going. There is a speculation, a lot of science being done on the beginning and ending of the universe. If you go far enough, you find yourself facing the expansion of the universe, dark energy increasing our expansion rate. Some writers are very ambitious, and it will take that kind of ambition to do realistic interstellar travel.

Q: I wonder how we can encourage this. Maybe it is a sign of my age, but a lot of science fiction seems less exciting now. I have a feeling that a lot of people are quitting, turning their backs on the possibilities precisely when they shouldn't. I don't see as much space advocacy either. I might reasonably ask whatever happened to the L-5 Society.

Niven: I believe you're right. We're losing our urge. And yet the reasons to go to space have become more by one. Meteorite impacts are a certain threat. Stopping the next giant meteor is very likely to require men in space. We don't know exactly what we're going to find.

Q: It used to be argued that you could go into space and get rich.

Niven: I think somebody is going to go into space and get rich. What I really think is that somebody needs to demonstrate that it can be done within the next few years. Up to now it is certainly true that the only people who have gotten rich out of space are the people who build the spacecraft. That's not the way you got rich off voyaging to the New World.

Q: But there was something in the New World which you could immediately steal, that is to say Aztec gold. We don't have the equivalent of that for space. You'd have to voyage someplace else and then *work* for it.

Niven: Right. Nothing to steal on the Moon, and nobody to stop you from taking anything you like. Getting water on the Moon is another matter. I was told this for my sense of proportion. If you were to find concrete on the Moon, it would be worth mining the concrete to get the water out of it.

Q: Only if you were living on the Moon. This gets back to the question of why you are living on the Moon.

Niven: I've been writing for forty-odd years and trying to tell people how wonderful space could be. If I've failed to do that, then maybe we don't get there. We still need a space program that will take out the next giant meteorite impact, and identify it first. Maybe it can be guided into orbit around the Earth, though I think maybe we would be stopped by various hysterics. Putting a rock in orbit around the Earth has a dangerous sound, and it probably is dangerous. You'd have to be quite careful.

Q: I think this gets back to the political aspect of it. All that tax money being spent on something that *might* happen in the next ten thousand years? How would you convince a politician of that?

Niven: Do you think politicians are what's standing in the way of the future?

Q: For funding purposes, yes.

Niven: Yeah. I think that's likely enough. It's our present political system, and maybe everybody's present political system that is stopping us from getting there. And yet that seems insane once you think about it. We have gotten from here to other places. We have taken the New World. The politicians weren't any brighter or less selfish then than they are today. We haven't seen an improvement in human nature. We haven't seen a degradation in human nature. Do you think that the Christian, Catholic Church is the key to having conquered the New World?

Q: I think the three things that made the conquest of the New World work were, first, stealing Aztec gold for the ready cash, then making colonies like Virginia pay by growing tobacco, which they did not have in Europe, and the third thing was that it was a great place to dump your religious dissenters.

Niven: Catholic gold I might admit. But if you're sending a lot of gold to the New World and hoping to bring back more, you're also hoping to convert some souls to Christianity. You're that kind of fanatic. That may be part of the impetus that gets ships to the New World.

Q: If we were to discover an extraterrestrial civilization, do you think our first impulse would be to evangelize it?

Niven: Somebody would certainly preach to the heathen. I am also thinking of the Chinese treasure junks, which could have conquered the New World, North and South America. Politicians got in their way. Actually bureaucrats burned the treasure junks in order to make life simpler in their books. That didn't happen to the Catholic missions.

Q: There are many science fiction angles in this. People have also written about what happens when the extraterrestrials try to evangelize us.

Niven: Yes, they have.

Q: On the subject of religion, I also note that you and Jerry Pournelle have recently come out with a sequel to *Inferno.* [*Escape from Hell*, Tor, 2009.] Why did it take you so long, to produce a sequel? Why did it take you over thirty years?

Niven: Forty years ago, when Jerry was trying to get me to write a second book called *Oath of Fealty,* I remembered that I had daydreamed of fighting my way through the Inferno without benefit of angels. I remembered that Jerry keeps lecturing on religion whether I ask him to or not, and I raised the subject with him. As I say, that was around forty years ago. I made him write that book. I mean the first one, *Inferno.* But we kept on thinking after we had written that book. It took him this long to come to various conclusions on religion so that he could persuade me. I already had a wonderful opening, and he picked up a co-star to participate in it. It just took that long. Some books take a long time to germinate.

Q: If you're going to make it a trilogy, I hope we don't have to wait another forty years.

Niven: I think you can safely say that it won't be a trilogy. I don't have much more to say. Jerry might, for all I know. I'd be surprised though.

Q: It seems that these books were driven by your daydreams and his theology. Could you describe how this collaboration worked?

Niven: As I say, I was the one who wanted *Inferno,* and I pushed him into it, and eventually he loved it. He was the one who wanted this second volume, *Escape from Hell.* Eventually I loved it. What more would you like to know?

Q: Well we could address the whole topic of how a hard science writer writes fantasy.

Niven: A science fiction writer writes fantasy by laying down some laws for how the universe works. They are of course going to be pure fiction, but they are going to be consistent and plausible if you close one eye and squint a little.

Q: In that approach to fantasy, ultimately nothing is very mysterious. You can understand it all.

Niven: Yeah. Fritz Leiber was quite different. Fritz wrote science fiction, but he wrote real pure-quill fantasy, and a lot of his science fiction resembles real, pure-quill fantasy. Making the rules was an optional thing for him.

Q: Isn't there something to be said for, say, Lord Dunsany's edge of the world? It is a great image, but hard to justify in terms of physics.

Niven: I spent a night reading Dunsany once, and then wrote an edge of the world story, with a dragon hovering at the edge of the cliff. You can get as fantastic as you like, as long as it's plausible and consistent, and the plausibility doesn't have to be very great. It's when you change the rules in the middle of the story that you look like a fool.

Q: Do you find that fantasy has the same appeal for you as science fiction, or is it a totally different activity?

Niven: I think it has a different appeal, and there is a different appeal for detective stories. I think all of us read detective stories in addition to science fiction and fantasy, don't we? Most of us will try to write some detective or crime fiction. I wrote five Gil the Arm stories, but I also wrote one which is present-time, about a hijacker trying to take a car away from a driver.

Q: You mean it had no fantastic element?

Niven: Right. There was no fantastic content.

Q: But if you wanted to become a detective story writer, could you make a career out of it, or are your strongest talents elsewhere?

Niven: Starting from now I don't think I could become a successful detective story writer. Starting from forty years ago, I might have gone that route and made it work. I think it's more lucrative to be a science fiction writer, though. We sell for longer. Our stories don't go out of date. Detective fiction goes out of date as soon as too many people know what the secret was.

Q: But doesn't detective fiction turn into period pieces? Science fiction can also go out of date. An old book that I read with interest recently was Heinlein's *The Door into Summer,* which starts in the future, 1970, and moves to the far future, 2000. It still reads wonderfully, but it's a very different experience than readers must have had when the book was first published.

Niven: *Lucifer's Hammer* is obsolete in the same sense. It took place around 1975, I think, before the Space Shuttle got going. We're back to no Space Shuttle. So some of it could be written now, without changing very much, but it's obsolete.

Q: It seems to me that the "future" a science fiction writer writes about is a dissociation from the present-day world, but it doesn't have to be ahead of us chronologically. The "future" of *The Door into Summer* is now behind us, but it's still appreciated in the same way. So in what sense is that, or *Lucifer's Hammer* obsolete, other than that they didn't happen in the years stated? I point out that *The War of the Worlds* didn't happen in 1898 either, and we still read it.

Niven: And *Nineteen Eighty-Four* didn't happen in 1984. There are still people complaining that it's the way we're going.

Q: So, does science fiction actually need an element of prediction? *Nineteen Eighty-Four* says eternal things about totalitarianism, which were true when it was written. There is nothing in it that Stalin wasn't doing, except maybe some of the stuff with television.

Niven: A story doesn't need to be an accurate prediction, or even an accurate description of reality. It has to be plausible enough to get you through the story. The shorter the story, the more implausible you are allowed to be. But it's got to hold the reader, or it will vanish. It's got to make the anthologies. It will never wind up on somebody's shelf for fifty years.

Q: One can write a "future" science fiction story which is set in the past. If you wrote *Lucifer's Hammer* now, it would be alternate history. Have you ever felt any desire to write alternate histories?

Niven: I wrote "The Return of William Proxmire," and that was alternate history.

Q: It was also political satire.

Niven: And political satire, and a paean to Robert Heinlein. Of course a story can be many things. Yeah, I have written that one, and probably other alternate history stories. I did a short story in which you follow all of the futures in which the timeline is split.

Q: I am sure you don't believe that science fiction is running out of possibilities. My own feeling is that it is about to renew itself. Every time you start hearing critics saying that science fiction is finished, something explodes. A new trend or movement happens.

Niven: I believe you are right. I have faith. I expect that I will see it myself. I will keep my ear to the ground and see if I can't get on top of this new trend we don't see happening yet.

Q: Alexei Panshin once came up with an elaborate theory of why science fiction is obsolete. There had been a paradigm shift and we could no longer live with the old assumptions, etc. Therefore science fiction could no longer be written. He explained it to me at great length about 1983, and William Gibson arrived the following year. Then everything was different.

Niven: In Europe now, they say Cyberpunk and they mean science fiction. Most of the science fiction they mean is Cyberpunk.

Q: Do they talk about Niven-style stories?

Niven: The people I am thinking of, don't. last year I went to France and Spain for conventions as one of the guests of honor. They know my stories. They know them well.

Q: I suppose that ultimately if we try to define a Niven-style story, we come back to *Ringworld,* which is the story of the Very Big Thing which is carefully extrapolated. I have to admit that the opening of *Ringworld* reminded me of the opening of *The Lost World* by Conan Doyle. It's about a bunch of people getting together and saying, "Hey there's a great adventure out there. Let's go explore this." Maybe this is a spirit we need more of.

Niven: Maybe that's the problem. The spirit of "let's go explore something" runs up against needing a lot of preparation. Also there is far too much news about the dangers of where you are going. You don't just go to Guadalajara these days. You read up on it and see whether there are riots happening, or whether there's a rash of kidnappings.

Q: Indiana Jones will just get in a biplane and go. We have a sense you could do that in the 1930s, but not now.

Niven: As if there were a loose Concorde around. Wouldn't that be convenient?

Q: There isn't any place left on Earth that is all that remote anymore. If you were on an expedition to the South Pole and you were injured or sick—you wouldn't be on such an expedition in the winter—somebody could fly you out of there in a helicopter in a few hours. There isn't any place that is too far away. Maybe interplanetary travel will restore that sense of the adventurer being out there on his own.

Niven: Yeah, and vast amounts of time spent getting there. It doesn't take months to get from Guadalajara to Seattle, but it takes months to get to Mars, however you do it.

Q: Maybe a lot of Americans are just too comfortable and the Chinese will go to Mars.

Niven: The uncomfortable people are often too poor to mount a space expedition. Science fiction writers need to work on that. The new revolution may be—Oh hell, I don't know where it's coming from.

Q: What we want is a revolution in which the older writers will be able to continue. Maybe what we don't want—for selfish reasons—is a another Campbell revolution, which put all the major writers out of business, with a few exceptions.

Niven: Did it?

Q: Yeah. Think of David H. Keller, Stanton Coblentz, Neil R. Jones. A lot of people who were big names in 1935 were really finished by 1945. John Campbell blew the whole field out of the water.

Niven: But he greatly improved the field. He improved the readability and the educational level of what of he was publishing. We all have the missionary urge. Science fiction writers and readers have the missionary urge. We want to improve civilization. We want to train people to run the world better. The educational factor of science fiction is impossible to ignore. Maybe that is what we are losing. If all the educators think that it's not really possible to conquer the Moon again…

Q: I wonder if it isn't that after too many *Star Wars* movies a lot of people think that going into space is just one more kind of fantasy.

Niven: They no longer believe in the ships any more than they believe in the power of the Force. It's all the same fantasy.

Q: It's the same as Harry Potter.

Niven: Yes.

Q: Gregory Benford has commented on this a good deal. He thinks that our society is losing touch with science. I argue that what we need is more compelling science fiction to lure the readers back.

Niven: Okay. I'm doing my best.

Q: Thank you, Larry.